About the author

My purpose for writing the series of Homewrecker novels extends above and beyond just wanting to write a gripping close to home story.

On occasions, I've picked up books and been unable to portray what the writer has so beautifully written for me. Then, when I've found a book I've loved and read it to the end, the sense of achievement is immeasurable. I believe everyone should embrace this emotion when they read.

My desire is for you to feel just as wonderful when you reach the end of this novel, as I've written this wholeheartedly for you!

HOMEWRECKER

A.L. Frances

HOMEWRECKER

Vanguard Press

VANGUARD PAPERBACK

© Copyright 2018
A.L. Frances

The right of A.L. Frances to be identified as author of
this work has been asserted by her in accordance with the
Copyright, Designs and Patents Act 1988.

All Rights Reserved

No reproduction, copy or transmission of this publication
may be made without written permission.
No paragraph of this publication may be reproduced,
copied or transmitted save with the written permission of the
publisher, or in accordance with the provisions
of the Copyright Act 1956 (as amended).

Any person who commits any unauthorised act in relation to
this publication may be liable to criminal
prosecution and civil claims for damages.

A CIP catalogue record for this title is
available from the British Library.

ISBN 978 1 784654 76 4

This is a work of fiction. Names, characters, businesses, places,
events, locales, and incidents are either the products of the author's
imagination or used in a fictitious manner. Any resemblance to
actual persons, living or dead, or actual events is purely
coincidental.

Vanguard Press is an imprint of
Pegasus Elliot MacKenzie Publishers Ltd.
www.pegasuspublishers.com

First Published in 2018

Vanguard Press
Sheraton House Castle Park
Cambridge England

Printed & Bound in Great Britain

Dedication

I wrote this for you...

A.L. Frances

The world that we are blessed to embrace with every living day, as one individual soul, seems so pure when you follow the positive teachings nature has to offer.

This colourful planet that beautifully homes our life as we know it, is populated by around 7.5 billion people. I'm sure you'll agree with me, that's one large number!

Every day, people meet new people; our human race is very trusting. We invite people into our lives, we invite people into our families, our homes, our businesses, without truly knowing them.

When we mix with new people, what I believe we should be asking ourselves is: what's this person's intention?

Are their intentions the same as mine, or do they appear to have a motive for being present in my life at this very moment?

What if I told you we are not the only race living on this beautiful planet?

Would you then ask yourself those questions indefinitely when meeting a new person?

We are all at risk of being used by people; if we, the adult, invite them into our lives, then so be it for us, agreed? Now the plot begins to thicken somewhat, as what if we, the adult, have a family living with us and we invite this new person into our family dimension, but hang on a minute, this is including an invitation into the lives of your very own dependants. Would you then agree that this changes things slightly?

A family is very complex; it's probably one of the most complex words, I believe, to be in the English dictionary. The top definition of a family according to an internet search is 'a group, consisting of two parents and their children living together as a unit'.

Well what about the family setups where one parent isn't present? I believe single parent is the correct terminology. What about those single parents? Are they and their children not classed as a family?

Single parents can be left wide open to people who may not have the best intentions. Single parents can be looking to fill the void at times with the missing family link, the other parent.

If it's within your desires, being a parent is a wonderful gift that the majority of the population are blessed to embrace. Having the ability to share this special gift with another, be that a biological parent or someone you feel that you've carefully selected to fill the void, should be a process we give gratitude for as our family unit grows. I'm sure you would agree to that one too.

Can you imagine? You've invited another person into your life to fill this void with faith, belief, and the trust that their soul is the right one for you. You share your life, you share your home, you share your journey, and you share the souls of your dependants with this person. Not only do you trust them to bring positive influences and kindness into your home, you may also expect them to fill the gap of the missing role model for your dependants.

Could you imagine going to all this effort and falling victim to this chosen soul? But hang on a minute, it's not just you who will fall victim, the dependants that you have in your life fall victim too, all because *you*, the adult, said yes to this person being a part of all your lives.

Here's how one family experienced just that, in the worst possible way.

Chapter 1
"The Honeys"

The day is bright, breezy and full of hope. Matthew's standing tall, proud and yet somewhat deflated in the living room of his luxury three storey home, which overlooks the beautiful serenity of a small, blissful, English beach and is positioned perfectly just outside the centre of Hythe, South of London in Folkestone, Kent. The room he stands in is grand, light and airy. Every object has its own place within the room, and not a single item leans so much as a centimetre out of place. This beautiful building with its strong structure stands out from the crowded beach front. Its unique, luxurious exterior was designed by the current owners of the property, Matthew and Lauren Honey. They had an image in their minds of the home they desired to raise their young in; from that vision, this magnificent building with its fresh brown brick and multiple strikingly designed huge windows was constructed.

Matthew Honey, forty-seven, an attractive, distinguished-looking young widow is wearing an expensive blue tailored suit, which has been designed to fit his slim and toned body to perfection. His dark hair, which has a slight curl to it, is slicked back, with strands of grey peering through on either side.

Standing with his back turned to the tall, immaculate, white living room door, he gazes peacefully out of the enormous uniquely designed window, which is overlooking the sea. Staring attentively, he looks up to the piercing blue, crystal-clear sky and begins watching as the delicate white clouds drift gracefully, a subtle symbolism that the world is continually passing with ease. A gentle smile begins to form on Matthew's handsome facial features as he sees the freedom of the beach-loving seagulls glide past his home. Reaching up to the collar on his white, crisp shirt, he corrects his tie. Once he has perfected this Matthew takes a deep breath, almost filling his lungs; as he exhales, he pushes the air to leave his body. At the same time, he releases a huge sigh: a sigh of relief, a sigh of despair, a sigh of forgiveness, who knows?

Partially deaf in his right ear, Matthew's sensitive to the feeling of vibration that presents itself in the man-made objects surrounding him and exists in the soundwaves circulating within the air.

Closing his eyes to embrace the moment, Matthew feels the vibrations from the floor move up his physique. With his body now absorbing the tingling sensation, his nerves react to the movement. With this new energy now present in his body, Matthew's weak sense of hearing begins to initiate. Turning gently to look over his shoulder, he hears and feels banging, stampede-like footsteps vibrating from behind him. Turning ever so slightly, he seems unalarmed and somewhat familiar with the noise, whilst also remaining cautious and unsure. With an inquisitive expression upon his face, he hears a voice as clear as day, and immediately, Matthew begins to smile; he knows exactly who these elephant feet belong to.

"There you are!"

Standing looking somewhat relieved in the doorway he sees his miracle, his blessing, his beautiful one and only daughter Eve. She's dressed extremely smartly for a sixteen-year-old girl and is wearing a deep grey fitted suit with a white blouse. Her make-up has been beautifully sculpted to her face and must have taken hours. With her hair shoved into a scruffy bun on the top of her head and a black pair of kitten heels on her feet, she's mastered the corporate look.

Almost instantly, Matthew begins to beam with pride as he looks directly at his lifesaver, who is still standing in the doorway looking somewhat concerned and slightly frustrated at her dad's lack of words. Waving her arms around in an is-anybody-home kind of expression, she says, "Erm, hello Dad... We're going to be late at this rate."

Walking across the room to Eve with a sincere smile on his face, he tucks her hair behind her ear, he looks at her and places his hand under her chin. You could spend an eternity searching the entire universe and you would struggle to find a bond tighter than this between a father and his daughter. With his eyes oozing love and his heart beginning to warm, he replies, "Eve, you worry far too much."

Tutting whilst raising her eyebrows and rolling her eyes, she responds, "Well, someone has to."

Smiling as his mind processes these mocking yet heartfelt words, Matthew glances down at the silver glistening necklace hanging beautifully around her neck and peering through the gap in her blouse. Closing his eyes if only for a second, he feels an immediate sense of discomfort and agony as he hears a pained scream in his mind; not just any scream, it's the high-pitched screaming of a suffering child, hurting internally and externally. Quick to open his eyes, Matthew looks to his daughter and begins to hold her tight. Eve doesn't question this and embraces the moment with her dad.

Releasing her from his arms, Matthew cups the heart-shaped locket that is hanging from a white-gold necklace, a vision of beauty in its simplistic elegance and oozing deep memories that are of the irreplaceable kind.

With his eyes forming tears of sorrow, he starts to relive a memory of Eve; she's with her mum once more.

In this vision, which has chosen to surface after being stored so sacredly away in his memory, Matthew sees Eve; she's delicate and tiny. Present only in the moment, he can see his mini creation standing on her tippy toes, balancing on a white-painted wooden chair, positioned safely next to the solid wooden-built mahogany island present in the centre of the kitchen. This chair she is standing on so innocently in her excitement is special and has been designed specifically for her.

With a beautifully detailed painting of a purple and pink unicorn looking magical on the seat of the chair, this personalised possession has been designed with hand-crafted excellence and, as an added extra, on the back of this, Evelyn Jade is carved into the wood, painted with luminous pink paint and sprinkled with what Eve would call her magical fairy dust, which is actually silver glitter. This was a very blessed child, who had two very loving parents.

Wearing a mucky pinafore, her facial expression is pure and sweet. With matching plaits draped over her shoulders, hanging beautifully either side of her tiny infant features, Eve's got her usual innocent and cheeky grin plastered across her face. As she begins clapping her tiny hands together, the dry white flour they are baking with fills the air and spreads around the kitchen. It's coating everything it lands on, like snow on a winter's night.

Still present in the moment, Matthew can see his wife laughing as she reaches out to their precious daughter and, using her fingers, she playfully presses cake mix on the tip of her nose.

Embracing this memory which has chosen to surface, and remaining deep within this, Matthew sees his wife looking her usual radiant, happy and beautiful self. Shimmering away, he notices the twinkle coming from the necklace positioned around his wife's neck. This very same necklace, Eve now proudly wears. He closes his eyes tight to embrace the memory but remove himself out of the moment; it's too painful for Matthew to relive. Eve, looking up at her dad, is filled with sadness; she says these simple yet heart-wrenching words: "I miss her."

She is aware of what's running through her dad's mind, she knows he's thinking of her mum. The only woman he has ever loved, the only woman who owns his heart, the heart she now wears around her neck.

"Evelyn Jade Honey, you remind me of her every day. Your mum will be so proud of the beautiful, courageous, strong young lady you've become, I know it."

Matthew acknowledges that he's been lost since he was forced to say goodbye to his wife, his soul mate. From that day on, he became nothing more than a wondering lost soul, destined to live an existence and no longer a life. Without this amazing woman, he felt he was nothing. Snapping out of the moment before he uncontrollably sheds tears, Matthew holds Eve and says, "Let's go to the café."

Regaining his composure, he stares proudly at his daughter, who is now looking confused, as she frowns her eyebrows and says, "But... your meeting?"

With his expression changing, Matthew smiles ever so gently. He's gone from resembling a man in the depths of despair, wondering why he's alive, to staring at his blessing, the reason he lives.

"Eve, you should know me by now. Two words: *extra hour...*"

Squinting her eyes, she reaches out and gently taps him on the arm in a cheeky manner; she knows what *extra hour* means. Every time he has a meeting, or an event, he tells Eve the time is an hour earlier than it actually is, or he has to deal with her chasing him. Matthew's view is taking your time is a much more productive and effective way to function. Since going through the traumatic experience of losing his wife, he doesn't like rushing, or being rushed. It's now a huge pet hate of his. With the recent realisation that life is too short, Matthew has absolutely no desires to spend any of his time stressed out, anxious or upset. Eve smiles; she knows he does this and yet every single time she forgets. Shaking her head, she hugs her dad and says, "Café it is then."

Driving through the country roads in his brand new, immaculate, shark-grey Porsche Cayenne, kitted out with full cream leather interior, Matthew looks to Eve. She has her elbow resting gently on the window ledge of the door; her chin is relaxing on her hand; and she's gazing up at the huge canopy of trees as they stand strong, arched either side and touching in the middle. A true vision of beauty. The sun's natural glow is peeping through the tiny gaps present in the branches; it's creating beams of golden sunrays that are spreading their magical surreal existence. Eve's embracing the view and all it has to offer.

Gazing to the sky, she sees small elegant birds graciously passing by – Mother Nature is the creator of all things picturesque and tranquil. These magnificent different types of birds spread their wings with ease and are such enchanting creatures. Present in the sky, they create a sense of empowerment and are a gentle reminder of the magical potential that's continually surrounding us. After all, what's more empowering than the ability to embrace the world from the highest point, where the air is clear and cleansed, within the clouds, flying free?

Eve closes her eyes – she becomes captive in the moment that's taking place in her mind. Just like those enchanting birds, she can see herself gracefully gliding down a beautiful strong mountain. The kind of mountain that makes the rocks that lie beneath it resemble one of nature's tiny creatures. She's falling free, no parachute, no safety net, no wings, just her arms out at the side of her body, flying, peaceful and alone. With every descent she smiles bigger, and bigger, with her eyes open, embracing each individual tickle of the breeze as it kisses her face. Trapped in the moment without a care in the world, Eve doesn't even attempt to remove herself from this vision. She's enjoying seeing the freedom she so desperately desires.

Eventually, opening her eyes, she looks across at her dad; the trees on the country roads are passing rapidly as Matthew picks up his speed. He glances to Eve as a life-fuelled, eye-twinkling smile surfaces in his expression. If only he knew her true inner desires, and that actually, she was peaceful and smiling at the thought of being free from life, whilst visualising the freedom of falling to her death!

The journey is serene, the roads are clear, for Matthew life is in the air along with a bright feeling, the feeling that anything can happen, endless possibilities, wonderful new beginnings. They've been through the worst thing any living person could imagine going through, losing a loved one; surely, life could only get better.

When you read the words *losing a loved one* you may begin to imagine losing your elderly relative or a family member/friend to a tragic illness, but this soul they so tragically lost was not just anyone. This loved one was once present in every daily activity, even the simple daily blessings of waking up, getting ready and watching TV. This loved one was very cruelly and abruptly taken away. No ability to say goodbye, no notification, nothing! A beautiful soul they were blessed with and was without a doubt the head of the family home, taken by circumstances out of their control; completely powerless, and worst of all, they had to stand by and watch. So, not only were they forced to learn to live a life without this kind, generous, strong woman – they had to relive the events that took place and continue to see the life leave her body; as the light went out, playing on a loop in their mind, each and every single time this horrific memory desired to surface. To know you have to continue your existence and live your life without this person's magic and beauty, every single day, really, what could be worse than that?

The relationship between both Matthew and Eve was very estranged; they never understood each-other, well, they never made time to get to know each other. As the years went by and Eve grew up, Matthew thought she was a complete pain in the butt, especially when she hit puberty. Eve's opinion of her dad was that he was old, uninteresting and a complete embarrassment.

Going through such a mentally traumatic experience whilst only having each other to lean on, mourn with and keep going for, had brought them closer than they could have ever imagined. Being physically and mentally dragged away from his wife, and Eve dragged in the same manner from her mum, both of them individually having to deal with the torture, the hurt, the pain, deep internal sadness, and unbearable loss, gave them a strong connection, once they finally pulled together. When one had no desire to live in this horrific, continued, pained existence, the other was the energy light that lifted their soul, and vice versa. They now understood the importance and value of having each other's powerful energy present every day. Father and daughter living every moment together, standing proudly side by side.

***

Eve flicks on the radio. A familiar song begins to play throughout the car. It's the greatest hits of the eighties hour. Instantly this music makes her smile. She begins to theatrically dance whilst singing the lyrics – admittedly, her dance moves aren't the best and actually, to be honest, they're kind of tragic. Nonetheless this has never stopped her before and it's y not going to stop her now as she continues a care in the world. Embracing the moment for the joy it's creating, Matthew glances to her as she's sat with her seatbelt strapped tightly and dancing on the spot. Her eyes are closed and she's singing the lyrics whilst moving around like no-one's watching. This young girl is beaming with joy and radiating happiness. Opening her eyes, Eve says, "I love this song."

"How do you know this song? This is mine and your mum's era."

Laughing cheekily, she continues to sing and once again with her heartfelt mocking words she speaks, "Don't worry Dad, I haven't been going through your lame music collection."

"Oi, leave it out you cheeky bugger. My music collection is classic."

Pretending to be somewhat shocked by her dad's choice of name calling, she continues, "We've been learning this in music – how cruel is this, right, did you know it's actually about a blind woman? I mean, hello, she's blind for God's sake. Not being funny Dad, but I think the guy who wrote this is a little bit sick."

Matthew laughs at her innocence.

"Our music group has been chosen to perform this song at the end of year concert."

Stationary at the traffic lights, Matthew quickly turns and looks to Eve.

Now, I think we can all agree that at some point in our lives we've all done this. The look he gave to his daughter was that *oh crap* look. You know the one: it's where your eyes begin protruding out of their sockets as fear begins to reveal itself on your face, and your talents win you the award for most forgetful person on the planet. Yes, that was this look. Eve said four words that had triggered a memory in Matthew's mind.

As clear as day, he can see Eve reaching into the fridge whilst he's sitting at the breakfast bar wearing his reading glasses and is deep in thought checking his accounts. Peering around the fridge door with a packet of wafer-thin ham in her hand, as she's munching away with a mouth full, she says, "Don't forget, it's my end of year concert on the seventh July, it's starting at two thirty and this year it's a... wait for it... Saturday. Yay. So, you should defiantly be able to come."

Sat looking stiff in the driver's seat, with both his hands on the steering wheel, Matthew's stationary at the traffic lights and as he's reliving this memory, his face suddenly begins oozing guilt. Eve's sat watching her dad's expression change.

"You are coming, aren't you?"

Attempting to look somewhat confident, Matthew fails miserably as his expression betrays him. He rarely gets to attend Eve's performances due to his demanding work commitments. Ordinarily, she's very forgiving, but this is her last ever end of year concert as she leaves school this year. A look of worry begins to spread across his face.

"Dad, you must be there, it's my last performance – you've missed every single one."

"Yes, of course darling – I wouldn't miss it for the world."

Satisfied with his words, and with the eighties hits continuing to blast loudly throughout the car, they both set about nodding and singing in sync with each other.

***

Arriving at the café, they park up in the car-park positioned at the side of the building. A huge sign stands at the entrance: Private Car Park – Customers of Sunnyside Up Café Only. The street is packed, people everywhere; they're all rushing past each other with bag, after bag, after bag, in their hands, no-one smiling. Children running at the side of their elders in a desperate attempt to try and keep up with their partially undeveloped legs. Parking in the visitors' bay, Eve hops out of the car and begins taking a deep breath in and is embracing the vision of her most treasured place to eat out. Both Eve and Matthew have a huge connection to the building and the land surrounding them. Walking round the back of the car, she's smiling and taking in the calming ambiance of the car park. Matthew shouts across to Eve, as she appears to be day-dreaming: "Come on then, kidda." Picking up her pace, she walks to her dad with a big genuine grin spread across her face. Linking arm in arm, they form a vision of strength as they make their way towards the café.

Chapter 2
"The meeting"

As they enter the café, the smell of cooking bacon, sausages and fresh coffee awakens their nostrils. They see the two young girls behind the counter looking flustered in their grease-stained pinafores. With their hair tied up tight, you can tell these two would rather be anywhere but behind the counter right now, as the café is starting to get busy. Whilst rushing around working on a customer's order, the girls notice Matthew and Eve and begin acknowledging them with sincere smiles. All the staff members at the café are extremely familiar with them both. They begin exchanging friendly nods of the head.

"Hi Matthew. Hi Eve."

"Eve! My god, I haven't seen you for ages – I'll come over and see you shortly."

"Okay. Hey Sophie."

"Hi Lucy. Hi Sophie. Is your mum or dad about?"

Sophie responds, "No – they're still on a cruise, ain't they?"

"Oh yeah – I forgot. Are they enjoying their exciting travelling experience?"

"They're lovin' it – last I heard they don't wanna come back. I told 'em they better, I want me life back. Suppose it's all right for some, aye."

"Ha, well, when you speak to them next, please let them know I was asking after them."

"Sure – will do."

The café is family run; it's really nothing spectacular and could probably do with an immediate lick of paint. Being a very wealthy man, Matthew could take Eve to any café or fancy restaurant in any location on the globe. They can afford all the lavish luxuries they desire. It's very simple; there is only one reason why they have no desire to venture anywhere other than here. They stand by this family run café and will visit until the day they are taken from this beautiful planet – as all those other cafés, restaurants, and luxurious locations don't hold the one irreplaceable thing that this café holds: memories. They weren't always wealthy; Matthew and Lauren built their empire together, and before their days of wealth, this café was where they would come to mastermind. The café to them was "The Creative Station." They were never mithered, always welcomed, treated like family, and so they continued to keep the connection which had been created.

The tradition remained, and they would often have business meetings together here, even long after the success of their companies. It was their lucky charm; a place of zen – I think we could all do with one of them from time to time.

Eve takes a seat in their usual spot, "The Mastermind Corner." As she sits, Matthew makes his way over to the counter. Lucy and Sophie are already preparing his order before he arrives; now that's what you call a regular customer – loyal to the service and the service loyal to him. Matthew's stood exchanging pleasantries with both Lucy and Sophie, blissfully unaware of anything taking place in his surroundings. Suddenly he feels a huge presence behind him.

I'm sure at some point you'll have experienced this. I often get this feeling within my soul; it mainly happens to me at night when I'm minding my own business and brushing my teeth, or when I'm switching all the lights and appliances off, and the room that was once beautifully lit becomes dark. I get this strong, daunting feeling, all my senses begin to heighten and no matter how hard I try to ignore this, I feel someone stood right behind me.

So – be honest now, which one are you? The brave ones immediately turn in the hope that no-one's stood there, or if you're anything like me, do you make no attempt to turn around, dodge the energy and run like a mad person to get away from whatever is potentially stood there, whether it's in your head or not? Well this moment was exactly like that. Matthew froze. Courageously, he turns around, only to be stunned by who is stood there staring back. Standing proudly, head held high, shoulders back, looking radiant, beautiful, and with a welcoming smile, is the most elegant woman whose energy beams brighter than a cluster of stars within the universe. Instantly, he becomes lost for words and can barely open his mouth as this dries up with nerves. This radiant looking woman with her flowing dark brown hair, slight freckles and natural enchanting beauty, has perfectly painted nude plump lips. She smiles, and although the situation is getting slightly awkward, she speaks, "Are you okay?"

Unable to reply, Matthew's gazing in admiration at this woman. She's wearing a low-cut cream blouse, dark skinny jeans, and matching her lips, like glass slippers, she's wearing fabulous nude stilettos. Hanging over her arm she has an oversized beige handbag, along with a pile of paperwork close to her body in the other.

Finally, Matthew breaks eye contact; as he peers down at her slim neck he notices a white-gold necklace. The movement from this has created a sparkle which caught his attention. Hanging from this delicate chain is a striking, silver, heart-shaped locket. This is so similar, if not identical, to the one Eve now has. Tucking her hair behind her ear in an attempt to distract from the awkward moment, she's now getting slightly concerned and once again, with her sophisticated voice, she asks, "Excuse me, are you okay...?"

Matthew finally speaks, although he probably wishes his brain would have processed the words first, but nonetheless they come out: "You are beautiful." *(I know, lame, right?)*

With an instant expression of regret plastered across his face, Matthew becomes slightly red with embarrassment by the words he's just blurted out. Blushing, she juggles her bag and paperwork in her arms as she puts out her hand.

"Hi, my names Jess. It's very nice to meet you."

Reaching out with his hand, Matthew replies, "Hi Jess – my name's Matthew. Nice to meet you too." Whilst shaking her hand, he's glaring at her perfection. Caught up in the moment, he again blurts out words before thinking: "Would you like to join me and my daughter for a coffee?"

Lucy and Sophie, who appeared to be working in the background, suddenly down tools. The coffee machine's screeching away as the boiling hot frothy milk starts to bubble over. Lucy was placing iced buns on a plate ready to hand to Matthew and even she's stood completely still. They're both resembling statues and look as though time has decided to stand still. Lucy and Sophie continue to look on in shock at what is taking place before their eyes. With a similar expression of astonishment on their faces, they make eye contact with one another and set about whispering. Matthew's standing just a few feet away and although he isn't looking in their direction, he sees them from the corner of his eye.

Noticing this sudden change, Jess is slightly puzzled as she looks towards them both.

"Oh, don't worry about the girls. I'm a regular and – well – in all the years I've been coming here, I've never asked anyone to come and sit with me and my daughter." He starts raising his voice slightly. "*That's why they're whispering...*"

Lucy and Sophie hear Matthew's words and jump with embarrassment. Under her breath Lucy says, "Oh, crap," as she drops the iced bun she was holding on the floor. Sophie jumps once more as she notices the hot milk frothing over the sides of the metal jug.

"Oh gosh, Lucy, quick, pass me a cloth."

Finally switching off the coffee machine, this instantly becomes silent. Having to clear up the aftermath, Lucy and Sophie are both kneeling on the floor cleaning up the mess they've both just made. The girls were solely present in the moment, and entirely unaware that their shocked reaction to Matthew's gesture was so obvious. Matthew, a few moments ago somewhat shy and bewildered with this woman's radiant energy, has now found his voice, "Please say you'll join us." Presuming she's going to say yes, he asks her, "What can I get you?"

Looking down to the floor in a flirtatious way, Jess begins twisting the ends of her hair; she looks up to Matthew and enchantingly begins to gaze into his eyes. Venturing into his sight, she becomes present in his mind and is embracing the power she has for this brief second.

"Matthew, thank you for the wonderful invite..."

Waiting patiently for a response, he's looking back at her, spellbound, and is completely engrossed in the present ambiance. He desires nothing more than to find out who this woman is. With her head held high she accepts his offer.

Internally bouncing up and down like a child with excitement, Matthew asks, "What would you like?"

Looking to the menu above the counter, she says, "Hmm, please may I request a hot chocolate, extra froth and no marshmallows?" She has a slight look of disgust on her face which confuses him. "I'm actually not a huge fan of coffee."

"Huh, you don't like coffee, how can you not like coffee?"

"Well, it's quite simple really – there's only one valid reason why I detest coffee and that is... It tastes far too much like coffee."

Immediately she begins to chuckle, and Matthew mirrors her actions. Knowing this sounds ridiculous, she's unable to explain it any other way. Captivated, Matthew begins to question if this is happening in his reality – and if so, if it is possible to magically stumble across such enchanting beauty inside and out and, well, not only this, but an instant connection whilst spontaneously going out for coffee, then why hadn't life helped him sooner?

Staring in amazement at this striking woman who has a strong presence surrounding her, along with an air of elegance and, as an added bonus, a sense of humour, Matthew feels somewhat spellbound. Granted, no-one could replace his wife, but this instant connection seems somewhat similar.

We all hear and read about love at first sight, but, is this true? Surrounded by beautiful women all day long at his company, external beauty alone doesn't impress him. So, what is this? Matthew feels a magnetic pull that's way out of his control. With their eye contact remaining, whatever this powerful presence is, it doesn't scare him, but draws him in.

Trying to appear cool, Matthew is now getting more and more nervous by the second, and instead of letting his handsome features and wonderful personality do the talking for him, he becomes out of sync with himself. Attempting to look somewhat unfazed by this woman, like the situation isn't at all a big deal, internally he feels like a rabbit in headlights. Leaning slightly on the window of the counter which has all the wonderful homemade pastries and cakes perfectly displayed, Matthew, trying to appear cool and calm, places his elbow on the glass pane, but almost immediately, his elbow slips off. Feeling slightly humiliated he tries to compose himself as Jess is holding back her laughter.

Lucy and Sophie look on in sheer embarrassment as they gently shake their heads and very subtly roll their eyes. Smiling at one another they begin to embrace the fact it's really quite sweet – he clearly likes this woman. Much to his relief, Sophie interrupts the awkward pleasantries: "Take a seat you two – I'll bring it over to the table."

Jess looks to Sophie and says, "How very kind. Thank you."

As he walks away, Matthew smiles and quietly says, "My god. Thank you."

Sophie mimes, "Stay cool."

Both Lucy and Sophie would love nothing more than to see Matthew once again sat in "The Mastermind Corner," happily sharing creative ideas and planning growth, happiness and a life with another person. Over the years they've watched the rise, fall and rise again of this incredible man. Their parents own the café and as they would often bring Lucy and Sophie to work with them, they've grown up with Matthew around. He's always been a regular customer, even long before the days of his wife, right back to being a single young man without a care in the world. Matthew would come in the café with treats and give these to Lucy and Sophie, but not before he pretended he'd found them behind their ears.

Alongside their parents, they've seen him develop into a husband with a loving family, whilst being able to play with Eve as she was also growing up. They've seen him a broken man at the depths of despair, trying desperately to live a *normal* life as a single dad, whilst having to keep the empire and legacy he built with his wife alive. They would love nothing more than to finally see him happily sharing his life, his adventures, his soul, with a perfect match.

***

Walking back to the table with Jess proudly by his side, suddenly, in a millisecond it dawns on him like a lightning bolt to the head, caught up in a giddy school boy mentality, that he didn't think about Eve. What was she going to think about this; how would she feel about him inviting another woman over to "The Mastermind Corner"? The very same corner he once shared with her mum. After all, this isn't just any table and chairs, or any café; it has meaning, it has purpose – it has memories. The sorts of memories you don't desire to replace or fade. With this thought process fresh in his mind, Matthew becomes more nervous than before. He literally has seconds to process this before they reach the table; he's now aware, there's no going back.

Feeling extremely anxious, Matthew has both his hands inside the pockets on his trousers and in order to distract his mind, he's fiddling with a tiny piece of pocket fluff. As he arrives at the table with Jess, they see Eve; she's sat arched over, leaning with her elbows firmly placed on the table and holding her phone in both her hands. Eve's completely unaware of the events that have taken place at the counter. Feeling a presence, she peers from the corner of her eye and can see her dad approaching the table. Looking up with a confused expression on her face, she notices a woman standing at the side of the table alongside her dad. Jess puts her bag and paperwork down at the side of the chair. Eve, wondering what she's just missed, is waiting for her dad, who is again for the second time today speechless, to open his mouth and explain who this strange woman is. Eve's facial expression begins to change and, as the silence grows, the energy circulating in the air becomes awkward. Feeling more and more uncomfortable by the second, Matthew's still saying nothing. Looking at Eve as he wipes his head, which is now forming tiny beads of sweat, he finally goes to speak, but before he can say a word, Jess puts out her hand.

"Hi – I'm Jess, your father has politely asked me to join you for a drink. I do hope this is okay?"

Looking at the hand in front of her and, as she glances to her dad, Eve showcases a very blank expression. In a complete panic as it's getting slightly embarrassing, Matthew sternly looks to his daughter and says, "Eve, don't be so rude!"

With the words fresh from her dad's mouth, Eve's developed from innocently wondering who this woman is, to full on rage. Her confused mind begins to race and the voice in her head is screaming out loud, *How can he call me rude? Why is he speaking to me like that; what the hell have I done wrong?*

With a frustrated look forming and, as the silence is getting more and more awkward by the millisecond, Eve's mind continues to race as she processes the current situation. Unable to comprehend her dad's knee jerk reaction, she's struggling. They were fine a moment ago. With a thousand words written across her face, Eve's trying to work out how her own dad could so carelessly call her rude – especially when he's the one inviting strange glamorous women over without so much of a thought to her, or her mum. Eve immediately becomes rebellious. Shutting down, she rudely crosses her arms and looks at Jess. Deciding to show her dad exactly what rude looks like, and without any attempt to shake Jess's hand, she says, "As you know, my name's Eve – enjoy your drink."

Eve gets up from her chair and goes to walk out of the café. As she reaches the edge of the table, Matthew puts out his arm to stop her from walking away.

"I apologise for my daughter's behaviour, she's normally very pleasant – aren't you Eve?"

Turning to his daughter, he looks at her with complete desperation and confusion, but Eve is now fast becoming even more infuriated.

"Don't apologise for me – apologise for yourself..."

Now at the mercy of his mind, Matthew's frantically trying to work out what Eve's problem is; he's practically begging her with his expression. Seeing the desperation in her dad's eyes and without wanting to create a scene, she reluctantly surrenders.

"A bit of warning: your inviting a woman to mum's corner may have been nice. You know that thing you always go on about, mutual *respect?*"

Sitting back in her chair, she puts her elbows onto the table once more, and this time she places her head into her hands. Matthew's relieved and before taking a seat, he pulls out a chair for Jess who surprisingly enough sits at the table. I can't speak for you – but personally, I would have run a mile, so why didn't she? It makes you wonder what this woman's true intentions are. Without seeming fazed by the horrendous attitude and disrespect Eve is distributing to her dad, as they sit down, Sophie comes over with a tray that's filled with hot drinks and cakes. Placing this directly in front of Eve, Sophie looks across the table as Eve peers through the gaps in her fingers. The pair make eye contact; Sophie smiles. Laying the cups out in front of her elbows, she whispers, "Don't worry it'll be okay."

Eve has confided in Lucy and Sophie for a long time. It's been over three years since her mum's tragic death and they've been there every single step of the way. She trusts Lucy and Sophie. Eve knows that they wouldn't encourage her to engage with anything that would disrespect her mum's memory. Bearing this in mind, she slowly starts to snap out of her arrogant and quite frankly disrespectful mindset. Removing her head from her hands, but with her elbows on the table, Eve places the palms of her hands together and begins crossing her fingers. She closes her eyes. As her energy calms, she looks as though she's praying. Taking a huge deep breath in, her mind drifts as she relives a flashback of a counselling session with her assigned therapist Josie, who she's very close to. She's been a life saver and without her professional and compassionate input, who knows, Eve may not be alive today.

After suffering the traumatic experience of losing her mum so cruelly, both Matthew and Eve are certain that if she didn't receive the help and support from this amazingly skilled woman, Eve would be lost. All Josie's lessons and techniques have helped her learn how to subside her aggression and free herself from pain, anguish and deep internal suffering.

Remaining present in the vision, Eve sees herself sat up straight on the comfy L-shaped burgundy fabric sofa. This was her usual spot. But if she'd suffered a relatively hard day, she would lie on the sofa and be oblivious to the session taking place. Sat up tall in her brown, high-back, Chesterfield leather armchair, with its extravagant gold metal detailing, Josie's content with the progress that's being made, and is proud of Eve's ability to embrace her sessions and implement them in her life. With her calming energy she says, "Now – close your eyes for me please, take a deep breath in, making sure you fill all the space within your lungs and then breathe out, feeling every last bit of breath leaving your body, as your lungs begin to relax. Now, what I would like for you to do this time is the same thing again, except whilst you're filling up your lungs, I would like you – in your mind only – to slowly start counting back from five, at a steady pace. So, five, four, three, two, one."

Eve begins following this.

"As you reach one and begin to breathe out, I want you to see the thoughts present in your mind and the anger in your body blowing across the room. Do you think you could do that for me please? Just imagine, right now, you're in a situation and you are out of control and fuelled by rage."

Eve's expression begins to change.

"That's it, now, counting backwards from five, begin to fill your lungs, fill them until you have no more room. Now, Eve, blow for me, as hard as you can, letting go of all that anger and frustration. Blow and push the negative energy out of your mind and your body."

Eve's blowing with all her might, her face begins to turn a shade of pink she's blowing that hard.

"That's it, well done."

Eve says nothing as she remains slightly red-faced and drained of most of her energy. She's sat looking depleted and suppressed. Josie remains with her comforting ways. She's desperate to educate this young girl's mind to ensure she no longer suffers.

"Eve, there are multiple reasons why this technique is so important – and also, there will be a large amount of challenges that *you* may face daily, where *you* can put this technique into action." Josie moves slightly forward in her armchair and begins raising her body, so her back is completely straight, and her head is held high. "You must sit up straight like this, and Eve, remember, this technique is for when you find yourself trapped in aggression, anger or despair and are feeling as though you have nowhere left to turn."

Once more, she begins leaning forward ever so slightly and continues, "Eve, if you find yourself in a situation where you are no longer in control, and you would like to regain possession of your emotions again, you *must* begin to initiate this technique. It is *so* important that you count backwards from five, *slowly*; this is what activates your brain's prefrontal cortex and distracts you from the choice you were about to make. The counting also gives you time to insert a new choice and change your actions, and don't forget on the count of one, as you release the air from your body, to see the negative energy and thoughts leaving with your breath across the room – then, when you feel ready, open your eyes and start again."

Back in her existing reality, Eve reaches one and exhales. Opening her eyes, she pushes the negativity out of her mind across the room and starts again!

Looking to the other side of the table, she sees her dad sat almost facing her and an innocent-looking Jess sitting beside him smiling, with a white-flag expression. A pure moment of surrender. Eve takes another deep breath in and as she exhales she stands up, straightens her jacket and puts out her hand as she reluctantly says, "Eve, nice to meet you."

Jess begins to smile and shakes her hand. Relieved, Matthew lets out a huge sigh as both Jess and Eve sit back in their seats. Satisfied with the pleasant exchange between the two, he begins passing them their drinks.

In the process of all the commotion and brief excitement, Matthew's forgotten one thing – I wonder if you have too. He's forgotten something very important: the clock still ticks even when you are so invested in a moment. Remember, time stands still for no man or woman. What did Matthew give himself an extra hour for this morning? Yes, that's right, his meeting. His phone starts bleeping extremely loudly from the inside of his jacket.

With Matthew's slight hearing loss, he doesn't always hear the phone and so he always has the volume and vibration turned up to the max. His condition is not something that is an issue, and lucky for him, Eve has the footing of an elephant, so he always knows when she's about. Looking embarrassed, Matthew reaches into his silk-lined pocket and takes out his phone; it's flashing like a strobe light in a nightclub. The alarm suggests that he only has thirty minutes left for his meeting. Starting to panic as he presses the screen on his phone, Matthew, for probably the third time today, speaks before he thinks. Blurting out words before processing any potential consequences, he says, "Jess, I'm so sorry, I've got an urgent meeting and we must leave now or I'll be late." Beginning to stand, he continues, "But please say you'll join us for dinner this evening at our home."

Originally looking smug and thankful that her dad has put an end to this ridiculous charade, Eve's now in shock as she hears his final words. At the end of her tether, her mind can't cope. She hears nothing but her own voice present in her mind. *Our home...! Really! Mum's home... What's going on with my dad.*

Eve's jaw drops, and her eyes widen as she continues to stare at her dad in disbelief. Matthew's not even aware of Eve's reaction. Patiently waiting for a response, the seconds turn into what feels like hours.

Tucking her hair behind her ear, Jess looks to Matthew and locks eyes with him. Cupping the locket around her neck she says, "Are you sure?"

"Yes, of course. Please say you'll join us."

"How can I refuse? Matthew, that would be amazing, thank you."

Eve shoves her chair back in anger and, as this scrapes across the floor, it creates a huge screeching noise. Pushing past Jess as though she isn't present, Eve doesn't make eye contact with her dad, or Lucy and Sophie behind the counter, who are now looking over to the corner, shocked, confused and extremely concerned. Lucy hurries out after Eve, whilst Sophie continues to serve the customers. Matthew, now unsure of what to do and where to turn, sees Lucy chasing after Eve and so he chooses to stay with Jess. Whilst exchanging numbers, he says, "I will text you my address shortly, it's on the beachfront. Do you know it?"

"Yes, I've been there once before. From what I recall it's very beautiful and tranquil there, which is perfect. One of my main pleasures in life is not being disturbed by others."

Matthew looks deep into her eyes and becomes captivated, unable to process his thoughts, or even ask questions like *what do you enjoy eating*? Matthew can't explain what is happening to his emotions, or why he is so fixated on this woman. In a desperate attempt to ensure she arrives, he says,

"I'll make sure Eve is on her best behaviour this evening."

Reaching out to Matthew, she places her hand on his arm and says, "Don't worry, I can handle a teenage girl."

Looking down to her hand, Matthew's embracing the moment as she touches him. He replies, "Thank you, but it's really not acceptable. You shouldn't be spoken to like that." With a pained expression appearing on his face, he continues, "I will try and explain this evening why Eve is troubled, but this is no excuse for her rude attitude, I know."

Matthew's so wrapped up in this woman's presence, her energy, her aura, what is it? Whilst standing like a love-struck dummy and gazing deep into her big brown eyes, he is totally unaware of the goings on outside of the café.

Chapter 3
"The awkward silence"

Fiercely stomping towards the car park, Eve is furious; she can't understand what's going on with her dad. Lucy catches up to her and in a fit of rage, Eve shouts, "You said it would be okay!"

Unaware of what's happened or taken place inside the café, Lucy looks at Eve, confused at her outburst. Eve's now stopped walking and is standing at the side of the car. Lucy approaches her with caution.

"Eve, what's happened?"

Responding with pure venom and aggression, Eve's beginning to express her anger in physical form, as her arms uncontrollably wave around in the air. She's no longer in control as a huge burst of rage begins releasing itself. Eve's shouting louder than ever in the car park. The streets are extremely busy, and her outburst is drawing lots of attention from passers-by, some of whom are shaking their heads in disgust at this young girl screaming aggressively. Youngsters standing across the way are looking over in shock as they begin whispering to one another and pointing. Breaking down, Eve's tears fall uncontrollably as she loses all self-control.

"I'll tell you what's happened." Slowly placing one foot in front of the other, Eve moves closer to Lucy, who's nervously stepping back. Continuing with her intimidating tone, Eve's pointing her finger directly towards Lucy's face. "Not only has he brought this woman to our table, my mum's table, he's invited her to *our* home!"

Lucy's gob-smacked, but not at Matthew's schoolboy tactics, at Eve's level of anger to this apparent innocent gesture. Appearing more and more upset by the second, Eve can't control it anymore and she falls to the floor. Rushing to heal her, Lucy cradles Eve tight whilst kissing her gently on the head. She whispers to her words meant from the heart, "Please calm down – Eve, I don't like seeing you this way and, well, do you not think you might just be overreacting slightly?"

Taking immediate offence to the spoken words, Eve stands up, pushes Lucy away and once again begins shouting. This time, her face turns red with anger, and saliva flies from out of her mouth as she loses control of her actions and emotions.

"Overreacting! Two minutes in her presence and he's forgotten all about my mum…"

Lucy, looking stunned, is riddled with nerves; she doesn't know what to say or do. She's never seen Eve this mad. Giving up, Lucy knows she's powerless to help. As she turns away, she says, "I'm going to get Matthew."

A fierce heartbroken Eve shouts, "Yeah right! Good luck with that."

Appearing from out of the café, Matthew's looking somewhat rushed and, as he turns, he sees Eve stood at the car. Admittedly, he was shocked at her appearance. Her eyes are completely swollen from the tears he can see falling down her face.

"Darling, there you are…"

Lucy passes him and says, "Good luck." Walking through the door and heading back into the café, she's feeling slightly relieved that she's no longer in the middle of such drama. Eve looks to her dad. He's seen this expression before, it's the look of doom. Pointing her finger once more, Eve says, "Don't you dare try, and act concerned about where *I am*."

Instantly devastated by these words, Matthew's looking across to his daughter, who is almost unrecognisable from the girl he woke to this morning, the girl who was so full of happiness and life; he feels at a complete loss. She's stood looking as though she's been possessed by the devil. Trying to calm the situation, but failing miserably, Matthew says, "Eve – please, we really don't have time for this."

With her blood boiling and her head beginning to hurt from all the rage and shouting, Eve no longer has any desire to engage in a conversation with her dad. She's filled with hurt and fury. Wiping her face with frustration, she gets in the car. The energy, the emotions, the atmosphere, is the complete opposite from earlier – and this time, when they both get in the car, there's no exchanging pleasantries. The doors are slammed, the radio is off and the vibrational energy that's forcing itself from their physical forms becomes present in the car. More distant than ever and with an awkward silence manifesting itself as they begin to drive past the café, they're both wrapped up in their own hurt and are totally unaware that Jess is at the café window watching them drive away.

She's peering through the gaps of the leaflets and posters stuck on the glass. With a somewhat cagey and proud expression upon her face, her eyes begin to spark. They're lighting up and appear to have an air of secrecy hidden within them. Holding onto the locket around her neck, she begins twiddling this between her fingers. Jess's expression is dark, mysterious, and satisfied, with a deceitful smirk presenting itself upon her face, as both Matthew and Eve are completely unaware of her empowerment over the magnetic pull she has. Embracing the level of negative energy, she's created between these two tightly bonded individuals, Jess appears extremely content – but why? As the car slowly travels past the window of the café, her sole attention and focus is on Eve. Her eyes begin changing as they darken. With an eerie mist forming spontaneously, Jess tilts her head conceitedly, as both Matthew and Eve go out of sight.

***

Meanwhile, in the car, both Matthew and Eve are deep in thought. It's extremely awkward and no-one desires to upset or hurt the other anymore than they already are, so they both choose to say nothing. As the clock ticks and the silence becomes somewhat deafening, the further apart emotionally these two are becoming. Continuing with a stubborn stance, it seems impossible for either of them to make the first move towards correcting this. Matthew and Eve are very much stuck in this process. Like a Mexican standoff, they've both decided to continue with their protest, shut down, switch off and dismiss one another. With their energy now supressed, you can see the confusion and the pain. How did they get to this point? They were fine less than an hour ago and now, you would think these two are strangers.

The birds are remaining at a great height flying freely in the sky and the only visualisation process Eve endures with this new tainted mind-set is seeing her mum's beautiful face present in the clouds as she's gliding down the side of the huge mountain. Embracing every drop as she's flying free, and making her way to the bottom, suddenly, with her final descent she *hits* the rocks, head first; she's feeling content at the sight of her death. Eve's filled with rage and hurt and has mentally taken ten steps back. Her sole desire is to free herself from this misery she must now call life. With her current dark thought process, Eve can't help but think this would be her best solution, at least this way, if she did free herself and commit suicide, she would once again be reunited with her mum.

The barrier lifts. Matthew pulls into the huge corporate-built car park. Driving round he eventually finds a space and parks up. Turning off the engine, Matthew looks to Eve, who hasn't even attempted to make eye contact with him throughout the whole fifteen-minute journey, which feels more like an hour. Matthew's looking to his daughter in the hope that she's snapped out of her mood as he says, "You ready?"

Eve, not warranting her dad the satisfaction of eye contact, is staring out the window; she says, loud enough for him to hear, "No – I'm staying here."

"What? This meeting was booked with the attendance of us both – Eve, as you know sometimes life throws things at us, but what you have to do is carry on." Leaning across to Eve he continues, "Darling, this is the real world now. Come on kidda, it's a simple meeting and I promise it won't take long. Just snap out of whatever this is and come in with me." Attempting to lighten the mood he says, "You can see what it's like behind the scenes of the Honey Empire, ready for when you take the reins one day."

"What, the empire you built with *my* mum? I said I'm staying here, end of!"

"Yes, me and *your* mum built this together. We did this for *you,* Evelyn Jade. So that *you* would have the best start and future." Feeling as though he's not standing a chance, Matthew continues, "Oh, Eve, why must you be so stubborn?"

"Stubborn! Just keep the insults coming why don't you, Dad? I said I'm staying here, I don't want to come to your poxy meeting, I don't want to watch *you* with another woman, and I certainly don't want to go in there and smile to a bunch of people I don't care about and watch *you* acting like everything's okay. Well, it's not *okay,* Dad!"

"Right, well this is what pays the bills, Eve, and your music lessons, and holidays and everything else you want —so I *must* attend this meeting. Like I said before, I won't be long."

Standing out of the car, Matthew *slams* the door and begins correcting his suit. Heading to the back of the car he grabs his briefcase from off the back seat, takes a huge deep breath in and as he, this time gently, shuts the car door he shakes his head. Matthew sets about crossing the busy car park and makes his way towards the building. Once again, Eve doesn't flinch in her dad's direction.

Now alone with her thoughts, she reaches for the cream, leather-covered glove compartment and pulls the catch to open this. Rummaging around, she begins lifting the papers present at the front. Moving them in no order, she grabs an old-looking, brown leather-backed book. Gazing at this in her hands, she triggers a memory which was stored away in her mind and for the second time today, she begins to relive a flashback of a counselling session.

Once again, she can see Josie sat in her usual high-back Chesterfield chair. This time, she's sat on the L-shaped couch across from her looking thin, pale, withdrawn and exhausted. Eve feels the moment as though she is living it for the first time today; her energy levels are low, and she just has enough oomph to listen to what is being said.

"Eve, there is huge importance when it comes to writing out your frustration. The pen to paper technique is the best process for everyone when it comes to healing – the idea behind using a pen, instead of typing, is that with every unique movement that your hand makes, you activate cells within your brain and, as these cells activate, your mind is caused to think. You are, in effect, distracting yourself and your mind from the aggression you have built. Once you have created this distraction, your mind will naturally begin to release the pent-up anger as you write each word. I encourage you, Eve, to always have a pen and paper easily accessible – this will help inspire you to write down any negative thoughts that you are either holding on to or creating within your mind. The best way to think of this technique is as though you are painting the picture that's being held in your mind. The images you see through your sight, and the anger you feel, you can let go of, but instead of painting the picture in a drawing you're painting the picture in words. Words create thoughts."

Ensuring she's getting through to Eve, who appears numb and trance-like, Josie continues, "Eve, it doesn't matter if only *you* can understand what's written – as long as you are thinking, hearing and releasing the words as you write them, you will begin to free the anger from your mind whilst at the same time letting go of your attachment to this."

In this vision, you can see Josie is once again desperately attempting to rebuild this broken young girl.

Opening the leather-backed book, Eve begins turning the pages, quickly flicking through. Flying by one after the other are multiple yellow pages with black lines and masses of writing on each page. Every word has been written in scrawling joined writing with blue ink. Without acknowledging the content on the pages, she reaches a blank page. Taking out her blue pen from the glove compartment she writes the following:

So, today's the day, I knew this would come, the day dad forgets all about you and moves on, like you never existed, like you're not a part of me too. Why should I have to sit and watch him forget that you were ever part of our lives?

If he carries this on Mum, I promise you, I'm coming, I will join you in the afterlife.

I can't be expected to live a lie whilst having to watch him playing happy families with another woman. I'm just not strong enough Mum, you know that, and you're not even here, so how can Dad not?

Argh, why's Dad being a complete dick? Mum why did you have to leave us?

I hate myself! Why did you have to go?

Dropping the pen on the page, she immediately raises her head to the sky. Getting teary-eyed, she knows her mum isn't coming back and unless she commits suicide and the afterlife is real, she isn't going to be reunited with her anytime soon.

An emotional wreck, Eve's now feeling powerless and broken. She's uncontrollably shedding tears. Each pear-shaped drop contains her pain and as these begin to fall down her face, quicker than the rain travels from the sky and hits the ground on a stormy night. Eve's becoming more and more inconsolable by the second. She picks up her pen, looks to the page, which is now holding her tears, and writes these four heart-breaking words:

It's all my fault!

***

Time passes quickly, and soon enough Matthew appears from out of the building. Eve becomes uncomfortable; she doesn't want her dad to see her this way and is desperately trying to hide her depression and compose herself. She shoves the book and the pen back in to the glove compartment, slamming the door shut. She flicks down the sun visor on the car, slides back the small cover and reveals the tiny hidden mirror. Staring at her pale blotchy face, Eve frantically tries to disguise the redness as she quickly wipes her eyes. Without success, she reaches to the side of the car door and pulls out her huge expensive designer black sunglasses with gold trimming; she places these on her face in a last-ditch attempt to disguise her suffering.

With her elbow on the window ledge of the car door again, this time she isn't full of life. She's resting her forehead in the palm of her hand. Hiding her inner expression of sheer hopelessness, Eve would love nothing more than for her mum to magically appear.

Matthew approaches the car; he can see Eve's wearing her sunglasses. Immediately, he's aware she must have been crying. When Eve would leave her counselling sessions with Josie, she routinely wore her sunglasses in an attempt to hide her sorrow. She doesn't think her dad noticed, but of course he did, he's her dad. Matthew gets in the car and endeavours to make conversation with Eve, but deep down, he doesn't hold out much hope. With his voice low Matthew says, "Evelyn Jade Honey – please speak to me." Looking across at his daughter with complete despair and helplessness, he continues, "Why did you react that way in the café?"

Eve's still withdrawn and not ready to speak as she continues to look out of the window. Matthew's trying hard not to copy her actions. He continues to look to his daughter.

"I can't help you if you don't open up to me..."

Eve's still listening to her inner voice.

Don't fall for it Eve, he's trying to sweet talk you. Remember, he didn't chase you out the café. No, he stayed and gave her your home address. You're right, he's wrong, don't answer him.

The inner voice, which is vulgar and present in Eve's mind, is getting louder and louder as she tunes in and receives the words it's feeding her. Choosing to take the advice, Eve remains withdrawn. Matthew once again attempts to speak to her, even with the present rebellion shut down; reaching out, he says, "Darling, please – you should know there isn't a woman in the universe who could replace your mum.

I ask you, Evelyn Jade, can I not have a female friend?"

Still Matthew receives no response from Eve. He begins to sigh as he looks down at the floor of the car, his head now hanging low and heavy. Matthew doesn't want to give up, but he also doesn't know what to do, or where to turn. What he is clear on is that his daughter is seriously unhappy at the thought of him potentially becoming happy. Is he supposed to be alone forever? Matthew starts the car. Reaching out to put this into first gear, as he looks up, small raindrops begin to hit the windscreen one after the other. The clouds suddenly become overcast and dark. Looking to his left with sorrow deep in his eyes, the same eyes which this morning were filled with life and love as he was sharing precious moments with his blessing, his best friend, his Eve, he can't help but feel an overwhelming surge of inner sadness. No more smiles, no more laughter. She's staring out the window and no longer acknowledging his existence.

Eve hasn't moved an inch since her dad entered the car. With her sunglasses on she appears to be looking into a dark abyss and is deep in thought. Matthew notices a tear roll down her cheek, which she's very quick to wipe away.

What does he do? He really hasn't got a clue; reversing out of the parking space Matthew prays the answers will be shown to him.

Chapter 4
"The arrival"

Back at the house, Matthew's decided he's putting all his energy into this evening; he's confident Eve will snap out of her mood soon. Getting excited at the thought of actually having a date, after being alone for so long, internally he's feeling amazing. Present in the airy, brand-new, bright white painted kitchen, Matthew's surrounded by pots and pans. He's got the radio on and appears to be dancing away in what can only be described as an embarrassing dad-like fashion. Wearing his relaxing casual clothes under his macho pinafore, he's excited, and he's immensely happy, even after the day's events, and he's completely enjoying the moment alone.

Making his way over to the fridge he grabs the grey metal tray containing four large seasoned raw chicken breasts. Reaching into the drawer at the side of the fridge, he pulls out his white latex gloves. Pulling these onto his hands, he sets about dicing the chicken on the red meat chopping board. With the oven being preheated, the accompanying ingredients have also been diced and are lay neatly on the black marble surface top, on the grey kitchen island. Matthew's a sufferer of OCD (Obsessive Compulsive Disorder); this means everything must be colour coded and have its own place. The red peppers are chopped with precision, perfection, and are organised into a neat little pile, as are the green peppers, mushrooms, herb-coated new potatoes and red onions. Grabbing a frying pan from the oversized matte black hanging pot rack, which is hovering at a distance above his head, he makes his way over to the huge modern built-in black Range cooker and begins frying the chicken. With his thoughts beginning to drift he wonders how this evening is going to progress. Would it get worse, would it get better, would they discover family life is again complete and live in blissful harmony? Who knows...

With the radio still blaring throughout the kitchen, Matthew's shaking his extremely toned butt, dancing and singing along. Whilst Matthew's showing his best Salt and Pepa tribute routine to the chicken in the frying pan, Eve's in her room; she's decided that she's taking no part in the charade her dad is creating downstairs. Sat in her room, which is bright, clean and filled with all her favourite things, she's remaining in complete silence. Each wall in her room is the same as every wall in the house. Painted only with the purest white. The only colour present within the room is on the curtains that hang off the pole; her floral bedsheets and the small mosaic of photographs she's created over her bed, of her and her mum in the shape of a heart. She also has a small en-suite in her room which contains a shower cubicle, toilet and a small white ceramic sink, which has a mirror above it, also in the shape of a heart. Next to the en-suite is a balcony which overlooks the sea.

Sat on her neatly made bed wearing her ripped jeans and grey casual t-shirt, Eve's holding a scruffy-looking brown teddy bear. He has a grubby red and white polka dot bow-tie around his neck. You can tell this delicate bear has been smothered with love by the wear and tear present on his fluffy existence. As she holds him tightly to her chest, you can see he has half his right ear missing and stuffing sticking out of his black button eyes. This is one of her most cherished possessions. The bear she holds so tightly and smothers with love was her mum's. His name is Gregg. This scruffy bear had known her mum longer than any of them; he was a gift from *her* grandmother when she was born. Her mum treasured Gregg always, and even when Eve was a child, she would never let her play with the delicate bear for fear that he would fall apart even more. When her mum died, both Matthew and Eve were sorting through all her possessions. Eve found Gregg tucked away in a shoebox, wrapped in gold tissue paper. As she lifted him out, she saw his features; they were a true reflection of her emotions. With Gregg lay in her hands looking sad, lost and lonely, she couldn't help it. Immediately she broke down crying. Gregg had lost his owner too. Eve's kept him close ever since. She now has her own personal strong connection with Gregg, just like her mum. Looking into his deep black button eyes, she says, "I never meant for any of this to happen."

When we think about losing a loved one, we instantly believe because we love them, we will have the opportunity to say goodbye before their life has gone, before the light goes out and they take their last living breath. Well, this is definitely a presumption that we hold in our minds. How would you feel if this perception was taken from you? What if *you* couldn't say goodbye to a loved one, a loved one you spent all your life connecting with? As an added extra, what if this person was the only person on the planet who helped *you* become who *you* are today? They taught you to walk, they taught, you to talk and they gave you every life lesson you had learned. Not only all of that, this person was supposed to be the main figure in every big event of your life. Including your wedding day, promotions in your career, or even the first time you would potentially have a child of your own. *You* never got to say goodbye, before their last living breath was taken...

Would you be angry, would you dislike the world and everyone in it?

Lauren Honey didn't die due to Mother Nature, she wasn't struck down with an illness, it wasn't a long process that everyone's mind could get used to before the inevitable happened. Lauren was in fact *killed*.

It's now seven thirty in the evening. The doorbell begins ringing loudly throughout the Honey household. Matthew's dressed casual/smart, with his dark denim designer jeans on, navy-blue shirt and deep navy-blue blazer jacket. Dressed to impress, he walks out of the kitchen. Slicking the sides of his hair back with both his hands, he appears to be in a slight fluster; his palms are sweating, and he sets about giving himself a pep talk whilst making his way to the door.

"Just be yourself Matthew. Just be yourself."

At the bottom of the stairs there's a grand floor-length mirror, which stands strong with its thick, metal-gold trimming, and is perfectly placed next to the front door. Lauren chose the majority of the decor items within the house; this item was her favourite. She had a very keen eye for interior design and she loved how this particular mirror opened up the doorway.

With just enough time to check himself out in the mirror, as he's straightening himself up, he can't help but look at his reflection and see the truth: he may be externally oozing confidence, but internally he's anxious, apprehensive and nervous. Still confused and struggling to work out what's so captivating about this woman, he can't help himself; Matthew feels like a teenager all over again. Butterflies in his stomach and hope in his heart. Hope, faith, belief that destiny and fate may not have forgotten about him after all. He understands and accepts that he will never have another soul mate, you only get one, but sometimes he gets lonely and longs for that wonderful adult connection. He knows Eve will one day grow and live a blessed life with another, and rightly so: this is what he desires for her to have, a life of freedom.

So, what would be left for him? Matthew would love to be able to share his journey with another person again; was this her? Before he knows it, he's answering the door.

With the darkness gently beginning to fall, standing there gazing back at Matthew with smiles on their faces and bright beady eyes, are two Jehovah's Witnesses. They're both wearing matching black and white suits. He can see the thick black straps hanging over each shoulder from the backpacks on their backs. They both have similar short-cut neat hairstyles. Matthew notices that not only is their appearance strangely mirroring one another, like identical twins, but they both appear to be holding the same items in the same manner in both of their hands. In one hand, they each hold a Bible and in the other, they hold an equal chunk of leaflets. One of the friendly looking gents speaks up. With his confident and loud tone, he says, "Sir, do you have a moment to talk about our Lord Christ the saviour?"

"Erm, sorry lads, I'm a bit busy right now."

"We promise sir, we'll only take a moment of your t..."

Before he finishes his sentence they both unexpectedly *freeze.* Standing as stiff as a board and in sync with each other, the silky leaflets they are both holding release from their hands and drop on the floor. Again, in sync with each other, they both instantly cling to the Bible and hold onto this tightly with both hands. Moving his head back slightly, Matthew's looking confused at this random unexpected action. Both the Jehovah's Witnesses now have their eyelids wide open. It looks as though their eyes are beginning to protrude from out of their sockets. Without any explanation, they slowly start to walk backwards and in an almost robotic-sounding manner, the Jehovah's Witness who hasn't yet spoken says, "We're sorry to disturb you sir. You have a pleasant, erm, evening now."

With their smart, immaculate, black shoes, they begin placing one foot behind the other and continue to *slowly* walk backwards. The pair, still clinging to the Bible, *do not* make any attempt to turn around. Without breaking eye contact with Matthew, they suddenly disappear out of sight.

"You forgot your leaflets." Bending down to pick these up, he begins shaking his head. "That was weird..."

He looks at the leaflets; they're pale blue with a picture of the clearest sky. Spread out in the middle of the clouds, in white bold font, is a slogan which reads: "Why you can trust the bible: One man died for us all." Standing strong and proudly towards the bottom of the leaflet is a white cross. Attentively, Matthew begins staring out into the darkness. Stepping backwards into the house, as he reaches to shut the door, he looks up and sees an outline approaching him. No longer concentrating and assuming it's the return of the Jehovah's Witnesses for the collection of their leaflets, he says, "Ah, here you go, gents." But he gets no reply.

Confused, he begins concentrating on the outline that's making its way towards him. He can see a single figure. It's Jess. She's standing tall and making her way up the path with a smile on her face. Her lips are painted red and her long dark-brown hair is beautifully styled and blowing in the breeze. Looking glamourous, stunning and wearing a tight-fitted red dress which sits perfectly around her waist and hips. The material is hugging her figure with perfection. This woman is oozing elegance; Matthew *is* captivated. I'm not sure there is anything at this point that could stop this man from falling in immediate love with this woman; like a love-struck boy, he's hooked.

As he locks eyes with Jess, again he's speechless. Her eye colour is the deepest shade of brown, but when she locks eyes with him, they go so intense, they spark and almost look as though they're turning an enticing shade of black. Completely unaware of this sudden change, Matthew's mesmerised. In an extremely flirtatious manner, Jess is standing looking back at Matthew who is again, for the second time today, staring at her.

"Good evening Matthew."

Obsessed, the only word his mind can process is, "Hi..."

Proud, confident and satisfied with his reaction to her presence, she immediately responds, "Well – are you going to invite me in, or are we eating outside?"

Finally, snapping out of his trance, with a slight stutter he speaks words of sense: "Sorry, erm, yes, please, come in."

Clutching a sliver clasp bag and wearing strappy silver three-inch stiletto heels, she elegantly places one foot in front of the other, and with an air of sophistication and empowerment, she enters the house. Her walk is captivating. As he closes the door Matthew says, "Eve has decided she won't be joining us this evening."

Not looking too concerned, she replies, "Don't worry, I'm sure she's seen enough of me for one day."

Matthew begins looking embarrassed.

"Honestly, she really is a beautiful girl inside and out. I know you two would really get on."

Staying quiet, she looks to him with a whatever-you-say kind of expression.

"She's never rude to anyone – actually, I haven't seen her like that before. Even after everything we've been through, she's never been that rude to another person."

Jess starts to laugh, "Should I feel honoured then?"

Matthew decides it's best to get off the subject of Eve and he invites her into the dining room.

"Would you like a glass of wine?" Trying to be funny, he makes a joke. "Or does this taste too much like wine?"

"Wine would be great. Thank you."

Entering the kitchen, he returns with a bottle of rosé.

"My favourite wine. Have you been secretly spying on me, Mr Honey?"

Blushing at this coincidence, he replies, "No, I only stalk people on the weekend."

In the midst of his schoolboy mentality, Matthew's missed one important thing. He failed to notice Jess referred to him by his surname. How does she know this? During their brief encounter today, he had only told her both his and Eve's first name. Is this a clue that things may not be as they seem, and he's just missed it? *Tough luck,* Matthew.

Suddenly, they hear a bang and immediately both Matthew and Jess look up towards the door they've just walked through. Matthew shouts, "Eve!" There's no reply.

Excusing himself, he heads over to the front door. Opening this, he shouts once again, "Eve..." Still he gets nothing back.

Matthew's standing on the grey cold concrete step outside the door. Wearing nothing but his black socks on his feet, he hears the sound of the sea coming from the beach as the waves gently flow one after the other. The tide's now coming in and the salty water can be smelt within the air. Looking out, Matthew can't see a single person.

Continuing her protest, Eve's now half way down the street. Marching down the pathways at a speedy pace, she's made her decision: she doesn't like this woman and can't explain why, all she knows is something just doesn't feel right. Eve has absolutely no desire to be in Jess's presence. She's got her backpack on and even though she knows it's going to get even darker very soon, she doesn't care. She's on a mission and nothing is going to get in her way.

When her mum died, to occupy her mind and feel a sense of meaning on this planet, Eve created "Lauren's Garden of Secrets" so she always has somewhere to go and be alone with her thoughts and alone with her mum. Each time she heads here with just one intention – to feel her mum's presence and speak to her whilst also, if required, letting off some steam. Eve asks for guidance, help, love and support from the presence of the spiritual world surrounding her, with belief and faith that it's her mum's spiritual influence. This healing process may not be for everyone and sometimes passers-by look at her like she's insane as she moves around in frustration, trying desperately to gain some form of understanding. She doesn't always receive the answers she wants, but this process helps her walk away with some form of clarity. Eve knew after today's events and what was currently taking place in the house, "Lauren's Garden of Secrets" is the only location she desires to be and so this is where she is heading at full speed.

Eve's on a self-healing mission. The street lights are shining brightly and as she passes directly under them they begin lighting up her face. Showcasing the truth, you can see Eve's features clearly: she's bright red, huffing, puffing, and fast becoming out of breath. Wearing her light denim ripped jeans, black school leavers hoodie and her hiking trainers, she's walking at a rapid rate with her backpack hanging low off her shoulders. Tatty brown suede with brightly coloured badges sown on the side, her backpack contains the following: her number-one treasured possession, a picture of her and her mum. This picture holds extra value. At least once every two months they would dedicate a day where they spent time together, doing anything they both enjoyed.

The jam-packed action days would range from paint balling and theme parks to spa days and fashion shows. Well, this picture was very special and irreplaceable. The camera flashed, and the picture was taken on their last ever mum and daughter day. It was *exactly* two weeks before the murder of her mum.

Present in the picture, you can see half of Eve's innocent, vibrant life-fuelled face. Half her smile and her bright, long shiny hair. She's holding the phone to take a selfie-styled image at their favourite spa and restaurant. In the background, her mum sat up high on a black leather massage bed, with her legs resting well and her feet off the floor – her dark chocolate long brown hair, which is styled to perfection, is draped over her shoulders and is complemented by the white fluffy night coat she's wearing. And, of course, *no* spa outfit would be completed without matching slippers. Eve's wearing the same.

Holding a glass of champagne in her left hand, the first thing you see when you look at this image, is Lauren's beautiful, white, beaming smile, full of life, full of hope and radiating love. You can't help but grin from ear to ear when you initially see this picture for its natural beauty. That all changes when you know the situation and the picture begins to represent something totally different. You suddenly can't help but feel an overwhelming surge of sadness over the loss of this beautiful woman, mother and soul.

Also present in the backpack and sitting next to the picture is the bow-tied teddy bear, Gregg, along with Eve's diary and a blue pen. Ideally, Eve didn't want to return to the house until Jess had left, but she must be home no later than ten p.m. With both her hands holding onto the straps of her backpack, Eve suddenly becomes full of an intense sense of anger and is raging with aggression; she can't hold the words in any longer, she begins talking to herself out loud: "Why is Dad putting me in this position? I don't understand. Was I not loud enough? I showed him. I am not ready to deal with the replacement of Mum. Why is he ignoring this?"

Taking a deep breath in and still without answers, Eve slowly begins counting back from five and calming slightly. Becoming less irritated with every inch she gets further away from home and closer to her destination, as she looks to the sky, Eve speaks to the stars, questioning the universe: "Is this how it's supposed to be? Am I supposed to sit back and watch my dad forget all about my mum – and then what, just move on like she never existed? Am I expected to play happy families with another woman? Oh, hello stepmum, yes, my day's been amazing what about yours? Yeah, right, like I care, just saying it doesn't feel right! Why are you doing this to me?"

Puzzled, alone and running out of energy, her aggression begins to subside her head throbs. Feeling a deep, inner sense of grief, Eve continues speaking out loud: "I've just lost one parent; do I really have to go through it all again? I've just started to have a *normal* relationship with my dad. A real father-daughter relationship; you should know I've not had that since being little. I ask you, universe – have you given him his wish, is my dad truly going to risk losing me for a woman he's just met?"

Eve's walking pace slows down with this puzzled question present in her thoughts. Staring at the floor as she's placing one foot in front of the other, Eve's mind begins projecting a flashback through the windows of her eyes. She sees clearly in her mind an image of her dad. He's a broken man sat on a brown, mahogany, wooden bench, wearing a black suit with a small artificial sunflower tucked in the pocket on the front of his jacket. This flashback that has chosen to surface is at her mum's funeral.

Her dad's uncontrollably sobbing. Reaching out, Eve begins holding him tightly in both her arms – placing his head close to her heart. She's wearing the silver chain and heart-shaped locket round her neck. Eve rests her chin in her dad's hair; she's almost cradling him, as tears begin to roll repeatedly down her face.

Sat in a huge church with its extravagant multicoloured stained-glass window panes, Eve is surrounded by relatives and loved ones. She's breathing deep and remaining in complete disbelief and shock; the harsh reality is, it's her precious mum lying lifeless in the box in front of her. Unable to control her emotions anymore and unable to console this broken man in her arms, she quickly releases him and begins to run over to the coffin.

This vision presenting itself within Eve's mind is extremely real; she can see every crease of her expression, which is pained – it almost looks nothing like her, she is that exhausted. Eve has allowed her emotions to take full control, and before she has time to process her actions, she's heading towards the coffin with tears streaming from her eyes and fluid uncontrollably gushing from her nose. Her face is entirely swollen. Eve can barely see the ground beneath her feet let alone what's in front of her. But what she can see, as clear as the daylight outside, is the white coffin which holds her mum's lifeless body. In utter desperation and not wanting to accept the reality, she kicks out and screeches, "Noooooooo…"

At the centre of the ceremony and the main focus of the church, standing strong on the platform, is the white wooden coffin. It's surrounded by beautiful, bright sunflowers and is beaming radiantly like the sun in all its glory. With yellow and orange luminous bouquets sharing their natural glow, the vision is stunningly warm, angelic, and yet, the energy, the mood, the vibration is the complete opposite. Approaching the platform, Eve begins reaching out and in her desperate attempt to grab the coffin, suddenly she's stopped. Being forcefully turned around, Eve sees it's her mum's twin sister. Her auntie Christina. Wearing black from head to toe, she has a black netted veil draped across her face. Instantly grabbing Eve, she begins holding her tightly in an attempt to console this young vulnerable soul. Whispering in Eve's ear. "Ssshhhhhhh…"

Collapsing on the floor, and falling with Eve, Christina is trying to stay strong and she's now more desperate than ever to help comfort this broken young girl. Whispering once more into Eve's ear she says, "Sshhh… My child, my precious Eve, I know your pain – she was once my only best friend too."

With these words, Eve is crumbled and starts rocking back and forth. She's inconsolable and begins screaming out in pain, "Why? Please come back to me. I'm sorry! Mum… I said I'm sorry – I never meant for this to happen… Please God, take me instead."

Quickly shaking this vision out of her head, Eve's back in her existing reality as she pushes this painful flashback out of her mind. Continuing to march down the streets, Eve wipes the tears off her face as she proceeds with her mission. Walking at an even faster pace, her breathing is getting quicker and quicker as her heartrate increases. Feeling a wrench in her stomach as her mental attention passes to another flashback, Eve begins to see a visual and again, it's of her dad.

They're at home in the day room. With a glass of red wine in his hand, Matthew's sat on the brown cosy couch surrounded by beige decorative cushions either side. He's talking away to Eve, as she's sat on the floor, but this time he has happiness in his features and a smile on his face. They are surrounded by pictures and boxes which have old photographs flowing out of them. She can smell the dampness of the boxes next to her and can see the scuffs on the edges where they've been banged about and stored away for years, transferred from home to home.

Embracing the moment with her dad, she sees and feels he's happiness as he's relaxing with a half-full glass of wine. The room is warm and cosy as the flames on the fire are flickering away spreading its natural glow. Getting excited and almost spilling his red wine, Matthew's on the couch sharing stories with her of the adventures he enjoyed with her mum. The photographs are endless. With so many memories and so many wonderful times, she's enjoying the vision of her dad looking extremely joyful and smiling away. She can see him reliving the moment in each picture, for its uniqueness, as though it was happening today. This makes her genuinely smile.

Snapping out of her vision and remaining confused, Eve looks to the ground as the memory disappears from her mind. Trying to work out why her dad is risking losing what they have built for some woman he's known for a matter of hours, Eve's unable to answer this. With her heart rate speeding up and completely out of breath, she's exhausted, and at the same time, relieved, as she finally arrives at her destination, "Lauren's Garden of Secrets."

A simple placement of a wooden bench, standing strong and positioned beautifully at the top of a hill, surrounded by nature's very own constructed unique rocks, the scene is simple, yet stunning. Crafted with picturesque varied shades of green, it's as though the creator of this huge earthly hill copied a patchwork theme design.

Ordinarily at the height of the day, you can see the clouds pass by if you stay still for long enough. The soil is mixed beautifully with different tones and shades of brown. In some areas, it becomes almost golden when the sun is out, spreading its glow. Mother Nature is such a calming resemblance of life – and this hill is a vision of our existence, it's presence gives us an awareness of the beauty that surrounds us every single day. If you truly look and take in the surroundings of nature, in one tiny snapshot of the world, you can't help it, you'll begin to feel a true sense of gratitude for how magnificent the planet we live on truly is, and how blessed you are to have been selected as a participant.

This is something young Eve never struggled with embracing. She knew she was blessed, she knew the importance of life, and, well, now she struggles to feel and embrace any part of her existence. Eve understood she was extremely lucky to have both her parents together. Not only did they remain together, they still shared love for one another as strong as the day they first met. A functioning, joyous, solid family unit and a true place to call home. She had friends that weren't so lucky and fortunate. Fate had different plans for their upbringing and most of them grew up in broken homes. They always adapted well; it was a normal way of life for them. They accepted that their parents didn't like each other, and it didn't faze them. I mean, of course they would have loved nothing more than to live a life with Mum and Dad, at least that way they wouldn't have to deal with the messy bits in between, but they couldn't change this.

The reality is, today it has become socially hard for two adults to form a relationship, share a strong bond, raise a family, all whilst building careers and attempting to live happily ever after. Eve would see her friends leave and spend the odd weekend with Dad, whilst living with Mum. Some, although rare, would live the opposite way around and live with Dad whilst spending the weekend with Mum.

Today's world is modern and many of her friends would have to deal with step parents, some of which, might I add, would see her friends as an inconvenience and didn't embrace the relationship they had with their parent.

When her mum died, Eve shut out all her friends. She felt they didn't appreciate how different her circumstance were to theirs. How could they even begin to compare to what she must deal with? She would often get annoyed and shout to her friends, "It is *not* the same!", as they would try and sympathise with her.

Okay, yes, Eve has a broken home – yes, she is no longer part of the two-parent family make-up, but this wasn't through her parents choosing to separate. They didn't have a huge falling out and the main point of all this is she doesn't have the opportunity to see both her parents – they do.

Eve, a young soul who once embraced life, felt blessed and was filled with gratitude, quickly slipped, and now with her present reality, which isn't a blessing, she feels cursed and bitter.

Sitting peacefully on the bench, Eve smells the purity of the air as she's looking out to the multiple shadows of the hills surrounding her. Slowly it begins to get darker. Visually she can make out the black outlines of the strong standing trees. It's still, quiet and not a tree leans out of order. Placing her backpack on the floor next to her, Eve opens this, removing the picture of her and her mum. Holding this tightly in her hand she begins gazing up at the sky. The stars align, forming a strong stance, and are beginning to glisten gently in the distance. The universe is such a beautiful place. All Eve sees is freedom. Speaking to the brightest star she can find she says, "Which one are you? – Hmm, I know – the one that shines the brightest, that's you, Mum."

Looking down at her mum's beautiful face in the picture she smiles as a tear falls on the glass that's protecting the image. She's been to 'Lauren's Garden of Secrets' more times than you could count in the past three years. Feeling cursed and suicidal, sometimes all she's wanted to do is run and jump off the edge of the hill.

Closing her eyes, she begins to visualise the surroundings she's present in, but it's daylight. Using her imagination, she can see a very clear image in her mind – it's her!

She's sat on the bench with the tatty brown suede backpack on the ground next to her. Suddenly, her body stands; holding the picture tightly in her hand and without a single tear down her face, Eve walks to the edge of the hill. She curiously leans over the side and begins to look down. The drop is at least one thousand feet and as the hill gracefully slopes, her vision is clear, and she can see how dangerously steep this is. The ground surrounding has rocks scattered all the way down and a huge amount are resting in a plie at the bottom. This beautiful vision has her captivated.

Becoming extremely intrigued as she's peering over, Eve's looking deeper and deeper as an abyss of the darkness forms in her mind. Heading back to the bench. Unexpectedly, she turns back towards the edge of the hill and without so much of a second thought, she quickly runs towards the edge – as she takes every step with a smile on her face, and as her feet hit the ground, Eve's shouting, "I'm coming for you, Mum!"

Using all her might she bends her knees, leans onto her toes and, bouncing like a spring, she jumps straight off the edge of the hill. Reaching up to grab the clouds present in the bright blue sky, she hasn't felt this free for so long. She's done it, she's over the edge and totally unfazed by the irreversible consequences of this action. Now diving head first with her arms out resembling wings, with the picture of her and her mum still present in her hand, gliding like a bird, Eve's finally free. Free from the life she'd been forced to learn to live. Smiling, laughing and embracing the air that's hitting her face, Eve gracefully glides down this magnificent hill and is accepting each second as the breeze gently kisses her face.

But, just before she hits the rocks at the bottom, she releases her mind from the visualisation process and opens her eyes. She's still sat on the bench, she isn't over the edge and it isn't daylight. Looking down at the picture in her hand, Eve feels sadness and sorrow. The only thing that has ever stopped her from committing suicide is the unknown impact on her dad. Surely, he would suffer even more. Unanswerable questions begin racing in her mind.

How will Dad cope, how will Dad deal with not only losing his wife, but losing the only person in his life who has a connection to her, me?

Eve cares so much about her dad she chooses not to kill herself. Although she closes her eyes from time to time and visualises the run and jump, embracing how free she feels in her mind as her body makes its way down to the ground, this is nothing more than a thought.

A sense of how to feel free when you're completely trapped in an existence you just want to run away from.

Chapter 5
"What happened?"

Back at the house, Matthew is unaware of how low his daughter is feeling and he's unalarmed about the severity of her current mental state. He's been here so many times before, where Eve's stormed out of the house, and he knows she will come back home no later than her curfew time.

With the food progressively cooking, Matthew's homemade specialty is thickening in the oven and the fragrance of chicken and casserole juices can be smelt throughout the whole house. This strong natural scent travels round the building, making it cosy, warm, and leaves it feeling once again like a family home. Present in the dining room, Matthew and Jess are surrounded by walls that have been painted with the purest white. The only colour present in the room is on the expensive, thick gold curtains, hanging heavy either side of the double doors, leading to just one of the many balconies they have overlooking the crisp English sea. Perfectly central and hanging from the ceiling is an extravagant diamond chandelier. With its strong structure, this magnificent unique interior-designed addition to the room is hanging and spreading warmth as the tiny reflections from the LED lights are scattering on the walls and are lighting up the room as they glow like stars.

Both Matthew and Jess are sat at the luxurious, solid wooden table, which is surrounded by six high-back, expensive, black-leather chairs. There's three on either side of the table and four of them are identically parallel to each other. Matthew and Jess sit comfortably on the other two and are enjoying each other's company. Perfectly central on this uniquely crafted, strong wooden table is an old-fashioned, white-laced, cotton doily. Standing on this beautifully detailed contribution to the table is a vintage, solid silver candle holder – this exquisite vintage piece holds six pure-white unlit candles as they stand individually in the arms of each holder. Matthew and Jess's wine glasses are also present on the table and placed on black and gold mats. The rest of the table is bare. Matthew's OCD, which has developed since losing his wife, means he is unable to have too many items laid out and surrounding him; his mind becomes confused and torturous as it feeds him words of destruction over the untidiness before his eyes.

Often, Matthew struggles when he finds himself within the vicinity of other locations: visiting family, or at other people's premises, if there's lots of dissimilar items out in front of him and placed in an unorganised fashion, his mind goes into overdrive, desiring nothing more than to place every item in an organised order with precision. More recently, he's started to move items around until he is content and satisfied with their positioning. Most people no longer question this and simply leave him to it. After all, this is an ongoing psychological battle that only Matthew can conquer himself, but at least when he's at home he can stay calm and remain relaxed as nothing leans so much as a centimetre out of place. The Honey residence is organised, and colour coordinated.

Captured in the moment and appreciating each other's company, both Matthew and Jess set about laughing as they discuss how embarrassing their initial meet was today at the café.

"Oh, Matthew, don't be so hard on yourself. I thought your response was cute, and I must admit I was very flattered. Personally, I think you are a very handsome man, and also, may I say, your style, Matthew, is exquisite. There is no greater attraction to me than a man who has his own style."

"You're making me blush, but thank you – and, well, I beg to differ. Honestly, I don't know what came over me, I couldn't speak. I felt a right daft git. I could only imagine what you were thinking."

With the wine flowing and the evening progressing well, Matthew's unaware and not ready for what's about to happen. The dreaded question is asked. "Matthew, if you don't mind me asking – what happened with you and Eve's mum?"

After the events that had taken place today and Eve's continued protest, he knew this question would be asked at some point – but he truly didn't expect to be answering this so soon. Closing his eyes if only for a brief second, Matthew sets about taking a deep breath in, almost filling his lungs, then as he exhales, and the oxygen begins leaving his body, he opens his eyes. Looking directly at him from across the table, with a captivating expression, Jess encourages him to speak. Reaching under the table she holds onto his thigh with a firm grip.

Somehow, gathering his strength, he begins to explain: "I met Lauren, Eve's mum, in my late twenties; we were both young and travelling around the world. We didn't know each other and yet we both set out on the same adventure, at the same time, with the same intention. We both wanted to take time out from education and work to embrace everything the world had to offer, including all the different cultures." Trying to remain strong, Matthew continues, "Not too far into our individual trips we both ended up staying in the same hostel in Thailand. It was fate that brought us together. Lauren was travelling alone, as was I – we were a pair of loners and loved it. I'm not sure if you know this, but when you're travelling, you stay in hostels, and more often than not you get mixed or single-sex dorms. I always chose the single-sex dorm, as did Lauren, but this hostel that we both arrived at was fully booked and we had to sleep in the mixed dorm. I was on the top bunk when Lauren arrived. I saw her huge smile from the corner of my eye as soon as she appeared in the room; her natural beauty completely blew me away. I remember lifting my head out of the book I was reading and just looking over like, wow, who is she? Instantly, we became best friends. Honestly, I've *never* had so much in common with anyone, let alone a woman. Every day was a brand-new adventure, we had so much fun together. I knew, within a matter of seconds, Lauren was my soul mate. A bold statement to make, but I just couldn't ignore the intense connection, it was super powerful. It was too strong for either of us to pull away, and actually, we didn't want to. We both decided to take a huge leap of faith – with multiple countries left to visit, we made a decision to only visit places that we'd never been to before. We spent the rest of our travelling days together. It was great and exceeded our wildest dreams.

"When I set off travelling I had absolutely *no* idea I would meet my future wife. My intention was to be free and to see the world – and yet fate had different plans for me."

Matthew stops speaking. He realises who he is actually having this conversation with. It's not a friend, or a family member, it's a woman he's only just met today. Does she really want to hear him declaring his love for his now deceased wife?

"Sorry – I didn't realise, I'm getting carried away with myself."

"No please, continue – you loved Lauren dearly. It shows you're vulnerable and sensitive side, and to me, Matthew, that just proves you are a man of integrity."

"Thank you, I think. I suppose sometimes I feel blessed to have found her and to have had the ability to share a section of my life with such a beautiful soul. It's also like a cruel curse at the same time. Maybe you're right I am slightly sensitive, but I'm still here and, well..."

Matthew looks to Jess as they begin sharing a moment; he stares into her eyes from across the table. Standing, he makes his way around the chairs. Positioning himself next to Jess, he leans in and tucks her hair behind her ear. Unable to hold the words in any longer he says, "You are so beautiful."

Jess smiles. "You're too kind. But thank you."

"What is it... I mean – why am I so drawn to you?"

"Well, I'm not sure what *it* is you are specifically referring to, but please, continue with your story..."

Coughing with a slight detection of embarrassment at his apparent rejection, he replies, "Yes, of course, sorry, I got slightly side-tracked, where was I?"

"You were describing how you decided to travel together, and how fate had different plans for you both. I have a question, Matthew, do you truly believe in fate?"

"Yes, I mean, most definitely. Fate is your life – and no matter your attempts, you can never change this. Unfortunate or not, the cards you are dealt through fate are the cards you must live with. I have visualised going back so many times to see if I could have changed my fate, changed what happened, and changed the tragic circumstance I now feel forced to live, and each time, there is nothing. Each time, I could say maybe this, or maybe that, but the facts are, if I went back it would all happen the exact same way. So why would I wish to go through such traumatic events all over again? Look at it this way, it was actually fate that I met you. I had a really important meeting today. It was to be Eve's first time attending an appointment with me as my assistant. She was so nervous, I could tell. We shared a moment this morning, thinking about Lauren, and so, to distract her and relieve some of the pressure, I suggested that we go to the café. Okay, so she didn't attend the meeting, and things took an unexpected turn, but I wouldn't have met you if I didn't make that choice. You see, it was fate that I should be there to meet you."

"Your perception of fate is extremely interesting. I guess your acceptance of this is what drew me to your family dimension. Sorry – now I'm side-tracking, please continue…"

"Why'd you ask?"

"No reason really – well, other than I have actually been waiting a long time for a family dimension such as this; now that I have you, let's just say, time will tell, after all, like you say, you cannot change your fate."

Matthew's slightly confused by Jess's choice of words, but she seems somewhat eccentric, so he chooses to refrain from digging into what she means by this.

"Please, Matthew, continue, I'm enjoying hearing your story."

"Erm, okay, yeah, sure, well… I think I understand what you mean. Would you like me to continue with how I met Lauren, or do you want me to skip to what happened?"

"I am enjoying watching your face light up as you speak about her. I'm sure you will explain what happened to Lauren in your own time."

Matthew smiles as he continues, "You're such a unique woman. This is always very hard for me and I truly appreciate your compassion and understanding."

"Thank you. I'm happy that you are able to be so open with me about such a sensitive subject."

"You just seem different; I feel as if I already know you, but I don't. I can't explain it, well, other than somehow it doesn't seem awkward telling you this. It's like you already know. I don't know. It's all very confusing. I mean, take for instance this. When we were travelling, we came across an old gypsy lady's stall. She was selling jewellery. Lauren instantly fell in love with a solid silver locket. It had a tiny little angel on it and was hanging from a delicate silver chain. I bought this when she wasn't looking and gave it to her that same night whilst the sun was setting. This was my special token of thanks for lighting up my life. Lauren never took this off and, well, since she, you know, passed, Eve's wore the necklace and she's never once taken it off. This necklace is very similar, if not identical, to the one you wear around your neck. Except, on your locket, your angel isn't smiling."

"Really? What a coincidence."

"Yes, and if I truly look into your eyes, and I mean deeply enough, it's as though I can see Lauren. Like she lives on through you. I'm probably freaking you out, now aren't I? See, I would never think about saying these things to anyone, *ever*, let alone a woman I've just met."

Jess can see Matthew's riddled with confusion. Trying to reassure him she smiles and says, "I'm here now. Maybe it's a good thing I remind you of Lauren. Everything happens for a reason; you agree with me, right?"

"Yes."

"So, we're both in agreement that this, right now, is potentially happening for a reason?"

"Yes. Why'd you ask?"

"I, too, have been alone for a long time. I, too, have been wandering the universe lost, waiting for the right soul. Matthew Honey, we have been placed together for intentions that are yet to appear in our lives. I'm intrigued, although you may think I know what happened to Lauren, I actually know nothing."

Matthew sighs a deep sigh; his expression changes. You can see the dread, the fear and the gut-wrenching pain plastered across his face. Jess feels the vibrational shift in his energy and moves closer to him. Placing her hand on his shoulder, she gently rests her chin on top of her hand and quietly says directly into his ear, "Matthew, what happened to your wife, what happened to Lauren?"

Closing his eyes, Matthew takes a deep breath in and as he exhales the oxygen, he slowly opens his eyes and begins, "It was just after six, evening time, over three years ago now. On the twenty-first of October, I'll never forget it, the date haunts me – I remember it too well. The day surfaces in my mind at least once a day, every day, since it happened. Myself and Lauren had collected Eve from her music lesson."

Matthew looks to the floor. He's struggling to hide his sorrow, as he appears less eager to speak. This is his least favourite subject to talk about; nonetheless, holding back his tears and regaining his strength Matthew continues, "We would always collect Eve from her tutor's home together. It was the same routine every Wednesday and practically like clockwork. Pretty much every step was taken at the same time every week. Anyone who was watching us would be able to predict our arrival time, it was that regular." He laughs slightly as he realises how fixed his routine used to be.

Jess can see Matthew's struggling, not only by the change in his voice, but by the emotions pouring from his eyes. His features are trying to resemble strength, but his eyes are completely giving him away. Coughing and attempting to resume his composure he continues, "We were making our way back towards the shops where we parked the car – Eve was telling us about the solo she had just learned."

Suddenly he lets out the biggest sigh.

"My phone began to ring. You've heard how loud this is, and so I stopped to take the call – I was standing still in the street, concentrating on what I was hearing. I'd managed to work out there was a problem relating to a work issue. One of the clients was requesting changes to the rough edit we sent across. Just as I was asking them to send confirmation of the changes to me via email, I looked up and could see Eve and Lauren had both carried on walking towards the restaurant. It was still light-ish outside. Eve was full of life, chatting away."

Shutting down with this image at the forefront of his mind, it's almost too much for Matthew to bear, as only he knows what's coming next. Immediately stopping himself from speaking, Matthew begins raising his hand and presses his thumb and two fingers into his eye sockets to deflect the tears that are about to fall down his face at any given moment.

Jess places her hand onto his leg; she doesn't request him to stop and she's willing Matthew to continue. Staying still for a brief minute, Matthew's face is becoming an extremely deep shade of red as he's holding on tightly to his emotions. Struggling to speak, he's stuck visualising random snapshots of that dreadful evening and is trapped in the moment; he hears the screeching of car tyres and Lauren's desperate scream over and over. He sees the fear on Lauren's face as she watches her baby stand in the middle of the road like a statue. Squeezing his eyes tight and shaking his head, Matthew's trying desperately to remove the visions and the noises from his mind.

Once ready, he bravely removes his hand from his face, clears his throat and once again, speaks: "I'd turned my back for a millisecond – the next thing, as I turned my head, I heard Lauren scream Eve's name at the top of her voice. I'm partially deaf in one ear and this was the loudest scream I've ever heard. I felt the vibration ringing through my ears. I lie in bed at night and sometimes I hear the noise as though it's been screamed only a few seconds ago; Lauren's desperate plea haunts me.

"Eve, without looking, had walked out into the road. A car suddenly appeared and was heading towards her at high speed. Eve was stood completely frozen in the road." With a huge lump in his throat, Matthew's voice changes slightly as he continues, "My wife – my soulmate – my beautiful Lauren, being the hero and the amazing mum, she'd always been, ran into the road without a thought or a care for her own safety. She grabbed Eve and instantly threw her out of the way."

Matthew becomes slumped in his posture with his head looking to the floor; he's relieving this moment, as he sits a silent and broken man. Aware there's now no going back, he clears his throat once more and is desperately attempting to be stronger than before. "Lauren was hit by the car with such force it snapped pretty much every bone in her body – as she came crashing down and hit the ground, her skull cracked, causing her immediate brain damage, and the amount of blood lost resulted in instant death. All I could do was stand by and watch as this happened. It was like my life had developed into a slow-motion movie scene. I could see the look on Lauren's face as she flew into the air. The car hit her legs with such a forceful impact, in milliseconds it had threw her up onto the bonnet and the biggest bang was heard – it was unbearably loud. By this point, Lauren wasn't even screaming, it was as though she had accepted her fate. She hit the windscreen, and I still hear the crack in my mind as it breaks into a thousand pieces – her body was thrown up into the sky. Immediately, my body went into shock, and I *couldn't* move. All I could do was stand still, in total disbelief at what my eyes were witnessing. My body remained entirely frozen. I dropped my phone to the floor, as I was helplessly looking at my soul mate, my Lauren, silently crashing to the ground. I did nothing to save my daughter or my wife."

Matthew's expression becomes numb and almost trance-like as tears begin to rapidly fall down his face. Remaining with a motionless expression, he continues, "Her face and her clothes were covered in dirt and stained with blood; all I could focus on, all I could really see, was the look of despair in her eyes as she collided with the ground. The immediate blow from the fast-paced vehicle threw Lauren into the air so high my heart broke instantly. I knew she wasn't going to be alive after her body hit the road."

"That night, I heard a noise, a noise I wouldn't wish anyone to hear knowing it came from their loved one. It was the loudest bone-crushing crack – and soon after this, a mist of red surrounded her head as Lauren landed in her final resting place on the road. Lauren's skull had smashed head first and bounced off the ground. The red mist was a mist of her blood as this was leaving her body."

His expression now slow, Matthew sheds tears as the lump in his throat is uncontrollable. It's formed so big he can barely swallow. Jess holds him tight and says nothing. She pulls back. The chicken casserole aromas are still circulating within the air around the whole house. Making her way into the kitchen she turns off the cooker. Suddenly she doesn't feel hungry anymore. As Jess turns off the oven, she grabs a handful of the gold napkins which are placed in a neat pile on the black, marble kitchen side. Heading back into the dining room, she puts the napkins on the edge of the table next to Matthew, who remains still and utterly broken with his head in both his hands. He hasn't flinched since she left the room. Sitting on the chair next to him, she doesn't expect him to speak, and yet he does.

"Do you want know something, Eve has never forgiven herself, and she's felt for years that it's *all her fault*. I know this is the reason why she gets angry: the poor child carries nothing but guilt. She's had counselling and I know she doesn't want to live. For years I haven't wanted to live either. I would've ended it all, but I know Eve would do the same and then what? Lauren sacrificed her life so that our daughter could continue to have one, what sort of respect for her ultimate sacrifice is that? I live for Lauren's bravery, I live for Eve, because I know that's what Lauren would want."

A brief silence takes place. His eyes are now red raw and almost closed through crying so many tears. His head is throbbing through revisiting the pained memories and reliving this emotionally traumatic part of his life. Matthew decides to break the silence and speak. "I didn't want to live for a long time – it should have been me that was throwing myself into the road for our daughter. I had to watch the only woman I've ever loved thrown into the sky like a toy – and come back down looking full of fear.

"It didn't end there: myself and Eve had to see Lauren lay completely motionless in the road. Her eyes were wide open, but you could clearly grasp the fact that Lauren's soul was no longer present – her skull was caved in on one side. Lay in a puddle of her own blood, not only was the ground coated, Lauren's clothes were also dripping as the blood just wouldn't stop gushing from her head. The horrific image of blood surrounding her body is the image that stays with me day and night. This image has embedded its unwanted existence deep in my memory. It lives at the forefront of my mind, appearing whenever it desires. As an adult, seeing such a horrific scene has impacted me massively, and has unlocked dark sections in my mind that I never knew existed. I can't help but wonder what impact this has had on my daughter. Eve's such a vulnerable young lady and at that time she was practically a child. When she was little she would always stroke her mum's face. Whilst Lauren was lay on the floor, Eve ran to her mum. Distraught, she was cradling her and stroking her face. This image kills me, it's hurts my heart to see my baby girl covered in her mum's blood just holding her and screaming out, suffering. My poor Eve is forced to live the rest of her life motherless at the start of her innocent journey and yet it is fate that has dealt her these hands; why? Her poor mind, without any warning, was left wide open to this horrific event, and now my once innocent, life-loving, adrenaline junkie, smiling Evelyn Jade, is riddled with aggression and bitterness. I can't blame her for this; I was the same for a long time. The only reason I didn't continue is, so that Eve can hopefully rebuild and gain strength from me. I live in hope that one day she will become strong again."

"Matthew, I'm speechless; how horrific for you both. As a fellow believer in fate, I'm sure life has its reasons for you both and, well, I'm here now, you are not completely alone just yet."

With these words, Jess's eyes suddenly spark and become an overcast shadow of grey. Grabbing Matthew by the chin, she locks eyes with him and says four simple words: "I will empower her."

Embracing Jess's words, Matthew is ready to get off the subject.

"Thank you. I understand everything happens for a reason – this soul-crushing tragedy has been aligned with our fate for a purpose, yet I feel we are still waiting to discover what the true intention of this is. The worst is, we have so many unanswered questions. Questions we will never receive closure on. I mean – why did we have to witness and go through the hardest thing anyone with a conscious mind could possibly experience, why us?" Pausing for a moment, as though he's waiting for someone to shout the answer, Matthew looks to Jess and with his final thoughts on the subject he says, "Fortunately, myself and Eve managed to regain some form of normality. But do you want to know what the worst part of this disturbing process is?"

"Only if you desire to tell me."

"What happened to Lauren was not an accident! I don't care what the police say, I believe this was done with intent, and one day, I will prove this. Both myself and Eve have never received closure for what happened to Lauren. It was a hit and run – the cruel coward behind the wheel didn't bother to stop. This devastating experience has never been closed. We have never received justice – and still to this day, we have no idea who killed our beloved Lauren." Suddenly the front door bangs.

Chapter 6
"Ring a' Ring o' Roses."

Matthew jumps, and wipes his face.

"Eve..."

Grabbing a gold napkin from the pile at the side of him, he quickly sets about wiping his eyes and makes his way towards the front door. As he walks through the dining room doorway, a relieved and slightly red-faced Matthew sees his exhausted-looking daughter. She's soaking wet, crouched down and taking off her shoes looking deflated, fatigued and full of sadness.

Without hesitation, he heads towards Eve, and as she stands, he begins hugging her tighter than ever. They're both embracing the moment. Matthew places her head towards his chest. With both his arms wrapped tightly around her, Matthew's holding Eve in a desperate attempt to make her feel safe. Holding back his tears and struggling to remain resilient to the emotions, he gently kisses her on the head and quietly says, "I love you, Evelyn Jade Honey."

Breaking down, Eve begins uncontrollably crying. She loves her dad more than anyone, after all; he's the only person she lives for.

"I love you more Dad – I'm so sorry."

At the doorway of the dining room, Jess emerges and begins leaning on the frame of the door. Observing the vision of a father and his daughter sharing their affection for one another right before her eyes, Jess's expression seems somewhat impure. The locket begins to glisten and as she holds this in her hand, Jess's eyes mysteriously begin to spark and transform into a dark shade of grey – without any warning, a thick, black outline begins spontaneously forming in her eyes, circulating inside this grey mist. The transformation has a resemblance to the black clouds you would see magically appear inside a storm at the height of its destructive takeover. Matthew releases Eve's head from his arms and, as he places both his hands on her shoulders, he says, "Are you okay? Kidda, where on earth have you been, look at you, you're soaking wet and shivering cold. Oh, Evelyn Jade Honey."

As Matthew says these words, tears form in his eyes. Making eye contact with Eve, he sees the truth: there's no getting away from the reality that stands before him. His daughter, his Evelyn Jade, this precious soul his wife gave her life to save, is standing right before him with a true expression of lifelessness. Her eyes radiate sorrow, discomfort and hurt; Matthew is devastated. What would Lauren say, looking down at her daughter in this state? Immediately he feels an immense sense of guilt. He's caused this. He's caused his daughter to endure such a traumatic event by inviting a woman back to the house, when she clearly wasn't ready. Instantly Matthew hangs his head in shame. He's emotionally deflated as tears gently fall down his face. Looking at her dad with her swollen eyes, Eve places her forehead on to his. As she too begins looking down, she quietly responds, "I'm home now – you don't need to worry."

Matthew, hearing her voice, is filled with relief; yes, she is home, yes, she is safe and yes, he never wants to let her go again. Matthew looks deeply at his daughter's appearance and as he holds her tight once more, he says, "Can I get you anything?"

Eve's temples are throbbing in her head. Peering to her dad with less than a fraction of her energy left she quietly replies, "No thanks, I just wanna go to bed – my head hurts, I'm tired, wet and cold."

Grabbing her soggy backpack from off the floor, she makes her way up the stairs and doesn't acknowledge Jess, who is still standing in the dining room doorway. Watching as his beautiful daughter makes her way up the stairs, and as she goes out of sight, Matthew hangs his head and releases a deep sigh of relief. He feels a presence at the side of him; he was unaware that Jess was observing. He didn't know she was standing in the doorway the whole time. Stood looking flirtatious and playing with the locket around her neck, Jess is unfazed by the height of the intense emotions within the room. Suffering with exhaustion, Matthew makes his way over to Jess.

"I'm sorry – maybe it's too soon…"

Before he can say another word, Jess stops him in his tracks; she grabs his chin and kisses him whilst running her fingers through his hair. Almost instantly, his body surrenders to this woman. Guiding his hands slowly, and moving these around her waist, up to her face, she places her forehead on to his, and whispers directly into his ear, "I will relieve you both."

With his eyes shut, Matthew's breathing heavy. What is happening to his mind, his heartrate, his emotions? He's not in control of any of them. With his tone controlled and almost robotic sounding, impulsively he says, "Jess – please, will you stay the night?"

As Matthew opens his eyes he looks to Jess. She says nothing! And slowly guides him up the spiral, black, metal staircase. Trying not to break eye contact, Jess stops mid-way. In her red dress, with her empowering energy, she's now standing looking proud, confident and in control on the higher step. Her resemblance is strong like a ruler. Her eyes remain overcast, with a grey and dark mist still present. On the step below, Matthew's looking up at her, withdrawn, lost, and has the appearance of a beggar. Leaning down ever so slightly, she begins holding his chin in both her hands. Breathing him in, her eyes now contain a deceitful energy and the grey mist is becoming the deepest thick shade of black. The colour is so deep, her eyes almost form a mirror, as you can see Matthew's innocent facial expression looking lost in the reflection.

With every second that passes, and as this powerful unbreakable connection remains, Matthew's surrendering a molecule of his soul to her. Completely unaware of this, Jess places her soft lips onto his – she kisses him gently – and any tiny seed of doubt that Matthew may have earlier had regarding this woman, has now vanished.

Embracing every second of this moment, Jess continues using the power she has. Not caring for Matthew's earlier confession of this being too soon, she leans to his ear once more and says, "Take me to your room."

Her breath is ice-cold, and this sends shivers through the nerves present in his eardrum. Fully aware of this sensation Matthew's completely powerless and trapped in the moment. He doesn't question her command, and instantly, he begins to guide her up the staircase. Entering the room, which is ordinarily filled with light and life, this now large space seems controlled by an evil unwanted entity. The four-poster bed looks sinister, and the dark vibration that's present is enough to make your soul abandon its physical form. Seeming self-satisfied, Jess shuts the huge, mahogany, brown wooden door behind her. Placing her head on the varnish stained doorframe, she stays in this position for a second or two. With a sudden sharp twitch, Jess turns her head, facing Matthew, who is standing in his room looking lost and unsure of what to do next, his expression blank and almost angelic. He's showcasing the innocent look a child will give his or her parent when they've been told off and will do anything for their forgiveness. Was this Matthew, or had this strange captivating woman taken over his mind?

"Shut the curtains!" she commands.

Her eyes are now blacker than the midnight sky outside. Matthew, without any fight or query, has made his way round the four-poster bed, approaching the window, he reaches for the expensive thick, floor-length, golden curtains. Holding one tightly in his hand, he suddenly becomes aware of his breathing rate which is deep and heavy. Feeling as though he may pass out at any given minute, the room is silent. Hearing only his own heart beating as he pulls the curtains together, his head drops as he sheds a tear, lonesome, long and lost. Is this Matthew showing a sign that he is himself after all and he truly isn't ready to play these flirtatious games?

Feeling a cold presence behind him, Matthew's nostrils are suddenly awoken by a pungent stench which is leaving a metallic bloody taste at the back of his throat. His eyes are battling against the darkness. He's desperately trying to make out what's placed in front of him, but he can't see anything, or anyone; he just feels a strange presence behind him. Closing his eyes, he says, "Jess..." He gets no response. Continuing, he says, "Jess – this isn't funny!"

"Do you like games, Matthew?"

"No."

Continuing her teasing ways regardless, Jess says, "That's a shame... I love playing games."

Appearing behind him, she begins to whisper directly in his ear, "Come on Mr Honey, play with me."

Instantly, he shudders. Her breath is ice-cold and the taste that is manifesting itself at the back of his throat has rapidly grown stronger. As it's development becomes formed its existence is thick and travels through his glands making him feel nauseous.

"Do you know why I am existent in your life Matthew, do you know your fate?"

Very blankly he replies, "No..."

With nothing but darkness present, Jess peers over his shoulder. She leans into his ear and licks this. His face remains blank. Her tongue is ice-cold and has a coarse feeling to it. A conceited grin begins to spread across her expression, as she teasingly says, "Good."

Stood as stiff as a board, he's too afraid to move. Quickly turning Matthew to face her, she makes a strong connection of eye contact with him and firmly feeds Matthew instructions, "Now, what I want you to do is sit on the bed – we're going to play a little game, you and I..."

Unable to break eye contact, or again question this order, he's walking backwards. As he reaches the bed Matthew's totally unable to bend his knees or control his movements. The calves on his legs hit the solid wood of the bedframe. His features stay motionless. He holds no expression on his face; his heart begins beating faster with every second that passes. His eyes fill with water. Unable to blink, the tears begin to fall unaided and sink into the slight stubble on his face. The black netted curtains which hang from the dark wooden frame of the four-poster bed begin freely closing one by one, with no assistance. These dark mysterious-looking curtains surround both Matthew and Jess. Suddenly, he feels an unwelcome force guiding him back and with one final powerful gust of energy, he's pushed and is lying back on the bed.

* * *

Wearing one of her mum's old nighties, Eve's fast asleep. She's resting peacefully in her bed and is blissfully unaware of the events which are taking place in the room down the hall. Her bedroom, which is normally bright, airy and full of life, suddenly becomes the complete opposite. Much like her dad's room a mood begins to surface. This dark, stagnant and gloomy energy is a mirror reflection. Lurking shadows appear in each corner. The rose gold floor-length curtains which are hanging heavy from her window are separated by white netting and this begins blowing forward ever so slightly.

The clothes she had on today are sprawled out in an untidy manner over the white wooden chair by her desk, which is holding all her coursework. Sat on top of all the papers is one of her most sacred possessions, her diary. This isn't one of the leather-backed, scrawling notebooks, which she uses to release her frustration, this is her actual personal diary! On its thick spine, a huge metal golden buckle is resting on top. Ordinarily, this is locked and secures the pages, which contain all her secrets. This deep red, rose, leather-backed book holds all her inner thoughts and true emotions. Her dad never enters her room and so Eve leaves the personal book around freely. Her backpack, with its contents removed, is looking deflated and has the zip open slightly. It's placed on the floor next to the bed. The picture of her and her mum is proudly positioned on the solid-white wooden bedside cabinet, and this is the first thing she sees every morning.

Gregg, the scruffy bow-tied teddy-bear, is on the pillow next to her head. She had fallen asleep with him resting on her face; Eve does this most evenings when she's experienced an emotionally challenging day. Gregg still has the sweet scent of her mum's favourite Chanel perfume resting on his fur even after all these years. Resembling an angel, Gregg looks as though he's watching over her whilst she's sleeping peacefully.

Suddenly, out of nowhere, a huge gust of wind flows through the room. Shuddering in her sleep, its presence becomes so forceful the hairs on her body begin standing to attention as she pulls the bedsheets up to her chin. She's still dreaming. Within a matter of seconds, this powerful gust of energy travels round the room and forces Eve's diary open. The thick, red, leather-backed book stands no chance as it flips to a page where it stays. Remaining asleep, Eve's expression is changing slightly. A look of concern, a look of fear, a look of neglect and despair, begins to surface on her face. Eve looks as though she's making a progressive transition and going from dreaming, sweet, pleasant dreams, to soul crushing, obnoxious, terrifying nightmares. As she turns, her face begins to sink into the pillow and she sobs ever so slightly.

The diary sat on her desk lies open and still. It's landed on a double page with blue inked writing neatly scrawled all over it. The pages read the following:

It's three years since you left me, three years since you were taken away from me. Today I met someone and the only person I wanted to tell was you.

I met him on the bus and for just a brief second, I forgot all about you not being here any more! A brief second passed and I thought... Shit, what's mum going to think about me speaking to him?

He's a lot older than me and yes, he made butterflies tickle in my tummy so much that I forgot all about you being <u>DEAD!</u>

Yes dead! You're DEAD and I must live with this! I must live with the fact that you're no longer here because of <u>ME!</u>

Your own flesh and blood!

You gifted me with life and yet I took yours from you!

Then it hits me! Eve, you don't have a mum and when this guy finds out why he will want nothing to do with you!

You're broken and cursed, Evelyn Jade Honey.
Why should you be happy...?
Why should you have a boyfriend and a life?
You killed your dad's soul mate! Your own mum!
I know I am not worthy of life and I understand that I am not worthy of death. Death would be too

kind. So, what am I worthy of? What is my purpose? Why am I still here?

A big group of girls at school call me a murderer every time they see me. I've been sat on the toilet before now and they've followed me in, reached over the cubicle and started singing 'Eve's a murderer.' I hang my head in shame and I don't go to the toilet at school anymore.

Why didn't I look mum, why did I just walk out? I can't cope anymore. What is it, why am I here to be punished in life and not worthy of being set free with death?

You can see the stains present from the water marks where her tears have fallen, smudging the blue ink as it's dried.

A brief whisper presents itself within the confinement of the room. It's so faint, if you weren't in complete silence you wouldn't hear it: "You're here for me. I have your purpose."

Eve, with her head remaining in the pillow, is sobbing louder and louder. She's dreaming deep and this was initially sweet innocent dreams, bright colours, rainbows and happiness, as she bounces through the fields holding tightly on to her mum's hand. They were skipping, laughing, and playfully rolling on the grass. Well, not any more. Now she's lost her mum and has ventured into the darkest forest; no one's present, not a soul in sight – the sound of snapping twigs and branches can be heard surrounding her. With her senses enhanced by the inner fear she feels and remaining trapped in this nightmare, Eve shouts, "Mum?" With no response, Eve's tone becomes shaky as she's allowing the unknown to control her primary emotions. She continues and shouts, "Who's there...?"

Again, with no reply Eve can't help but realise she's trapped. Everywhere she turns it's the same. The trees are the same. The brown soil on the floor is the same. The sky is black, without a star in sight; it's as though the universe has disappeared. The energy radiating through her body is like a surge of electricity and is making her heart race even faster. Feeling a strong aura, as though *she's not alone,* and that something evil is within her presence, Eve stops and remains extremely still. With only her chest moving as she breathes in deep, Eve's looking up to the midnight sky which is still without a single star. Feeling more vulnerable than ever, she shouts, "Help!"

Completely unaware that she's trapped inside her own mind, Eve falls to the floor. Her hands are cupped, holding her heavy head as her sobbing gets louder. In the emptiness of the forest, Eve's cry begins echoing its way throughout the identical, haunting-looking trees and is circulating within the air. The ambiance is still. There isn't a mist or a presence of any living existence to be seen. The eerie, dark trees are motionless. Eve reluctantly opens her eyes and glances through the gaps in her fingers; she sees nothing but darkness surrounding her. Any animal present would have a huge advantage over the current situation and the ability to sniff her out by the fear she's oozing. Hearing her own heart beating and the sound of her breath leaving her body, Eve's thoughts become clear, loud and present. They're thoughts of sheer panic along with an intense rush of overwhelming anxiety as her mind goes into overdrive.

Accepting her fate, Eve curls herself up on the cold earthy floor surrounded by dirt and twigs. Suddenly, the senses in her ears pick up a vibration of sound. Lifting her head slightly, she begins holding her breath. Again, she hears and feels the same vibration. Desperate to work out what this is, Eve is deep in concentration. The sound is faint; struggling, she manages to hear the tone. It's a female's voice; the sound is distant and almost sounds like singing. With her senses the strongest they've been, this enchanting voice is becoming established with every millisecond, and is now getting closer. Closing her eyes, with her sight gone Eve's hearing is now stronger. She's almost certain it's a female voice. She appears to be singing a familiar song or nursey rhyme. Eve speaks out: "Mum?"

With no response, she focuses all her sense of hearing on the sound. Closing her eyes tighter than ever, Eve's desperate to make out what this familiar song is. Suddenly, she hears the words – this mysterious enchanting voice is singing Ring a' Ring o' Roses, but the words aren't quite right. Still present on the ground, Eve wonders if this is, in fact, her mum. Sitting, covered in dirt and autumn-looking leaves, moving in the same spot, she frantically begins searching her surroundings. She's desperate to see her mum again, even if it is in a dark haunted forest in the middle of nowhere. At the top of her voice Eve shouts, "Mum!"

Echoing round the parameters of the forest, she suddenly hears the words of the nursery rhyme. The voice doesn't at all sound familiar. Lauren loved to sing this to Eve when she was a small baby girl, and yet this tone seems quite depressing, daunting and soulless. Still holding hope in her heart that this is her mum, again Eve speaks: "Mum, please, if it's you just answer me, I'm scared."

Instantly she hears, "Ring a' Ring o' Roses – your soul is mine. Ring a' Ring o' Roses – you've been chosen for the dark side."

With these final words travelling through her ears and becoming present in her mind, Eve shoots up off the ground – the nightie she's wearing gets caught round her ankles and she stumbles slightly. Picking up the pace, Eve's now running faster than ever through the forest, and is making no attempt whatsoever to watch where she's going, as multiple twigs begin snapping under her feet. At the height of scarcity, with her adrenaline rushing around her body stronger than ever, Eve no longer feels pain.

Waving her arms frantically in front of her, she's desperately attempting to whack the branches which are hitting her in the face out the way. Her arms and face are continually scratched. It's as though the trees and bushes are alive, reaching out to restrain her. One of the branches scratches her left arm so deep, she begins to instantly release blood. Slowly becoming out of breath, but with no desire to stop, Eve hears a loud female laughter surrounding her and no matter how far she runs, it's as though the voice is travelling in the air – embedding its existence into her pores and resonating deep within her mind. The voice is stalking and taunting her. Again, Eve clearly hears the words of the daunting nursery rhyme which are being repeated, over and over and over.

Exhausted, she finally stops. With no more fight left in her, she helplessly surrenders and falls to the ground sobbing. Her lungs feel raw. Sore, and with nowhere left to go, she's lay on top of the dirt, twigs and leaves. Reluctantly, Eve sits up and turns to face the darkness. The trees she's just frantically ran through appear haunting.

Instantly, Eve's eyes begin protruding out of their sockets. Appearing from out of the dark eerie mist, she sees a black, female silhouetted shadow. She's elegantly flowing and making her way towards her. Eve instantly makes a connection with this female form. Enticed by her grace and presence Eve is unable to break free. Embracing every individual word of the possessive nursey rhyme, Eve's captivated.

"Ring a' Ring o' Roses – your soul is mine. Ring a' Ring o' Roses – you've been chosen for the dark side."

Physically frozen, Eve's mind continues to race. She's traumatised with the horrific image her eyes are portraying into her mind.

"Why are you following me... Mum... Please, is this you?"

Without an answer, the only words Eve can hear are the continual repetition of the nursery rhyme being sung in the same dulcet tone. Submissively surrendering herself on the cold earthy ground, Eve's screaming out louder than ever: "Argh..."

With her hands covering her ears, she's folded herself into the foetal position whilst persistently rocking back and forth. Her face, her energy and her body are expressing pain, agony and desperation. With tears gushing and exhaustion in her tone, making her sound hoarse, Eve shouts one final time, "Mum – please stop... I'm sorry."

With a sudden gasp of air, Eve shoots up from her pillow. She's soaking wet from head to toe with sweat. Immediately, she touches her head and chest to ensure she's in one piece. Relieved and wanting to run to her dad, Eve jumps from off the bed and attempts to head towards the bedroom door. But as soon as both her feet hit the cold dark wooden floor, she loses the use of her legs and falls to the ground. Hysterical, she screams out, "Help!"

Almost straightaway, she hears someone heading towards her room. Still traumatised and in distress, Eve, not knowing who this is, begins to silently drag her limp, heavy body across the floor and heads towards the desk in order to hide under this. In a matter of milliseconds, a gust of wind presents itself within the realms of the bedroom walls and once again, this encourages the curtains to begin blowing. Suddenly, the female silhouette shadow from the apparent nightmare is present in her room. Only this time, Eve can see her clearly. Her jet-black hair hangs heavy and straight, and travels past her thighs. It's separated equally and hangs with precision either side. Her hair is soaked with a thick black substance. The sinister-looking liquid travels down each strand and lands on the floor where she's standing. Her eyes stand out through the gap in her hair. They're as red as the blood that's leaving Eve's body. Not a speck of white can be seen. Remaining more fearful than ever, and embodied with deep shock, an overwhelming surge of anxiety travels through Eve and begins taking over. Eve's unable to cry. She sits, silent in disbelief at the image her eyes are projecting into her mind.

Slowly, embracing the power she has, this female form begins making her way across the room to Eve. With every step she takes, the black substance drips from her existence and lands wherever she surfaces. Eve's eyes transform and become dark as she gazes at this seemingly evil, impure entity. Completely engrossed and fixated on her presence, Eve remains in a solid trance.

"Ring a' Ring o' Roses – your soul is mine. Ring a' Ring o' Roses – you've been chosen for the dark side."

In these spilt seconds, Eve's embracing the words as she feeds these to her. The rhythm and vibration of this possessive rhyme is felt entering into her mind. It's forming part of her blood flow and embedding deep within her DNA. This apparition travels through Eve's internal organs as it makes its way towards Eve's eyes and is taking over her sight. Every individual sense can be felt as her eyes begin changing. Her nerves are tingling. With this unfamiliar sense, Eve feels as though someone is repeatedly stabbing tiny needles into her eyeballs. This sadistic possession is taking over her body and is claiming her soul. Her innocent soul, which is now accepting its fate.

A huge *bang* sounds in the background. This breaks eye contact between Eve and the unknown female. Screaming even louder than before, Eve, this time, doesn't stop. In an attempt to silence her, the female unexpectedly appears under the desk and is right in front of Eve's face. This time, Eve sees the truth. She sees her full expression. This evil entity's skin is entirely grey, she's covered with black cracks which are spread all over her physical form. These deep embedded rips present on her body are dripping the same sinister, thick, black bloody substance from each individual laceration. Thick black blood drips from the surroundings of her mouth and from the centre of her grey soulless-looking lips. Placing her grey forefinger, which has deep marks upon it, to Eve's mouth, she signs, "Shh...."

The black substance gushes out of her mouth and continues its decent down her chin, landing on the floor. Her temperature is ice-cold. The skin-crawling texture of her finger stays on Eve's mouth with it's hard, rough and neglected existence. Eve's nostrils are awakened by a pungent stench which leaves a metallic blood-stained taste as it begins to make its unwanted way to the back of her throat. Its manifestation is growing at a rapid rate. Thick, unwanted and oozing neglect, Eve is powerless to remove this substance from her internal body. It's taking over. Her mouth is wide open, but no sound is coming out. Matthew's now violently kicking the bedroom door, but this sturdy fixture with its strong structure isn't going anywhere. The solid golden doorknob is beginning to shake on the inside as he's desperately trying to get to his daughter. He's repeatedly shouting, "Eve... Unlock the door, Eve..."

The doorknob turns one final time. Losing the support from the door, Matthew's feet begin to trip over one another as he stumbles into the room. Wearing nothing but his green and white checked pyjama bottoms and a white-gold chain which holds a solid silver cross hanging around his neck, Matthew's standing in the dark and mysteriously eerie room, completely alone. As he gains control of his balance, he stands still between the bed and the desk.

"Eve..."

In a state of panic, his breathing is getting heavy as the sense of fear he feels begins to heighten. Observing the room, he looks straight to the bed. It's messy, empty and no-one can be seen. Hearing a knock come from behind him, which sounds like the tapping of bone, Matthew's breathing rate increases rapidly. The room's developed a sudden sub-zero temperature and he sees his breath leaving his body. The hairs on his skin begin standing to attention. With every deep breath he takes, the sub-zero atmosphere present in the room can be felt travelling around him. Noticing a familiar, disturbing, nauseating stench, this develops into an equally disturbing taste at the back of his throat. Feeling unwell, he remains alone in the middle of Eve's dark, shadowed room. Standing still, the fear of the unknown has taken over his mind.

"Eve... Is that you...?"

Arriving from out of the hallway, Jess suddenly rushes into the room behind him. Standing at the doorway, she remains only a couple of feet into the room. Covering her naked body with Matthew's black silk night jacket, she speaks, "Matthew, what's going on?"

He doesn't answer. His eyes are now the only part of his existence that's moving. Suddenly, his ears twitch as he hears a shuffling sound and feels a vibration coming from under the desk. Immediately, he makes his way towards the sound and without so much of a second thought, he reaches out and pulls back the chair. The same chair which was holding Eve's clothes. Matthew drags this so hard the chair and all the contents it's holding flies across the room. Leaning down onto his knees, he moves towards the gap under the desk. His levels of anxiety are shooting through the roof. As he bends and looks to the floor, he notices tiny spots of black liquid leading like a trail underneath the desk. More anxious than ever, Matthew's now wondering not who, but what, is actually hiding under the desk. With his body shaking, he suddenly feels an immense sense of relief.

"Eve... There you are."

Putting out his arms, he reaches under the desk to hold his frail, timid-looking daughter. Eve instantly screams. Releasing the most horrific sound, which continually travels up her vocal chords, as this leaves her body the noise becomes established and circulates its ear-piercing tone within the soundwaves in the air.

"Ahh!"

Matthew leaps back in shock and almost instantly, Eve jumps, banging her head on the wooden desk top. The sound she's released is so piercing, even her ears are unable to withstand the vibration from the noise. In desperation, Matthew shouts, "Eve it's me. Dad."

Peering back under the desk from a safe distance, he's instantly horrified. Eve's eyes are jet-black; *no* white can be seen and she's laughing insanely at nothing. Her skin tone is changing with every second that passes. She's turning a sinister shade of grey. Focusing her attention towards her dad, Eve's head begins to move closer to him. The energy oozing from her has a strong psychotic existence surrounding it. Matthew once again leaps back, except this time, he leaps so high he practically throws himself as his spine hits against the wooden frame on Eve's bed. Full of shock, and riddled with fear at what he's witnessing, Matthew turns to Jess who is stood in the doorway. She has her hand on her chest and is holding the locket round her neck. Her expression seems unnatural for the current situation. She's calm and unnerved.

Eve slowly appears from under the desk, looking directly towards her dad who is motionless. Matthew's face is still and radiates fear. His slightly hairy chest is seen expanding with every deep breath he takes. Reaching out with her right arm, Eve places each of her fingertips onto the floor, one by one. They land still and are arched. Her thumb is the last to land. With her hand now resembling the long legs of a spider, Eve begins to drag her heavy body from under the desk. As the oxygen is hitting her physical form, Eve's skin tone continues to be taken over. This once innocent-looking young girl is now losing possession of her soul, as she slowly turns a deeper shade of grey.

Watching this transformation take place, Matthew remains still. Whispering, he's praying for himself and his daughter. "Please Lord – save our souls... Please Lord, I beg you, save our souls..."

Reaching out with her left arm in the same manner, this time, Eve's head follows. She looks down at the blood leaving her body as it's dripping from the deep cut on her arm. Appearing red as this seeps through the rip in her skin, this thick substance begins to drip and, as the evil energy circulating in the air takes possession of each drop, it turns sinister and changes to black. Eve suddenly stops. Slowly she turns to face Jess. Their eyes lock and the pair connect. With this mysterious takeover, Eve's skin changes. As she stretches out her face, deep cracks begin forming sporadically. You can see each rip presenting itself through her flesh. Every rip is black and appears as a gaping hole in her body. Jess seems unnaturally content and slowly she steps backwards out of the room. Gently placing one foot behind the other, being careful not to break eye contact with Eve, Jess's expression is oozing pride as Eve's face turns venomous.

With Jess out of the room, Eve turns her attention back towards her dad. She's lay in an army crawling position and, as she drags her heavy, limp body towards him, black blood begins dripping from her mouth and smears across the floor. Speaking Italian, with her tone deep, she's repeating the same words, "*Darmi la tua anima e non ucciderò, darmi la tua anima.*"

Matthew's panicked; he's unable to process the words she's saying as she moves closer to him. Having a full panic attack, Matthew's head begins to spin. He's petrified, frightened and riddled with extreme terror as he's continuing to pray. His body is stuck in a mysterious trance. Remaining still, he has an item in his hand, which he's holding onto tightly. The white-gold chain no longer hangs round his neck, it's now hanging from the creases of his hand – slowly he opens his fingers and reveals the item. It's the solid silver cross. Matthew has imprints from the edges of the cross embedded in the palm of his hand. Noticing the cross shimmering, Eve immediately stops dragging her body towards her dad. Her facial expression is confused. Unexpectedly, she feels a presence behind her. It's the evil entity. A gust of wind presents itself within the realms of the walls and the bedroom door *slams* shut locking Jess on the other side. Looking down to the floor, Eve receives instructions: "Your soul is mine!"

Within a millisecond she lifts her head and her eyes are filled with pure hatred along with a dark evil energy. Raising her leg in an acrobatic manner, her toes are pointing perfectly to the ground. Eve's expression is getting darker and darker. Her eyes are completely black and remain without a shade of white present. They sit like bottomless holes in her face and are wider than ever. Dragging her soulless body, Eve picks up the pace as she moves faster and faster towards her dad, leaving smears of thick black blood on the floor behind her. Matthew remains frozen. With tears of faith falling rapidly down his motionless face, he's completely immobile. His breathing is becoming intense. He's holding onto the cross so tightly it no longer creates imprints as it cuts through his skin. Deep red blood begins dripping from the cross, falling from the creases in his hand as this substance hits the floor.

Revealing the cross and holding this out, as Eve reaches her dad she instantly collapses. Her arms fall, and her legs go flat. Her body lands in a heap. Eve begins uncontrollably shaking and convulsing on the ground. She's foaming a black substance at the mouth, and her eyes are now cloudy.

As the cloud descends, her eyes begin returning to their normal colour. The movements in Eve's facial features begin twitching. It's as though you can see the evil entity leaving her physical form and letting go of her soul. With every second that passes, her expression becomes less demonic and is returning to her normal tone.

The deep rips in Eve's flesh begin healing on their own. The black blood dripping from each limb begins absorbing into her skin. Foaming from her mouth, this travels down her chin and also begins to disappear. The transition from grey to her natural skin colour is changing before Matthew's eyes. Lay with her eyelids wide open, Eve is now motionless. Feeling his heart beating as his own daughter is extremely close to him, Matthew's filled with terror.

Without knowing what to do next, he hears a creek and turns to the door as this catches his attention. It's beginning to open. Jess, who was standing in the hallway, peers into the room from a distance. Once again, she's proudly holding the locket around her neck. Matthew doesn't speak. His breathing has got so heavy and erratic he looks as though, at any given moment, he's going to pass out. Attempting to create some distance between him and Eve, as a precaution, he pushes his limp, stiff body onto her bed. Eve's lay lifeless on the floor; she hasn't moved since her body stopped. With a resemblance of her mum when she died, it looks as though her soul has left her physical form. Matthew whispers, "Eve..."

Suddenly, he feels an overwhelming surge of breathlessness as his head begins spinning round. Feeling as though he's been spiked with drugs, his sight goes blurry, his hearing fades and his head becomes heavy. The room is spinning at such a rapid rate he feels queasy and as though he's about to throw up. Matthew's having a huge panic attack. Feeling the nausea circulating and travelling up his stomach he becomes extremely light-headed. The last thing he sees is an outline of Jess heading towards him. She's looking somewhat pleased with herself. Hearing his own voice one final time, he says, "Eve..." Slowly, this begins to echo inside his mind.

He's out!

Chapter 7
"The games begin!"

Matthew's trembling, half-naked body lies collapsed on Eve's bed.

Completely unaware that he's been mentally trapped in the depths of his own mind, a terrified Matthew hesitantly opens his eyes. He sees only darkness surrounding him. Jet-black to the left and jet-black to the right, no fixtures, no fittings, *nothing*. An eerie energy begins travelling through his pores, into his veins, and resonates within his mind. It's telling him *he's not alone*.

Feeling a strong evil presence surrounding him, Matthew's desperate to discover where he is. Riddled with anxiety, which enhances with every second of the unknown that passes, he slowly reaches out his hands and places these directly in front of his body. Looking as if gravity is no longer a privilege to him, Matthew slowly moves his arms around with a floating resemblance. He's anxiously attempting to feel for anything that could be present within the vicinity of his confinement. But still he sees, and feels, nothing.

As his sight adjusts he places his hands a few inches away from his face. Waving them slowly, he sees his tiny freckles, hairs and the scruffy-looking nails he bites. Turning these around, he looks into his palms. Immediately, he's *shocked*. In his right palm, he sees dark red, thick blood, along with four deep imprints spread out, but still quite close. The blood dripping from each cut travels together and forms a cross. Feeling his stomach turning, he's no longer able to hold this as he vomits next to where he stands. Almost instantly, this evaporates. With a sickening acid taste remaining at that back of his throat, Matthew's feeling ill and scared. Spitting in an attempt to remove the taste out of his mouth, before he vomits once more, he bravely shouts, "Hello, can anyone hear me? Eve?"

With no response, his eyes become overcast and heavy. The temples in his head start to throb and the fear of the unknown is getting too much for him to bear. Feeling more vulnerable than ever, Matthew looks dead ahead; still he see's nothing but darkness. It's exceedingly quiet and all he can hear is the sound of his breath as this leaves his body. Trying to bravely suppress the fear he feels and without surrendering, Matthew finds his inner courage, and again, he shouts, "Hello, can anyone hear me?"

He doesn't know whether to feel relieved at this deadly silence or even more fearful as the evil presence surrounding him appears to be getting stronger. Without knowing who, or what, owns this energy, but feeling as though it isn't the blessing from the Lord Christ himself, Matthew breathes in and closes his eyes. His legs become weak. Desperately trying to dig deep and locate every inch of his inner courage so he doesn't collapse, Matthew looks down at his appearance. He's still wearing the green and white checked pyjama pants and he can just make out the flesh showing at the bottom from his bare feet. Looking beyond his body, he appears to be standing on *nothing. No* floor. *No* ceiling. It looks as though he's floating on a jet-black blanket of air, standing singly and alone in the universe with no stars, no planets, just an abyss of nothing, as though life itself never existed.

Imprisoned by his own thoughts, Matthew's absorbing the fear this evil entity is feeding his mind. Closing his eyes, reassuring himself, he says, "Come on Matthew, it's all in your head. You just need to wake up."

Opening his eyes, he fiercely begins shouting at the top of his voice, "What do you want from me?"

Surrendering to the darkness, he lies a broken man and is completely unaware of the deception to which he has so cunningly been thrown into. Such a calculated and scheming trap. Unknowingly, Matthew's converted to this evil entity's desires. This once strong man is now a victim to the shackles of his own mind. Sobbing gently and holding his head in his hands with his eyes still closed, he unexpectedly hears a female voice echoing towards him.

She very teasingly says, "Do you like to play games, Mr Honey?"

Lifting his head from out of his hands, the only desire Matthew has *right now* is to break free and find his daughter. And so, he chooses to say nothing.

Again, he hears, "Do you like to play games, Mr Honey? Ring a' Ring o' Roses..."

Irritated by the suggested games, and with saliva flying uncontrollably from his mouth, he interrupts, "What do you want from me?"

A long pause takes place. Suddenly, he hears an echo resonating in the distance. This calms him slightly as his aggression subsides. Closing his eyes and tuning in his ears, he soon works out, it's *him*. His own voice is very mockingly echoing within the parameters he's confined to and is quickly surrounding him. Placing his head back into his hands, he closes his eyes. No sooner had he shut off his sight, Matthew's mind begins to project a disturbing undesired flashing memory. He hears the screams of his innocent young Eve. He sees her face as she watches her mum collide with the ground, covered in her own blood. Distraught by this vision, he covers his ears and screams out in agony, "Eve!"

A pungent stench once again begins to take over his nostrils and is making its presence known as this explores the back of his throat. Choking, Matthew suffers as this substance leaves a strong metallic blood-stained taste. Curled up, he feels as though someone has taken a blade to his organs and they're slowly ripping through each one. With nowhere to turn and not a glimmer of hope in sight, eventually the teasing female voice reappears.

"Don't cry, Mr Honey, your purpose is aligned – you will soon receive your fate."

With these final words, the female entity releases a psychotic laughter. She's embracing this helpless soul surrendering to her desires. The insanity of her laughter begins embedding itself inside Matthew's eardrums, and as this circulates, it implants its unwanted existence deep within his mind. Screaming louder and louder, in a desperate attempt to drown this out, Matthew has tears forming in his eyes which begin to fall down his face. He's repeatedly screaming, "Let me out… Let me out… Let me out…"

Feeling exposed, weak and vulnerable, he's lay on his side, with his knees tucked to his chest and his hands stuck to his ears; he's desperately attempting to prevent this psychotic laughter from entering further into his mind. Squeezing his eyes together tightly, he feels as though he's crying thick tears of blood. Matthew, for the second time, passes out.

***

With a sudden *gasp* of air, he leaps forward. He's back in his room, soaking wet from head to toe, undressed, wearing nothing but his boxer shorts and is unexplainably back in his bed. Attempting to shout, "Eve," Matthew's unsuccessful as he's lost his voice.

The room's empty. The perfectly painted white walls appear bright as the sun peers through the gap in the curtains. The mood in the room is calm and still.

Touching his face and wiping the sweat off his head, Matthew lies back and coughs as he's struggling to clear his dry throat. Reaching for the glass of water which has been left on the bedside table, as he drinks this, he considers if he's in fact losing his mind. Completely alone, Matthew's breathing heavily and confused as to how he's got into bed. Still in a daze, he begins to wonder where Eve is. Pushing his legs out from underneath the bedsheets, they suddenly appear stiff and heavy. Shuffling to the side of the four-poster bedframe, Matthew's retaining a very low level of energy, as he slowly slumps to the floor. His sight becomes blurry. Gradually he raises his head. Feeling pathetic, Matthew's lay with his head on the edge of his bed. He's so tired. The entrapment begins to replay in his mind; he hears the psychotic laughter of the female and her teasing words as they play on repeat in his head, like a scratched disk.

Another undesired memory surfaces. He sees Lauren's soulless face and cracked skull flash in his mind. Closing his eyes tight, he shakes his head in a desperate attempt to remove this image from his mind. As soon as he opens these, Matthew's mind projects another image. It's Eve. She's curled up on the ground next to her mum – who's lay dead – uncontrollably crying. With salvia running down her chin and fluid gushing from her nose, she's screaming, "Mum, come back to me, I'm sorry. Mum please, don't go, somebody do something, Dad, *save* her."

Reliving this horrific moment, suddenly he sees himself, and he's not helping or doing anything to save his wife; he's frozen on the ground next to her battered body and isn't moving. Again, closing his eyes to remove the image, Matthew's determined this time he isn't going to surrender and become frozen with fear. Pushing himself up using all the upper body strength he can, slowly he rises off the ground. Now standing on his feet, he manages to steadily take one step at a time as he gradually makes his way across to the bedroom door.

Exhausted and fragile, finally he reaches the wooden doorframe. Instantly, he loses his balance and collapses whilst still holding onto the golden doorknob. Mentally drained, he quietly begins to sob as he presses his head against the wall. Surprisingly he hears voices clearly in his mind. Female voices. But the tone, isn't haunting, sad or full of sorrow, it's laughter; it's happy, joyous, female laughter.

It's *Eve*. He can hear her. Hearing her voice is like an injection of life has been squirted directly into his veins. Dragging himself up, he attempts to stand once again and this time he triumphs. Gathering enough strength, he reaches out and successfully opens the bedroom door. Feeling a sharp pain shoot up his right arm, Matthew lets go of the golden doorknob and looks into the palm of his hand. Right before his eyes, and in his reality, he sees the four deep cuts which are spread out and shaped like a cross.

Matthew glances down to his chest. The white chain along with the cross is *gone*. All that remains in its place are tiny spots of what he believes is his own blood mixed within a small amount of his chest hair. He hasn't taken the chain off since the day Lauren gave this to him almost four years ago, on their final Valentine's day together.

Hoping this has come off in his bedsheets, Matthew's now standing in the hallway. The mood is the complete opposite of the last time he stood in this very same spot. It's now bright, airy and filled with life. The pure white painted walls are complimented beautifully by the exquisite bright pieces of art hanging perfectly parallel with precision.

Suddenly he hears Eve. She's laughing away downstairs. Still uneasy on his feet, he slowly places one foot in front of the other. Feeling slightly weaker than before, Matthew approaches the top of the spiral staircase.

Standing like a statue looking to the task in front of him, he sees each step beginning to stretch out. His breathing rate changes, becoming out of sync with his body. With an overwhelming sense of nausea, instantly Matthew becomes light-headed as the ground beneath him spins. Daunted by the challenge the staircase presents him with, he suddenly hears Eve's voice getting closer. His heart begins to warm and his eyes form tears of relief as he sees her. She's appeared from the kitchen looking cheery, well rested and full of life. Satisfied now that he's seen his daughter, and thankfully she's okay, Matthew collapses on the only step he'd managed to step on to. Grabbing the metal rail as he falls, he places his head on the cold, metal bars. Quietly, Matthew says to himself, "It was just a dream."

Eve immediately runs to her dad's aid. With his hearing becoming slightly fuzzy, and as the relief he feels sinks in, he hears Eve shout out to someone, "My God, Dad. Help, quickly, he's collapsed..."

As he opens his eyes slightly, daylight beams through the glass surrounding the front door, and glows like a torch into his eyes. Squinting and in somewhat of a daze, he can just make out Eve's worried and concerned face. With his vocal chords still refusing to resume to their normal tone, he sounds as though he's losing his life.

"Eve, there you are. Please, I've been looking for you."

Again, he hears Eve speaking to someone in a panic. But he doesn't know who this is.

"Help me, please, I think we should take him to the hospital. Dad. Can you hear me?"

Matthew hears a familiar voice in the distance.

"Matthew..."

Peering through the tiny slits in his eyes, he sees a woman walking up the staircase and heading towards him with a sliver shimmer. He notices a beautiful star-like glisten around the woman's neck. Almost instantly, his expression becomes happy. With his voice remaining hoarse, he says, "Lauren," reaching out his arms. "Lauren – it's really you. You came back."

Eve panics. "What's happening..."

The woman he believes is Lauren kneels at the side of him on the step. With a smile still beaming on his expression, Matthew turns to face her. The daylight isn't so bright any more and as he opens his eyes fully, he sees the truth. It's *not* Lauren, it's *not* his soul mate, it's a very concerned-looking Jess, with a locket around her neck glistening away, and next to her kneels a scared and concerned-looking Eve. Turning to Jess, looking confused, Matthew says, "I don't understand, what's going on?" Looking to his daughter he continues, "Eve..."

But, before Eve has time to answer, Jess says, "It's okay, Matthew, don't worry, you just had a bit of a strange turn last night. I think it was a bad dream. You were randomly shouting in your sleep and dripping with sweat."

"But I don't understand, Eve, you... weren't you... your skin turned grey, and you were in trouble. Eve, your eyes. They were black, and you had black blood down your face."

Eve stops her dad. "Dad, honestly, I'm fine, like Jess said it was a bad dream – nothing to worry about with me." Holding her dad's hand, she continues, "It's you I'm worried about."

Confused, he's in a slight panic as both Jess and Eve are practically confirming that he's, in fact, losing his mind. Matthew turns to Jess in the hope of receiving some form of reassurance.

"Jess, you were there, you were just as petrified as I was."

Immediately, Jess turns to face Eve. She nods her head and Eve, again, speaks up. "Dad – seriously, it was just a nightmare. I'm fine, you're fine, Jess is fine—"

Matthew interrupts. "Hang about... When did you two become best friends?"

Still kneeling on the staircase, Eve, who was staring at Jess, turns back to look at her dad; she stands and begins reaching out to lift him from off the step.

"Dad, come on, don't worry about that, we're fine, you need to concentrate on getting better. Now, let's take you back to bed. Time to rest."

Helping her dad to stand, Eve carries him up the stairs.

Reaching his room, she guides her dad and places him on his bed. Positioning herself at his bedside, she gently begins to stroke his face.

"Dad, I love you. Please rest and promise me you'll stay in bed."

"Okay, darling, I promise."

Matthew's just as concerned for his own wellbeing; he's confused, exhausted and simply desires nothing more than to feel himself again. Slowly surrendering to the bed, he can feel himself about to drift off.

"Will you be okay?"

Stroking back her dad's hair, Eve whispers, "Of course I will. Jess is all right, and, well, to be honest, you really gave her a fright last night. She was so scared." Attempting to lighten the mood, she continues, "And, well, between the pair of us, Dad, I'm kind of surprised she's still here."

Now more confused than ever, he begins to question himself. Was it really just a nightmare? It felt so real. Looking down, he can still see the cuts on his hand. Seeing the confusion spread across her dad's face, Eve begins holding him tight. As she lets go, she cups his face and says one final word, "Sleep."

Sinking into the mattress, and with the soft Egyptian cotton from the sheets gracing his skin,

Matthew's eyelids begin to close as all his energy leaves his body. With one final glance, he sees Eve leaving the room and as she closes the door behind her, he notices a bandage on her left arm. But it's too late. He whispers, "Eve." *He's out...*

Once again, Matthew's falling back into the darkness. With his eyes firmly closed, no sooner has he escaped the traumatic nightmare when he's *back*. Locked within his own mind. Falling deeper and deeper into the abyss of his inner soul, he becomes paralysed with fear. His physique is falling into the jet-black surroundings and the movements of his body are no longer in his control. Resembling a helpless, merciful individual who drowns at the hands of the vicious parts of the sea, Matthew's actually drowning at the hands of his soul. Appearing as though his spinal cord has been removed from his skeleton, a motionless, deflated, collapsing Matthew surrenders himself. Within a few short seconds of his helpless submission, a powerful force awakens around him.

With one final descent, his body has sunk. He's no longer falling. His physique lands and is confined to a seated position. With his eyes closed, Matthew's trapped with an overwhelming surge of anxiety regarding his fate. Frozen to his surroundings and feeling suffocated, Matthew once again feels an energy surging through his veins as this surrounds him. This powerful sinister energy field is letting him know, yet again, *he's not alone.*

The sensitivity of the nerves embedded into his muscles slowly begins to activate. This enhances his ability to feel pain. With his eyes remaining closed, he's breathing deep. His lungs stretch and aren't even close to their maximum capacity, when almost instantly, Matthew's chest becomes tight. Feeling as though someone's sat suppressing his ribcage as he takes each breath, the strong sensation from the movement of his chest feels extremely intense. Matthew's in agony. Feeling as though each individual rib is snapping and piercing its way through the layers of tissue surrounding his lungs, he's struggling to breathe.

In excruciating pain and, at a huge disadvantage as he is unable to influence, or control, any movement of his body, the powerful presence he has surrendered himself to is leading all his senses. Suddenly, the muscles and nerves behind his eyes begin twitching. His eyelids uncontrollably flicker. Paralyzed, Matthew's aware he isn't creating this spasm. In a desperate attempt to remain with his eyes closed and wanting to stay away from the reality that's present before him, Matthew tries to battle against the movement, but he's unsuccessful. Feeling as if someone is stood over him ripping his eyelids apart, he's unable to fight this any longer. Each wriggling blood vessel in his eyes can be felt making an appearance, as his pupils dilate and adjust to the light that is appearing in the distance.

Regaining his sight, Matthew's only ability is the manipulation of movement from his eyes. Putting all his focus on the light that's forming in the distance, this strange single beam has the resemblance of a small star that is present in the sky at night. Unwillingly Matthew begins to accept his fate. But before this acceptance takes over, he unexpectedly hears a voice present in his captured mind. Entirely restrained at the hands of this torturous, evil presence, he turns his attention to the voice he hears so clearly. He's quick to realise, yet again, it's him. Hearing the vocals, he feels no connection to the words, or the tone, whatsoever. The characteristics are almost unrecognisable. The words Matthew hears himself speaking are, "Whatever my fate, I ask you to free me – if death is in my cards, please let my soul know she's gone with no return. If life is in my cards, please let my soul live free and tell me how I can bring her back."

Remaining completely paralysed and unable to speak, Matthew's thoughts begin to question what this could mean.

Feeling as if he's receiving some form of unwarranted clues Matthew's attempting to piece this together, "Bring her back to me. Lauren's gone."

Remaining quiet as though he's waiting for the answer, with no response, Matthew's powerless. Having only just broken free from one entrapment, he has absolutely no desire to go through the same games all over again. With his previously traumatic experience still fresh in his mind, he begins to slowly piece together that his current situation is far more concerning than the last. At least he had the ability to move freely. This time, he's completely unable to control, or influence, any of his movements. The only advantage he has is the ability to move his eyes, which given his current state, doesn't seem so much like an advantage to him.

The light that is appearing from the distance is getting brighter. Desperate to regain possession of his body, he begins staring attentively at the enchanting beam, trying to work out what this is. Suddenly, he develops a new sense of feeling. This uncontrollable feeling is resonating within his lower body. With aches in his feet, and pain in his legs, Matthew's physique unexpectedly begins to move, in a very controlled motion. But this movement is once again not in *his* control. Every rock forward is timed to perfection, and each movement back is in sync with the next. The continual sequence feels calculated as the motion of his body moves back and forth. Matthew's completely incapable of stopping this, and he feels as if he's under a deep state of hypnosis. With the light getting closer, he sees his surroundings. This unexplainable radiating beam is brightening his parameters. A strange presence appears at the side of him, which doesn't *at all* feel friendly. Petrified, Matthew's breathing rate becomes faster.

Unaware of who, or what, is present in the darkness with him, Matthew reluctantly plucks up his courage. Slowly he begins to focus his sight to the space at the side of his rocking body. The movement is big, and yet he can't hear a single thing. Visuals are forming on their own. The experience is supernatural and strange; it's as though a scene is changing at a theatre production except there's no-one around. There's no-one present moving the stage props and pulling wires to change the backdrop. Peering from the corner of his eye, a pain shoots through his nerves. Natural daylight begins to beam towards him. Squinting his eyes in an attempt to adjust his sight to the bright vision, Matthew's stunned. He sees a window has mysteriously formed. Straining to see the view out of the mysterious window, he's at a huge disadvantage, but for some unknown reason, Matthew feels a weird sense of familiarity with the structure. He recognises this but it's too far away to make out the specific details. Straining one final time, he's convinced he's seen this before. It virtually looks, and feels, as if he's seeing the window in his dayroom. The very same window he stands in front of most mornings.

Looking deeper and deeper, Matthew's eyes can't take the straining any longer and he turns his sight away. The pain becomes too unbearable. Still paralysed, he remains unable to move his head, which makes him incapable of confirming if this is, in fact, his window. The visual is just out of his sight's capacity and it almost feels like a cruel intentional trap. The light appearing in front of him becomes brighter as Matthew's body continues to rock back and forth.

Looking dead ahead, he sees a mirror has appeared. It's full-length and standing tall. Again, this object feels *familiar*... It's extremely comparable to the one standing proudly with its gold trimming at the bottom of the staircase at home. Matthew begins to centre his focus on the reflection in the mirror. In the reflective glass, he sees himself. He's sat in a dark wooden rocking chair, and is silently rocking back and forth, in a controlled motion.

With an overwhelming surge of emotions running through his mind, Matthew begins feeling a deep internal sense of loss, depression, lifelessness and evil revenge. Caught off guard, he suffers an intense amount of uncontrollable agony. He feels his heart actually *break*!

Unable to shout out, Matthew's breathing becomes rapid. He feels each blood vessel of his heart crush. Tears begin to form in his eyes. Once again, he hears his voice. The words he speaks. "I will find her..."

No sooner had this circulated around his mind, Matthew hears and sees himself showcasing an insane laughter. In excruciating pain, and more confused than ever, Matthew questions what he's hearing.

Chapter 8
"Premonition... Maybe?"

Looking deep into the mirror, Matthew sees his body is top-heavy and slumped with his head hanging low. His jawline is resting on his chest. With the slight resemblance of a patient that's been sedated by medication, he begins directing his attention to the bottom of the mirror. Engrossed by what he can see, Matthew's wearing a pair of black boots which are dirty and covered with grey dust. This look is not representative of his usual immaculate and smart appearance. His feet are placed perfectly parallel on the floor and are moving in synchronisation with the rocking motion. With possession of his sight and the advantage of the mirror, Matthew now sees each rock forward, and each decent back. This experience seems surreal as the movement of his body remains totally out of his control. Looking either side of his feet, he sees the flat, dark, wooden rocker rails on the chair; the movement of these slats of wood are mirroring the slow rocking.

In an act of desperation, he gradually begins to make his way up his body. Observing the items of clothing he has on, Matthew's wearing the faded ripped jeans Eve purchased for him as a joke one Christmas. On the tag she wrote, "Welcome to the twenty-first century, Dad". He's only wore the jeans once, and yet here he sits, looking as though he's been wearing these for the past several months. Dirty, faded black material. Matthew can see his flesh peering through the rips on his knees. Midway, he notices both his hands are crossed and resting on his lap. This instantly grabs his attention as he never sits this way. Focusing all his energy on this spot, he becomes aware that he's securely holding on to something, but he can't quite make this out. Getting frustrated, Matthew desires nothing more than to understand why this is happening to him. With what little amount of internal strength he has to fight against this entrapment, he shouts, "Move Matthew, please, *just move*."

Instantly, he hears his voice circulating round in his head, but the harsh reality of this is it was only in his head. Looking into the mirror, Matthew sees his mouth hasn't moved, and neither has his body. Running out of options to release himself from this trap, Matthew's only hope is to piece together the puzzle of his current unfortunate state. With his eyes continuing to rock back and forth Matthew feels nauseous. Determined to succeed, he looks into his lap. Matthew sees he's holding a picture frame. Once again, he feels a sense of familiarity with this item. Attempting to make out what the image is inside the frame, immediately, he's unsuccessful. Being unable to move his head places him at a great disadvantage and so he has no chance of seeing the image, it's *too* far away. Working out a piece of the puzzle gives him internal strength. He's determined he's not giving up and brings his attention to his other hand. With a very firm grasp on the item he holds, Matthew squints his eyes to reach his sight; straightaway, he works out, what this is.

Staring in complete shock and disbelief, his breathing gets heavier as he becomes riddled with panic. Resting on his lap, and held tightly in his hand, he sees a black 9mm pistol, and attached to this is a protruding black silencer. As soon as he sees this, his mind sets about racing.

"Please Lord, forgive me, what have I done?"

Now more scared than ever, Matthew's thoughts have become a mist of combined madness. He suddenly hears insane female laughter. Extremely worn out, he questions his purpose; he's never held a gun in his life. Desiring answers, but not receiving them any time soon, he begins an attempt at piecing together the image he sees via the reflection of the mirror.

"I've got a picture in one hand – and a lethal weapon in the other."

With his eyes beginning to feel pained through straining and blocking out the screaming and unbearable insanity circulating within his mind, Matthew recalls something he said. Something he now considers an important piece of the puzzle.

"I said I'd find her. Find who... who is she?"

Remaining helplessly trapped and no closer to freeing himself, Matthew's almost ready to submit and surrender to the demands of whoever or whatever is taunting his innocent soul. Looking deep into the reflection he can't help but grieve for the man he once was. The same strong Matthew Honey who now seems like a distant memory. Thinking of Eve, instantly he internally feels a sense of happiness, be it for a brief second; it doesn't matter. In this snapshot moment, Matthew isn't filled with discomfort and rife with pain. He sees his best friend and an intense sense of power generates inside him, making him stronger. He must break free; he must fight for his daughter.

A voice begins echoing within the realms of the room. The words are unclear, but nonetheless, this voice is present. Ready for the next challenge, Matthew's alert. Is this Eve? With his ears finely tuned, he hears and feels himself breathing deep, every inhale and exhale. He frantically begins searching his parameters through the reflection in the mirror.

He notices a grey mist, which has spontaneously begun to seep around him and begins surrounding his feet, along with the rocker rails on the chair, this grey unnerving mist has not entered alone. Travelling with this substance is an evil and deceitful energy. Looking deeper into the mirror, there's not a soul present. But the mysterious dark mist is getting thicker. Surrounded by a suppressive, devious energy, which appears to be binding the mist together, Matthew feels as if this is it: this is his final command of fate.

Making its presence known, this dark energy begins to originate and reveals its true self, becoming strong, overpowering and dominant. This energy field has full advantage over the situation as it rises in the room. Becoming established and surrounding him with its unwanted manifestation, this energy is ice-cold and, as the mist thickens, it circulates inside his boots. The sub-zero temperature gives him a sense of feeling in each of his toes; it's a tingling pin-like sensation. Thousands of tiny nerves can be felt wriggling around, sending signals to his brain registering their survival. The pain is strong and unbearable. With its existence forming thicker as this feeds from Matthew's fear, the mist slowly moves round his physique.

Feeling an ice-cold, stinging sensation, with every section of his body this maliciously forces its presence upon, the sub-zero temperature travels through the arches in his feet and circulates around his ankles. The pain is so intense. It feels as though someone is constantly spraying liquid nitrogen everywhere this evil and viscous energy lands. In a desperate attempt to distract himself from the agonising pain, Matthew decides to refocus his attention back on his reflection, when suddenly he notices a change in his features. His mouth begins to move ever so slightly. Again, this is completely out of his control. Matthew unexpectedly hears a voice once again. This voice is him.

"I won't lose you... Eve."

Instantly his breathing becomes heavier; his chest feels as though someone is sat suppressing his lungs. Now he's in sheer panic mode.

"What have I done – where's Eve?"

Unable to answer his own questions, Matthew's staring into the mirror; he's focusing all his attention on the 9mm pistol he holds so calmly in his hands. The rocking motion speeds up. Staring at his face as he rocks back and forth, the lifeless expression remains on his features. Movement begins to slowly present itself on his mouth. Matthew's again powerless to stop, control, or prevent this. A smile appears on his face. This smile is in no way a symmetrical symbolism of the emotions running through his body and circulating within his mind. Looking more psychotic with every second that passes, he's beginning to question his sanity.

No sooner has he questioned this, he sees a female silhouette has spontaneously appeared within the mirror. Frozen with fear, Matthew's staring at this female figure as she gracefully moves her way around the reflection. Unable to blink, he's captivated by her existence. Her features slowly begin to make an appearance. He sees her smile. She's enhancing, prerogative and begins luring him into a false sense of security. Distracting him from the reality of the pain he's in. Matthew's almost breathing this woman in.

"Lauren... You came back..."

Trapped in the moment, he feels an intense state of euphoria and is embracing each second of this enchanting possession. Staring intently, he's now convinced it's Lauren. Surrendering himself to the female entity, no sooner has he surrendered his soul, captivated, he's failing to notice the progression of the mist. It's surrounding the mirror, becoming thick. Eventually losing sight of the mirror, Matthew gets in a fluster.

"Lauren... Lauren..."

Once the mist descends and begins to ease away, the female, still present within the reflection, unexpectedly leaps out of the mirror towards Matthew! Her existence is nothing like Lauren. Jet-black long hair hanging heavy either side of her face. Dripping a deep black substance. Her skin is the deepest shade of grey, with deep rips present sporadically upon her flesh. These sinister gaping holes ooze the same black substance. As she attempts to absorb Matthew's soul with her demonic eyes, they become the deepest shade of red as her power grows stronger with every second that passes. Her lips are grey and gushing from her mouth; the thick black substance rolls down her chin. Matthew's heart feels as though it's about to burst as he sees her grey, stained teeth stretching out aggressively. Forcing herself towards him, she's reaching to pull him into the mirror with her.

With a sudden *gasp* of air, Matthew leaps forward. He's back in his room, soaking wet from head to toe, undressed and wearing nothing but his boxer shorts and is, once again, unexplainably back in his bed. Touching his face, his mouth, and patting his hands all over his body, relief begins flowing round his facial expression as he realises it was, as Eve suggested, just a bad dream.

Collapsing back onto his pillow and breathing heavy, Matthew's staring at the bright white painted walls and beings to ingest the purity of the air that's circulating around him. The bedroom window is open slightly and the fresh sea breeze is gradually blowing into the room. Embracing the safety of his home, he reaches to the bedside table and grabs the small white alarm clock. The time's flashing green. It's five thirty a.m. Falling back on the pillow to rest, no sooner had his sight adjusted to the fact he's home, his eyes begin protruding from their sockets. Matthew is sure he'd made the transition from nightmare to reality, yet here he lies in shock. Frozen to his confinement and once again unable to move, he's stuck. His eyes tell no lies. Matthew sees the female shadow; she's appeared and is present in the corner of his room, staring directly at him. Matthew sees this isn't the Lauren he remembered at all. Placing her grey forefinger with its deep marks present upon it firmly to her mouth, she mimes, "Shh…"

Opening his mouth in a desperate attempt to scream, Matthew's quick to find out he's unable to achieve this. Blinking his eyes, he sees she's suddenly disappeared! Still unable to speak, he's lay in a panic.

But no sooner has the unknown female disappeared, she returns! Except this time, she's closer than ever and sat on the side of his bed.

Seeing her true form, her true existence and the reality of her horrific presence, Matthew remains in disbelief. With her head low, she's facing towards the window and is dripping the same mysterious black substance all over his bed.

Remaining still, she's feeding from the fear radiating off his soul and is gaining strength with every second that passes. Matthew lies paralysed with terror, tears begin to fall down his motionless face. Unexpectedly, she rises off the bed. Matthew doesn't move and is holding his breath. For a brief moment, he believes this evil entity is about to disappear. Standing with her back turned to him, she's once again luring him into a false sense of security. Quickly turning she throws out her arms in an attempt to grab Matthew, who instantly screams out, "Help!"

With the words fresh from his vocal chords, he sees a flash of her demonic features as these disappear into his face. Thankfully she's gone!

Chapter 9
"New eyes."

Parking at the front of the huge steel school gates, Eve looks across to her dad.

"Are you sure you're okay, you've been very quiet this morning, Dad?"

"Yes darling, I'm fine. Please don't start worrying about me." Leaning over and tucking his daughter's hair behind her ears, he continues, "I'm lucky I have you, Evelyn Jade Honey."

Taking in the moment, Matthew's living each individual second as though he runs the risk of never having the privilege again. Smiling back, Eve, now satisfied with her dad's response, turns to get out of the car.

"Darling, where's your mum's necklace?"

Eve immediately replies, "It's here."

"Sorry, panicked for a second then, I couldn't see it."

"Dad, maybe you shouldn't go into work today, I think you need time out."

"I'm fine, now go on, get into school before you're late."

Jumping out the car Eve shouts, "Love ya."

With her final words, she slams the car door shut. Matthew sits watching his daughter walking off in a world of her own. As he sees Eve enter the school gates, he notices a group of girls closely following her. Their intentions seem impure and they appear to be laughing and mocking Eve behind her back.

Four young pretty girls, each with long blonde hair. They're walking along in perfect synchronisation with each other. They hold matching handbags over their shoulders, matching grey socks are pulled up to their knees and each wear make-up which has been perfectly sculpted to their faces. All four of them are pointing, laughing and pulling mocking spiteful facial expressions. With a rage building up inside of him, Matthew's now completely unable to control his emotions. He stands out of his car and shouts across to the girls, "Oi, you lot, leave it out."

The girls turn around to see who has just shouted. With the words fresh from his mouth, Matthew's aggression levels begin to rise as his blood boils. Not content with the warning words he's shouted, he makes his way around the front of the car. The girls jump as they realise who's yelling. Instantly he recognises one of the young girls, and so Matthew shouts once more, "Stacey, don't think I won't have a word with your dad!"

Upon hearing her dad, and being completely unaware as to why, Eve puts her head down and runs through the huge dark-oak double doors. She's turned red with embarrassment. The girls instantly begin sharing the same expression. They've been caught out. Straightaway, they all stop their taunting ways and, as they scurry off putting their heads down, they set about whispering to one another. Matthew looks round and sees all the astonished faces of the young adults who are casually making their way to school. No longer in control of his actions, he shouts once more, "Show's over."

Storming back into his car, he places his head on the steering wheel. With his adrenaline racing throughout his mind and body, Matthew closes his eyes. Taking in deep, singular breaths, he's desperately attempting to regain possession of his emotions once more. Focusing on the purity of the air he breathes so deeply, as he begins embracing this, and feeling alive, whilst he's caught off guard, Matthew's thoughts slowly begin to drift. Unexpectedly his mind projects a flashback from his recent nightmares. In this one horrific flash image, he sees the demonic woman. With a pained expression upon his face, Matthew's quick to shake this traumatic vision out of his mind. As he opens his eyes he shudders.

"It was just a bad dream."

Looking up, he stares at the clear blue sky. The serenity of nature helps to calm his thoughts and soothe his mind. The world appears bright and the freedom of the birds gracefully flying free gives him a sense of empowerment.

Attempting to shift his mood back into his usual, happy vibration, and desiring to heal his mind, Matthew breathes in deep one last time and smiles as he turns up the stereo. His favourite chill-out collection is playing through the speakers. Feeling slightly more relaxed than before, he's confident the weekend's events are not going to have a negative impact on his precious mind-set. And so, with his new eyes, and gratitude for life, Matthew shakes off the incident and begins driving to work.

As he pulls up to the entrance of the huge gravel car park surrounding his offices, the sun is at its height of the morning. The security staff lift the barrier.

"Thank you."

With a slight Jamaican accent, a voice sounds through the security speaker, "You're welcam' Mr Honey, and gud mornin' to you."

"Good morning, Eric."

Finding a spot, Matthew parks up. He doesn't have a designated space at the front of the building; he firmly believes in equality. He is equal to everyone who works at the company, all eighty-seven of them, first come, first serve. The only parking policy is that all staff must park their vehicles one after the other. Matthew strongly believes that first impressions count. Reaching into the side of the car door, he grabs his phone. Placing this inside his silk-lined pocket, he grabs his briefcase, and, for a split second, Matthew sits back, and this time, he carefully allows his mind to drift. Taking his phone back out of his pocket, he checks his messages. With multiple missed calls and messages from all different people, Matthew has not one missed call or even a message from the one person's name he desires to see, Jess. With disappointment and confusion fast spreading across his face, he pulls up Jess's contact number.

"Where did you go?" With a slight pause, Matthew remains deep in thought.

Suddenly, he feels a slight sense of guilt for losing his cool this morning and embarrassing his daughter. He decides to text Eve: *Darling, I'm sorry.*

As he steps out of the car and walks towards the building, he begins to make a mental note of the registration plates, which are neatly lined up in the car park. He smiles. Matthew knows exactly who's in the office. He enters the high-rise, brown brick building through the rotating glass doors; the simple external structure is deceitful to the interior magnificence you're presented with. As soon as you enter, you're greeted by huge silver letters which hang on the wall. Honey Productions is centrally positioned and standing proud. The internal design of this amazing building is unique and unlike anything your eyes have ever seen. After all, this has Lauren's irreplaceable stamp all over it. Sitting at the huge modern curved glass reception desk, Matthew's greeted by his charming, friendly, and often hyper receptionist, Daniel. Who sometimes comes across as though he's had way too many E-numbers.

"Good morning, Matthew."

"Good morning Daniel. Any messages for me?"

"Yes, you've got an urgent call from Mr Hews. Erm, something about voiceover issues. Then, another from Vera, Bill Hades's PA. She wants you to call her back when you get the chance. What else was it, oh damn, erm." Tapping a pencil on his head, Daniel's trying to remember the final message. "I'm sure I wrote it down somewhere..."

"I tell you what, email me."

"Okay, will do, Matthew."

Grabbing a newspaper and placing this under his arm, as Matthew makes his way over to the lift he presses the button. Whilst standing waiting patiently for the lift's arrival, Daniel shouts one final message.

"Ah ha, found it. A lady called Jess rang for you this morning. Let me see, let me see, nope, she didn't leave a message, just a name."

Matthew immediately heads back to Daniel.

"Jess?"

Pausing, Daniel looks at his notepad and begins quickly flicking through the pages.

"Yes, erm, she said her name was Jess but, she didn't want to leave a message."

Grabbing the pad, Matthew himself begins flicking through this.

"Did she say anything else, anything at all?"

Becoming confused by Matthew's frantic reaction to this woman, Daniel replies, "No, but I have her number. I wrote it down whilst she was on the call. Would you like me to call her back and find out what she wants?"

"No! It's fine. I'm sure she'll call back."

Ripping the page out that contains the contact number, Matthew makes his way back to the lift and puts the piece of paper in his pocket. Hearing a *ding* as the glass lift arrives, he steps in, presses five, and as the doors close he shuts his eyes. Now alone with his thoughts, Matthew feels an overwhelming surge of guilt. Leaning with his back against the glass lift, without warning, a very significant event appears in his mind. With his eyes remaining closed he smiles. Matthew's back at his wedding day. The room is white, fresh and he's surrounded by orange and yellow flowers which are reflecting in the room, creating a radiant glow. Standing tall in his navy-blue suit, the only sound he can hear is each deep breath he takes as he's waiting in anticipation for the arrival of his soul mate. Beaming brighter than the stars, he is the proudest man alive. Not once has he endured nerves; he couldn't wait to commit his life to Lauren.

Embracing every second of this vision, Matthew sees the two, giant, brown mahogany doors as they begin to open. With his hands placed behind his back, he looks down and takes a deep breath in and, as he raises his head, there she is. Standing strong and beaming with pride in her white lace, fitted wedding dress, is his soul mate. Her smile is brighter than the stars. Tears of pride, tears of joy and tears of love fall down his face as she's gracefully gliding down the aisle making her way towards him. Still captured in the moment, Matthew once again hears *ding* as the lift arrives at his floor. Feeling a slight bounce, this shifts him out of his vision and sadly back into his reality.

Regaining his posture, he steps out of the lift and begins to walk past the desks of his fellow colleagues. Greeting each of them with a smile.

"Good morning, Matthew."

"Good morning, Sarah."

"Good morning, Mr Honey."

"Ha-ha, good morning, Jack, what have I told you, Matthew is fine."

"Sorry, Mr Honey, I mean – Matthew."

"Good morning, Matthew. I've sent you an email regarding filming at the Tattoo Convention in Surrey."

"Good morning, Esme. Oh, that's great, thank you. Did you manage to get some quality footage for me?"

"Yeah, oh my God, the event was great. Just you wait till you see what me and James captured on camera. You're gonna be jealous that you didn't go."

"Ha-ha, I'm sure I will. Thanks again, covering for me at such short notice."

"No problem, just don't you go forgetting my Christmas bonus."

"Never would."

Smiling, Mathew approaches his office; he unlocks the door and as he's about to enter, he's stopped.

"Matthew, is everything okay?"

"Morning, Christina. Yeah sure, why'd you ask?"

"Well, Eve text Melissa the other night, suggesting she was going to..." She lowers her tone. "End it all. She's only just told me this morning when I drove her to school. I thought she'd been acting weird all weekend, but I just assumed it was, you know, that time of the month."

"Oh, Christina, I'm so sorry, yeah Eve's fine now. Well, I say now, what it was, well, I... erm, keep this to yourself."

"I promise."

"I actually got chatting to a woman the other day."

Christina interrupts. "A woman! Matthew, really?"

"Yes, a woman, shh, keep ya voice down. Well, I invited her for tea and after that pretty much the whole weekend's a blur."

"How was Eve about it, do you need me to talk to her?"

"At first, she was horrified. Actually, she was furious and then, strangely enough, she was, I think, just fine with it."

"Matthew, what do you mean, you think?"

"Listen, Christina, you wouldn't believe me even if I told you. Thanks for letting me know, I'll have a chat with her later. You busy today?"

"Well I'm here if you need me. I'll let Melissa know in a minute, she's been worried sick about her. Nope, not particularly busy today, just passing through to try and book some new appointments and check me emails."

"New appointments, that's what I like to hear. You and Lauren always were the twin sister queens of sales."

"Ha-ha, you know this. See you later."

"See you later. Oh, tell Dave the rave I said hey."

As he enters his office, Matthew places his briefcase down on the floor at the side of the two-seater black leather couch next to the doorway. Walking over to his solid oak desk, as he places the newspaper down, he notices the light on his office phone is flashing. Pressing the hands-free button and play, he hears:

"You have three new messages and seven saved messages. To listen to new messages, press one. To listen—"

Matthew interrupts and presses one. He makes his way to the window. Placing his hands behind his back, the voicemail messages begin playing out.

"First message received today at seven forty-five a.m. *Beep.* Matthew, it's Bill, call me when you get this. *Beep.*

"Second message received today at seven fifty-eight a.m. *Beep.* Hi Matthew, it's Laura calling from TLC Operatives, could you please check the edits I've sent across to you? Many thanks. *Beep.*

"Final message received today at eight thirty-six a.m. *Beep.* Hi Matthew. It's Vera, Bill Hades's PA, can you give me a call when you get this please? Many thanks. *Beep.*

"End of messages. To listen to these messages again, press one."

Making his way over to his desk, Matthew lifts the receiver and puts this down to end the call.

As he peers out of the huge uniquely designed window from the fifth floor, he's surprisingly disappointed. Matthew thought at least one of the messages might have been from Jess. Standing alone with his thoughts, he hears chitter chatter and laughter coming from his colleagues outside his office;

he smiles at their happiness. Reaching into his pocket he pulls out the piece of paper containing the number Daniel wrote down, walking over to his desk. Much like his home, the layout on this is immaculate and not a single item leans so much as a centimetre out of place. Putting the piece of paper containing Jess's number down, he peers across to the family photograph of him, Lauren and Eve. Suddenly he feels an overwhelming surge of sadness.

"God only knows how much I miss you."

No sooner has he spoken these words, Matthew feels his phone vibrating inside his pocket. Without having to remain with a feeling of disappointment for too long, he sees Jess is calling. Her name's flashing like a strobe light. Before he knows it, he's answering the call.

"Hello, Matthew Honey speaking."

"I was worried about you."

He smiles.

***

Oblivious to what's taking place in the outside world, Eve's sat at the front of the class in her English lesson. She's daydreaming about nothing of any significance. Suddenly her teacher, Ms Phelps, *bangs* a book on her desk. Jumping with fright, this unexpected movement shifts a distracted Eve back into her reality. Flicking through the pages, she's desperately trying to work out where the class are up to. English isn't her favourite subject. She considers herself a creative, free spirit, and it doesn't help that Ms Phelps is extremely strict. She believes children should only be seen and never heard. Ms Phelps's classroom has the same eerie energy as her gloomy appearance. She looks as though she's never been loved and gets dressed in the dark every day. With lipstick continually plastered across her teeth, this isn't her only attractive trait; she always has an overbearing stench of coffee breath. It's disgusting. During Ms Phelps's classes, pupils are *not* permitted to speak unless she authorises them to do so.

"Now, in complete silence, this means *no* reading out loud. I want you all to read the following highlighted passages on your worksheets. Make notes on the grammatical errors, as I will be testing you on this in the next five minutes, before the end of class."

There's a sudden tap on the window of the classroom door and Ms Phelps instantly leaves the room. Once the door's shut, and, Ms Phelps is out of sight, Eve hears mocking words and laughter coming from the girls at the back of the class. It's the same group of cruel girls who were taunting her this morning.

"Oh, my name's Eve. I get my daddy to stick up for me."

"Ha-ha, yeah, even though I'm a murderer and I killed my mum."

"I know, he probably doesn't even know he's next, am I right girls, ha-ha."

The girls, in sync with each other, begin laughing loudly as they become satisfied with their bullying intentions.

Eve, in a fit of rage with her head down, shouts, "Enough!"

Ms Phelps immediately bursts back into the classroom.

"Evelyn Honey, how dare you shout in my classroom!"

Eve, the girl who would normally cower away and hide in the corner crying until her eyes were sore, is now the complete opposite. Much like her dad earlier, she's unable to control her emotions. Unable to stop the rage from growing inside of her. The pencil she holds in her hand snaps. Blood slowly drips from the cuts which this now sharp piece of wood has created. Completely oblivious to this, Eve's digging the pencil further into the palm of her hand. As her fury grows, her grip continues to get tighter. Eve's chest begins pulsating up and down as her breathing rapidly increases. Her eyes suddenly become overcast. As this new energy takes over each blood vessel, her sight has been overpowered, and her eyes are now jet-black. Not a patch of white can be seen. With her head remaining down, Eve's thoughts are in one place only. Her mind and all her energy are completely focused on the girls at the back of the class. Again, in sync with each other, the girls begin to place their hands over their ears. Creating suction and pressing them tightly, it appears as though they're desperately attempting to block out sound, but no sound can be heard within the confinement of the walls of the classroom. Each girl has a pained expression on her face and they individually set about screeching at the top of their voices. This group of cruel bullying girls, who all ordinarily remain strong and feed from the evil energy they all share, are now lay looking more vulnerable than ever. No more do they look as though they should be feared. No more do they look strong. These bitchy cruel girls are weakened, as their mind is being taken over by the unknown.

All the other pupils present in the classroom panic. Without being restricted, they each jump from their chairs. Most of them make no attempt to look back and leave their belongings. Once every single innocent pupil has frantically burst out of the classroom, a gust of wind presents itself within the confinement of the walls. The heavy brown door bangs, and with no visual help, the door locks. The girls, now curled up on the floor, are still covering their ears as they set about individually screeching louder than ever, one after the other.

The view from the window of the classroom, which was bright and the sky clear, is no more. Deep grey clouds materialise, and the outside world appears to be within complete darkness. Much like the resemblance of the storm forming outside, the angrier Eve gets, the darker the mist in her jet-black eyes becomes. Digging the pencil, she holds tightly into the table, Eve begins to drag this towards her. From nowhere, the horrific demonic grey lady appears behind her. Her long jet-black hair hangs heavy. With eyes that retain the deepest shade of blood-red, her grey sinful face is impure and is to be feared. A sinister black substance drips from the deep cracks surrounding her mouth. Leaning over Eve's shoulder, this evil entity is embracing every second of her possession over this once innocent soul.

With each internal sinister manifestation, and the wilful acceptance from Eve, her body is no longer pure. As her rage builds, and the possession reigns, Eve's unaware that she's surrendering to the desires of the demonic creature. A tiny section of her soul is being retained and locked deep within this evil entity's deceitful black heart. Her black heart which no longer beats. Her black heart which oozes neglect, and a strong supremacy, whilst it holds this carefully selected soul captive; this same unnerving organ is now absorbing Eve's DNA, making them connect as one. Now there's no going back. Like a magnetic pull, they both stand closely together. Eve feels her soulless breath brushing past her skin. Every exhale is felt, along with its sub-zero temperatures. The sinister black substance which drips from the cracks surrounding her mouth begins gushing as she separates her lips. Leaving its sickening presence wherever it lands, this black liquid has the stench of death attached to it. Content with the progression of her calculated possession and the acceptance from Eve, spitting the thick black bloody substance, she begins whispering directly into her ear, "Ring a' Ring o' Roses – your soul is mine."

Like a command, Eve instantly stands and with a sudden twitch of her head, the girls who remain in agony on the floor now each have their hands fixated around their throats. Gasping and struggling for air, they individually begin choking. Turning and making her way towards the back of the class, with every step closer Eve gets to the girls they're continuing with the battle of life they've been presented with, and their ability to breathe becomes even more restricted.

Ms Phelps, frozen with fear, stands overseeing the disturbing unnatural events happening in her reality. This strong, overpowering, woman has, much like the cruel bullying girls, lost her voice. Like a statue, she remains stiff, standing at the blackboard next to the book cabinet by the doorway. Ms Phelps, unfortunately, didn't make it out of the classroom before the door was locked. She's been forced to watch the events taking place as her soul has been violently frozen against her own will. Not so much as a twitch presents itself on her facial features, or throughout her body. Ms Phelps is immobile.

Reaching the girls, Eve bends down. Her eyes remain jet-black, so black, they form mirrors, and the girls can see their desperate reflection in Eve's eyes. Uncontrollably choking and unable to beg for release, each girl sees the fear plastered across her face as they become unrecognisable. Not only this, each of the girls sees the effect of the possessive energy, ligature, which is tightening around their necks, as their eyes begin protruding from out of their sockets. The struggle to breathe gets too much as the lack of oxygen to the brain begins taking its toll; their eyes start to roll slowly towards the back of their heads. Eve's now satisfied with their suffering and, just as they're all about to pass out, she leans across and says, "*Ti libero per ora.*"

The girls, along with Ms Phelps, who falls to the floor, instantly lose consciousness. The demonic evil entity embraces an intense, euphoric and orgasmic sense of satisfaction at Eve's ability to receive commands and willingly surrender her soul. Receiving this young girl's DNA and embedding it deep within her existence warrants her empowerment to grow stronger. Making her way over to Eve, she leans to her ear once more and whispers, "Welcome to the dark side."

With her final words spoken, the evil entity disappears. Eve stands. The girls remain in the same position. They are entirely motionless and silent on the floor. Their eyes are wide open, bright red and swollen. Appearing on the surface of their skin and around their necks, a faint line begins to originate. As the oxygen once again circulates around their bodies, this faint line manifests and develops a deep red bruised tone. This internal damage is showcasing, exactly, where the possessive strangulation has taken place. Feeling a sense of euphoria herself, at the confirmation of her bullies' intense suffering, Eve calmly makes her way back towards her desk, collects her belongings and walks towards the classroom door. With every step she takes, her eyes start to revert to their normal tone. As the mist sets about leaving her sight, you can see the intense effect of the possession leaving Eve's body.

Making no attempt to look back, Eve steps over Ms Phelps and glances down at the bullying teacher. Lay in a trance-like state, Ms Phelps is flat on her back, with her head facing up. Her eyes are wide open, but you can see there's no-one home. This once strong woman is frozen with fear. She looks as though her soul has left its physical form as a tear slowly ventures down her motionless face.

Content with her actions and leaving the aftermath behind her, the door unlocks, and Eve exits the classroom. As she steps out onto the corridor, she closes the door behind her. The energy is still and quiet, not a single soul can be seen. As the bell begins ringing loudly throughout the school, Eve places her backpack over her shoulder and makes her way towards the front entrance. Her eyes are now, once again, her own.

Chapter 10
"Suspicious or paranoid?"

"Table for two, usual spot please."

Standing next to the island in the kitchen, Matthew's on the phone to his favourite Italian restaurant.

"Time, eight thirty. Brilliant, thanks Daniela, see you then." He ends the call.

"Hi Jess, yes, it's all booked. So, I'll meet you out front. Shall we say twenty past eight?" He continues, "Great, I look forward to it. See you later alligator."

Putting the phone down, Matthew says, "Alligator, what the f—"

Shaking his head and laughing to himself, he places the phone into his pocket, turns, and makes his way towards the day room. With the television blaring throughout the house, as he enters, he sees Eve sat on the couch with her feet tucked up. She's watching telly and laughing away at her favourite American TV show, *Friends*. Walking over to the couch, he sits right beside his daughter.

"Oh, is this the one where Monica has a cold?"

"Yeah, I'm in the pribe ob libe. Ha-ha. Classic."

Laughing, Matthew pulls Eve in tight. Kissing her on the head he whispers, "I love you, darling."

Eve smiles as she looks up at her dad.

"Love you too, Dad."

"You will always be my priority. My number one and my right-hand lady, no matter what, I will *always* take care of you."

"I know, Dad."

Eve begins to snuggle her dad tight. The silence created says it all, and both father and daughter are enjoying the moment together whilst watching TV. With Eve in a world of her own and giggling away at the telly, Matthew looks to his watch. He has four hours before his date with Jess. Glancing out of the huge window he sees the sun's shinning and the sea's still out. Turning to Eve, he says, "Fancy a walk along the beach with me, kidda?"

"Sure, but why... Hang on, what's going on?"

"You're always suspicious, Evelyn Jade." Laughing, he continues, "Honestly, it's nothing, I promise."

"Hmm..."

"Look – I cross my heart. I just thought it would be nice to go for a walk along the beach together. Clear mind's a healthy mind."

"Okay then, lemme just get my jacket."

Daydreaming about nothing of any importance, they both walk hand in hand along the beach front. Matthew and Eve are quietly enjoying each other's company. The huge, grey and white beach-loving seagulls are out on top form this evening as they begin circling above them. Once these magnificent but greedy birds realise both Matthew and Eve serve them no purpose, as they have no food present in their hands, they quickly flock off looking for anyone within the vicinity who might be able to feed them.

Over the crisp, English sea, the waves begin slowly mounting, one after the other. The sound of this is calming. Not too far out into the distance, you can see the outlines of the boats as they gently float on the water top. Matthew stops walking and begins stretching out his arms. He takes in the biggest deep breath, filling his lungs.

"You feel that, darling?"

"Huh..."

"This is what being alive feels like in one single moment. Try it."

Eve laughs as she copies her dad's actions. The fresh salty sea water can be smelt within the air. It seems cleansing to the lungs and almost euphoric as it enhances their ability to feel true inner happiness.

"Feels good. Am I right, kidda?"

Laughing, she replies, "Suppose so."

"You know something, the minute you were placed into my arms, I looked at you and I couldn't believe it. I had gifted this beautiful little girl with life. Okay, your perfection is mainly from your mum's genetics, but nonetheless, you are half me, too."

Eve smiles. Without thinking she grabs her dad's hand. Feeling a pain shoot up her arm she jumps and instantly let's go.

"You all right, darling?"

"Yes, sorry, I fell at school today and cut my hand, it just hurts a little, that's all."

"Here, let me take a look at it."

"No, it's okay, honestly I'm fine. Come on."

Grabbing her dad's hand once more, Eve begins dragging him closer to the water.

"Eve... What are you doing?"

"Just shut up and run with me."

Dipping her hands into the freezing cold sea water, she cups this and chucks a handful directly at her dad, who it hits in the face.

"Oh, really – so you wanna play, do you kidda, right, well it's game on."

Instantly, Matthew starts laughing and mirrors her actions. These two, now behaving like innocent children, begin having what can only be described as a water fight. Passers-by are laughing as they look on at the fun and joy they're both creating. The dogs who are playing freely on the beach have heard the laughter and have run off from their owners, ready to join in the fun. Heading straight towards Matthew and Eve, this innocent playful group of dogs begin barking with excitement and wagging their tails, trying desperately to play.

Matthew's still got his suit on and so this snapshot, family-fun image looks even more angelic than normal. Giggling away, Eve can't help herself as she creates waves of water and begins throwing them her dad's way. They're both soaking wet, but radiating love, joy and happiness. Eventually, accepting defeat and running away somewhat theatrically, Matthew heads back towards the man-made, grey brick wall. He's surrendering. Eve's not too far behind him. She shouts, "Come back, you wimp."

Seemingly out of breath, Matthew rests on the low wall with his hands in the air.

"I give up. You win."

"Yes. I win. I'm a winner, Dad!"

Laughing, they both sit side by side staring out at the tranquil surroundings. This is home. This is where they belong. Taking off his jacket and placing this on the wall to dry, Matthew grabs Eve and tucks her under his soggy arm.

"Eww."

"You know something, kidda, when I went to see your mum in the Chapel of Rest, I made a commitment to her. Have I ever told you this story?"

"No, go on, what did you say?"

"I made a commitment that I would never let you go. Her sacrifice would be my strength to protect you always in life and, if for any reason I lost you, I vowed that I would never rest, and I would search the ends of the earth to find you."

"Aww, Dad, that's so sweet. But honestly, I'm going nowhere."

"I spoke to your auntie Christina today at work. Melissa is very worried about you."

"Oh. Now I understand. Dad, look, I'm sorry, I didn't mean it, well, I did in that moment. I was at Mum's 'Garden of Secrets' and I was just so mad. But, I'm fine with it."

"Eve, I have something to say, I'm—"

Eve interrupts. "I know. Go on your date with Jess, like I said I'm fine with it. I just want you to be happy, Dad."

Matthew smiles, "Are you sure, kidda, you would tell me if it got too much? You're always my priority."

"I know, Dad, it's fine. I like Jess, she's all right. When I'm around her, it's weird, she kinda makes me feel... what's the word I'm looking for... that's it, she makes me feel empowered."

Tapping her on the head gently, he says, "Erm... Hello... Can I have my Eve back, please, clearly this is an imposter. I'll never understand women. You all literally confuse the life out of me."

***

Standing in the cold but extremely organised garage, Matthew's frantically searching for something. Reaching high on the shelves and pulling out the contents inside the drawers, cabinets, boxes and anything else he can see within his proximity, Matthew begins scratching his head.

"I'm sure it was here somewhere."

Reaching up high on the final top shelf he grabs a box.

"Ah ha, found it."

Firmly in his hand, he holds an immaculate box containing two micro-sized cameras. Being a professional film-maker/technology nerd has its perks, and he always has the latest equipment in cameras and gadgets. Taking the box up to his bedroom, he places its contents on the bedside table. Out falls two teeny tiny cameras. Holding these in his hands, as he's trying to work out where to put them, Matthew's mind begins to drift. He starts to wonder if he's actually being overly paranoid, as both sides of his brain begin having a debate.

Putting cameras up in the house, really? It's a bit extreme Matthew, after all, it's only a bad dream.

Yes, but it's a weekend's worth of bad dreams, not just one night. There's no harm in putting them up. What's the worst that can happen, you'll either see something or you won't. No-one needs to know, and no harm done.

With his mind desiring answers and this looking as though it's the only logical way he's going to receive them, Matthew's content with the outcome of the debate circulating inside his head. He sets about placing one of the cameras at the end of his curtain pole. The other, he places in the hallway on the corner of the picture frame, facing Eve's bedroom door. These wireless, genius inventions, to the naked eye, cannot be seen.

If this demonic woman is real, or if she isn't, and Matthew is, in fact, just experiencing nightmares through guilt, then the cameras won't lie. But maybe, just maybe, something strange is going on and the cameras will confirm this. What if Lauren *is* revisiting him in the night, what if she's expressing her disgust at him bringing another woman into Eve's life, or what if he is losing his mind? Either way, the outcome for him is one of great intensity, and Matthew's extremely nervous about the result. He's even more nervous about the outcome of this than he is about his date with Jess, which is now less than one hour away.

In his favourite navy-blue suit, white shirt, and navy-blue bow tie, looking as handsome as ever, Matthew's hair's slicked back and tiny deep silver strands peer through his slight curls on either side. Standing outside the entrance of the restaurant, he's waiting in great anticipation for the arrival of his date. Looking to his watch, as he peers back up, she's there. He is speechless. Walking across to the taxi, he opens the car door. With elegance Jess places one foot after the other and steps out.

"Why, thank you, Mr Honey."

Handing the taxi driver payment for the journey, as he turns, he sees her clearly. She's standing in a floor-length red dress which has lace beautifully detailed around the neckline and down the sleeves. A silver glisten can be seen from the chain and the locket, as this hangs close to her chest. Her hair is styled to perfection and, as this thick full head of deep brown hair sits over her shoulders, it begins flowing ever so gently in the breeze. Jess's eyes are radiant and enchanting, so enchanting, in fact, Matthew finds himself locked into her sight. With utter admiration, and a trance-like expression upon his face, he speaks: "You really are so very beautiful."

Captured by her aura, he's locked into her energy. Standing gazing, Matthew's completely unaware of the awkward silence he's once again creating.

"Shall we?" Jess says.

"Yes, erm, sorry, after you."

Entering the restaurant, which appears rustic and romantic, they smell the fresh bread, pizzas and tomato-based sauces cooking throughout the whole building. This fabulous restaurant is family run. Authentic Italian music plays gently in the background and multiple pictures with fairy lights can be seen hanging on the walls, giving all their customers a true taste of Italy.

Standing in the beautifully lit and warming reception area, Matthew and Jess are shown to their table for the evening by their waiter, Daniela. With his Italian accent and broken English, he says, "Ciao, Mr Honey, so good to always be seeing you again. I will be your waiter for this evening. If you will be needing anything, please let me know. I am always being happy to be helping you, and your beautiful lady friend." He passes them both a menu. "Today we have the specials for you, a calzone of your choosing, ravioli, mussels, fillet steak pepe and polo crème. Now, whilst you browse at your timing, can I be getting you any drinks?"

Matthew replies, "I've got this. Daniela, we'll have your best bottle of rosé wine please."

"I'm impressed that you remembered, Mr Honey."

Matthew's feeling slightly proud of himself, as this is probably the only thing he can remember from the time they spent together. His ego collects the brownie points he's just been rewarded with. Both Matthew and Jess begin smiling in sync with each other as they look down at their menus.

Making conversation, Matthew says, "Out of interest, what is your favourite place to eat out?"

But before she has chance to answer, Daniela approaches the table with their wine. Pouring this into their glasses, he explains, "This is a Chateau d'Esclans, Les Clans and Garrus, from the Esclans range. This is our most popular of the rosé wines."

"Thank you." Jess says, as she reaches out with her left hand and elegantly grabs her wine glass. She begins swirling this and smells the wine.

"You're left-handed?"

"Yes..."

He sits back in total disbelief. "Lauren was left-handed." He laughs. "How did I not notice? So similar, this is just weird."

"Really? I would never have known. How peculiar."

Jess looks to Matthew and, as she places her wine glass back on the table, she says, "In answer to your question, I don't really have a favourite place to eat. You see, I'm fairly new to the area and so I'm unsure of the best places, or indeed any places, to eat out at."

"Oh, really? So where are you from then?"

"Well now, here's a question for you, Mr Honey. Would you, in fact, like to know where I am from, or where I currently live?"

"Erm, I've never been asked that question before. But, well, I guess I'd like to know... Hmm, can I say both?"

Laughing, she responds, "Of course you can. I just wasn't too sure if you were interested. Well, I'm originally from a small village called Gehenna."

Matthew interrupts: "I've never heard of it."

"You never will, it's a very small village. Now, Mr Honey, I live wherever I desire."

With his dry sense of humour, Matthew laughs. "So, you're homeless then?"

"Do I look homeless?"

Embarrassed, he says, "No, sorry, I was joking."

"You're lucky I like you, Mr Honey. You're forgiven. It's meant metaphorically. I am what's known as a free spirit."

Taking out his phone, Matthew says, "Gehenna, you say, how are you spelling that, is it G—"

Before he has time to finish, Jess takes the phone from out of his hand and erases the internet search he was about to complete.

"No phones this evening, Mr Honey. I want your full attention to be on me."

"Please, call me Matthew. So, come on then, enlighten me, how come Eve's now your biggest fan?" He places his hand on his head. "What did I miss whilst I was out of it?"

"I told you I would empower her. You see, Matthew, I know how the complicated mind of a teenage girl works."

Once again, with his dry sense of humour, Matthew replies, "Me too, I was a teenage girl once too, you know."

Laughing awkwardly, Jess replies, "Ha-ha, yes, you are funny, aren't you?"

Coughing as though he's clearing his throat when he's actually trying to distract from the discomfort he's created, Matthew says, "Really, though, I'd seriously like to thank you."

"Thank me?"

"Yes, whatever you've said to Eve has made a huge difference; she seems calm again. I can only imagine it's your influence that's created this."

"Oh Matthew, don't worry, I'll always help. I'm here for Eve."

"Well it's greatly appreciated. As you can imagine, after everything we've both been through, Eve has to be my priority, and it's a huge relief to me that she's been able to build a connection, of sorts, with you."

"You don't need to thank me for that. She's a precious soul and has the ability to be a strong, powerful woman. I can see her making an unforgettable influence on the universe. Call it a prediction."

"That's very kind of you to say."

"I only speak words of truth."

It's Friday evening and the restaurant is packed. The Italian music's playing gently in the background, and as Matthew's beginning to relax, the conversation develops from awkward to engaging. These two individuals both begin resembling flirty innocent school kids. The smiles, the giggles, and the chemistry begins to show. As the night progresses, they're both enjoying each other's company, so much so, a spotlight may as well be present on their table and everyone else frozen in time.

Chapter 11
"It's... Showtime!"

Arriving back at the house, as both Matthew and Jess enter, they notice Eve. She's making her way down the stairs and heading in their direction.

"Hey darling, look who's come to say hello."

Bypassing her dad, like a magnet she makes her way across to Jess and without saying a single word, she stands directly by her side.

"Aye, kidda, where's my hug?"

Standing with her head held high, Jess looks empowered by Eve's seemingly impulsive action.

"It's so lovely to see you again, Eve. I've had a wonderful evening with your father; it's a shame you couldn't join us."

Saying nothing, Eve remains with a blank expression, peering up at Jess, and is yet to make any form of contact with her dad.

"Erm, earth to Eve."

Turning to her dad, she speaks. Her voice sounds broken, and, in a robotic and timed manner, she says, "Hello Dad."

"Hello Eve. What's gotten into you...?"

Not only does Eve choose to ignore the question her dad has just asked, she turns back to look at Jess as though he doesn't exist.

"What the f—You avin' a laugh?" Puzzled, he continues, "Kidda, tell you what, it's getting late, time for you to head to bed."

Remaining with a strong stance of eye contact, Jess and Eve are locked tight. Suddenly, Jess gently nods her head. Without any warning or sound, Eve makes her way across to her dad, kisses him and heads up the stairs. Not a question raised, or a kick off heard. Continuing as though nothing has happened, Jess says, "Shall we have a nightcap?"

Following her into the kitchen, Matthew's confused. "Hang about, what was that?"

"What was what?"

"That, just then – that with Eve?"

"I don't know what you're referring to, Mr Honey."

"Jess, don't try and mug me off. And it's Matthew. You know exactly what I'm on about, my daughter has just ignored me like I don't exist."

"She didn't. Matthew, you're over-reacting."

"*My* daughter hasn't walked past me like that for a long time."

"So, what you're saying is, we can't win with you? Eve no longer gets angry at my existence, and this – what – angers you? Shouldn't you just be happy that we're getting along?" Walking across to Matthew, Jess wraps her arms around his neck. "Matthew, I don't know the answer, maybe Eve's drawn to me because she's not had female company since her mum died. Maybe she's just missed having a woman around."

Pushing her away, Matthew's in shock and unconvinced by Jess's words.

"I'd rather you didn't speak about Lauren like that. She may be gone in body, but she's still very much a big part of our lives."

"Matthew, relax; here, drink this. I told you, I'm here for Eve. We've had a lovely evening; do you really want to spoil our time together because *your* daughter actually likes me?"

Sipping his wine and thinking about the reality of his kick off, Matthew begins to slowly surrender. Although it pains him to admit it, he knows she's right. With a hint of embarrassment, he submissively reverts back to his usual understanding and rational thinking self.

"Jess, I'm sorry, it just took me by surprise. I'm not used to seeing her so distant from me. After everything we've both been through... it made us stronger. We've been forced to adapt to our new family dimension, just me and Eve, against the world. I suppose I've got so used to not having to share her with anyone, I lost my train of thought for a moment. I'm sorry."

"I know it's probably strange for you, and Matthew, these moments are going to happen; I ask you to just please take them with a pinch of salt. She's a daddy's girl and I'm sure deep down she always will be. Eve must have been happy to see me. I think it's a great step in the right direction."

"I really appreciate that, and once again, I'm sorry, and I thank you for being so understanding. I truly don't know what came over me."

"It's my pleasure. You're just being a protective father, which I respect. I expect you to be that way, it's all new to you both." Leaning in, she says, "But believe me when I say your family dimension was worth the decades of waiting."

The beachfront is dark and still. You can no longer see the outlines of the boats in the distance. Night's beginning to fall. The glisten from the street lights can be seen as they start flickering on and off, becoming established alongside the darkness. Standing on the balcony with a glass of wine, Jess is embracing the moment as she's looking out at the tranquillity of the sea. The waves are flowing gently, and the breeze is calm as the tide has now come in. The view is symbolic of the comforting energy surrounding them and is serene. Matthew joins Jess and, as he stands by her side, he places his chin on her shoulder.

"This is my favourite time of day."

There's not one person present, not even a bird in the sky. Gazing at the small cluster of stars that have made their existence known, both Matthew and Jess are listening to the soothing sound of the sea and enjoying each other's company.

Turning to face Jess, Matthew once again speaks. "Can I ask you something?"

"Of course."

"Why are you here? I mean, I don't actually mean that the way it sounds. What I actually mean is, why haven't you run a mile; my life must seem chaotic to you, what makes you stick around?"

Jess remains silent for a brief moment and appears to be deep in thought, staring out at the darkness of the night.

"Do you like to play games, Matthew?"

"What sort of games?"

"Games that strengthen your mind."

"Suppose."

"Well, when you play, let's say, a board game. You have your piece and you move around the board. Yes?"

"Yes."

"Well, when you play any game, you don't know the outcome, and it's exciting, do you agree?"

"Yeah, suppose so."

"Well, what is it you do with your excitement?" Pausing as though she's waiting for Matthew to answer her apparent question, but without giving him enough time to speak, Jess continues her teasing ways. "It becomes your energy. You put all that enthusiasm into winning the game. The thrill of the chase enables you to focus, and *you* will literally do everything you can to win. Only you know that you're not going to give up. That's the way I live my life. It's like a constant game. I can predict what I desire the outcome to be; do I always get it right? Yes. Do I always win? Most definitely. I'm a winner, Matthew."

"So, I don't understand... What's that got to do with why you come back and don't run a mile?"

"You see, Matthew, Eve's precious mind is wide open. She's like a lost piece on the board, just wondering around waiting to see the outcome of her fate. I'm the master of my mind and the leader of my board. I am here to empower her." Turning away, she continues, "Don't worry, though, you should know one important thing about me, Mr Honey, or Matthew as you like to call yourself. I always take good care of my pieces."

With these words spoken, Jess turns to him and pulls his body onto hers. Locking deep into his sight, and, with their eye contact now fixated on each other, Jess whispers on Matthew's lips, "*Mi temono.*"

The mood instantly changes, and a powerful vibrational shift can be felt within the energy circulating around them. The waves of the sea are no longer calm as they set about surfacing high off the water and come crashing down one after the other. This dark eerie energy is strong, overbearing, and leaves both Matthew and Jess feeling as though *they are not alone*. Remaining tightly bonded together, from out of the distance, a spontaneous and loud squawk presents itself. Jess and Matthew, oblivious to this, remain locked together by their sight. Her eyes become overcast, with a grey mist. Matthew, now breathing her in, is unaware of sudden changes circulating around him.

The loud squawk becomes established as it makes its existence known, travelling closer with each second that passes. No sooner has this sound journeyed through their eardrums, and embedded deep into their minds, a huge, black raven, bigger than your eyes have ever seen, circulates above them at a great height. Flapping its beautiful and strong glossy wings. Matthew and Jess haven't so much as flinched. They are unaware of this magnificent and great bird that's within their proximity, remaining totally entrapped within the moment and aware of nothing more.

***

Oblivious to the goings on outside, tucked up in her bedsheets, Eve's blissfully dreaming. Looking extremely angelic, she's sleeping with Gregg lay on the pillow, resting next to her head. Surfacing itself through the cracks surrounding the door, a deep, eerie mist slowly seeps its way into the room and sets about corrupting the innocent energy, which almost instantly begins to change. The mood within the room is much like the transition which is taking place outside: the shift is dark, gloomy and seemingly suppressive. The curtains spontaneously begin flowing as this unwanted, cruel and haunting mystified breeze manifests and presents itself within the confinement of the room.

Much like before, Eve's leather-backed personal diary is lay in its usual position, closed flat on the desk. This mysterious energy travels past Eve as she shudders in her sleep. The mist circulates around her diary, taking over its secrets. The gust from this deceitful energy is so forceful, the diary stands no chance of remaining closed, and is once again forced to flip open. The pages become out of control, blowing faster than ever one after the other, and are continually flicking without any visual assistance. Eventually the fluttering pieces of paper rest and land still on a double page where it resides. With the same blue-inked scrawling writing, the pages read the following:

"I thought about you a lot today. Me and dad were driving on the motorway to auntie Christina's house and we ended up driving past the place where me and you went paintballing. I started laughing to myself and dad asked what I was laughing at. So, I told him.

"I told him about the time where you were lay behind a hay stack and I was high up near the tree top. You couldn't see me, but I could see you. I heard you shout, 'Evelyn Jade, I'm going to win this game, I just know it.' Then I shouted, 'Don't be too sure Mum,' and shot you about five times. Dad started laughing, and he said that was one of your greatest qualities of all, your ability to have fun no matter what. He said he wouldn't go paintballing with me. He's too scared of getting hurt. But not you mum. You had no fear.

"The drive was very much silent after that. But I could still see you. I could still see your smile and hear your laughter. I relive the days we spent together a lot. I will never lose them, after all, it's all I have left of you.

"Don't worry, I'm looking after Dad and Gregg. I just wish I could speak to you one last time, see your smile one last time. I miss you Mum. I miss having a mum. Someone I can go to. Someone I can share my days with. Someone to go shopping with. I miss everything about having you. I miss mum.

"You will always be my queen. I'm sorry I was your daughter; you might have lived if you had a different one."

Unaware of her revealed thoughts and true inner emotions, Eve remains in her peaceful trance-like state. Sleeping, using only the unconscious section of her mind, she's oblivious to the events taking place in her room, along with the grey mist which has presented itself. Lay face up, Eve's expression is pure. Surrounded by the softest, white cotton bedsheets, with rose-gold detailing, her innocence beams bright. This vulnerable young girl is entirely unaware of her chosen fate; not only this, she is unaware of the practicality she is soon to face. Eve's been elected for a great purpose. Selected from billions of souls. This wisely chosen rhyming possession is slowly taking over tiny sections of her soul. Carefully wrapping its evil charm and vindictive energy around her existence, each word is overpowering her identity, removing one tiny section at a time, so it is not to be detected, until the moment is perfect, and the possession is complete. But at who's control?

As the mist begins to thicken within the confinement of the room, it gradually travels and makes its way towards Eve. Reaching the legs of her bed, this slowly moves up the frame and embeds itself in the wood. Rapidly, the atmosphere within the room changes. Once enlightened by innocence, once embracing purity, this very same room has now been taken over by a deceitful existence. Now formed, the mist begins circulating Eve's body outside of the bedsheets. Resembling bonds, this thick grey mistiness wraps itself around the outline of her physique and travels through the gaps in the sheets. It sets about surrounding her body, which is covered only by her late mother's nightie. Securing its existence, these bonds appear to be restricting Eve from moving. Travelling at a slow rate, this mist is preparing the room for the arrival of the unknown. The arrival of its master, the leader of the dark fate, whom Eve has so carefully been selected by. The Dark Empress.

Continuing the take-over and making its way up her body, the thick grey mist circulates around her sleeping facial expression. This expression is no longer pure. Her features are slowly changing. Her skin tone is being taken over. No longer natural, no longer pure, this shade is unknown to the existing world. Eve's changing to a light shade of grey. Transitional twitches are present upon her features. No sooner has this mist taken over Eve's body, you can no longer make out her presence. The room is now empowered by the deep and deceitful mist, as it's now ready for the arrival of its owner.

Without a living person in sight, not a single soul can be seen, and yet a voice very quietly joins the vicinity of the room. Echoing within the parameters and radiating throughout the bedroom walls, the words which can be so faintly heard are: "*Non temere di me.*"

With the final soundwave disappearing, the mist begins to gradually descend away from Eve's face. The transition has started to take place. Impure, unknown and unexpected, from out of the mist a grey wounded hand rests at the top of Eve's head. No longer able to visually see her features, the hand has entirely taken over Eve's appearance. Along with this neglected and unloved body part, a slight female humming can be heard. With its traumatic existence, and tainted manifestation, black blood begins oozing from the deep rips which are present. As this horrific visual becomes formed, the humming turns to singing, and the implantation of the possession, once again, originates.

"Ring a' Ring o' Roses – your soul is mine. Ring a' Ring o' Roses – you've been chosen for the dark side."

The rhyme is very gently being repeated, over and over. As this tainted, unloved hand moves around Eve's face, the lyrics begin embedding and taking possession of her brain's living cells, one individual, cell at a time. A dark, evil energy circulates within Eve's blood flow and quickly sets about changing its natural, pure, human tone to a sinister, thick, black, substance, with every part of Eve's DNA this fixates itself onto. Black, razor-sharp, dirt-filled, pointing nails travel down Eve's face. These thick, black nails have the ability to rip the flesh from your bones with ease. As this sinister body part descents over her features the reality of the transition begins to show. Eve is no longer Eve. Her skin tone is the deepest shade of grey. Her lips are black. Deep rips begin sporadically appearing upon her once innocent and beautiful face. Once formed on her flesh, these evil impure additions begin oozing the same black sinister substance that has taken possession of her DNA.

"Ring a' Ring o' Roses – your soul is mine. Ring a' Ring o' Roses – welcome to the dark side."

With the final lyric sung, the grey demonic hand pushes Eve's face at force and throws her into the dark abyss of her own mind. Eve, no longer grey, is now showcasing her natural skin tone. She's falling slowly. Her physique looks as though her spinal cord has been removed from her body. Surrounded by darkness, this evil and unknown entity continues to drag Eve's innocent soul deeper and deeper. Remaining trapped, she's powerless and no longer the master of her fate. Being taunted by the unknown and, entirely unaware that she's sinking further and further into the abyss of her own mind, Eve's petrified.

Once satisfied with the depths of this evil entrapment, the Dark Empress commands her final decent. In the final resting place, Eve remains completely still. Hearing only her heart beating and, as her sense of fear heightens, Eve can feel each individual pump as this pulsates throughout her body. Frantically searching the parameters, she sees there's nothing, and no-one, there. She's sitting in complete darkness.

Being the brave young lady, that she is, Eve shouts, "Hello?"

Suddenly, she doesn't feel alone. Breathing heavily, as her heartrate begins to speed up, she bravely shouts once more, "Who's there?"

With yet again no response, she cups her head in her hands and begins to sob. Gently under her breath, Eve says, "Please Mum, just say it's you."

Music begins playing from the distance and it is making its way towards her. Slowly removing her hands from her face, Eve tunes in her ears. Without the lyrics, she hears a clear tune being played. It's, Ring a' Ring o' Roses.

No sooner had she recognised this piece of music, Eve's thrown into a sudden flashback. Standing in the corner of the day room, she can see herself as a small child. Looking around the room in amazement at all the decorations, lights and presents, Eve works out it's Christmas day at home. The kind of Christmas day she used to share with Mum and Dad. Suddenly, she sees her mum walk into the room. Little Eve, who's sat by the tree, looks up and her face lights with joy. Mummy has a present in her hand. Big Eve, completely forgetting that she's currently living in a flashback, runs over to her mum and, as she goes to throw her arms around her, Eve in fact passes right through her body. Falling next to the wall, she awakens to the awareness that it's not actually her reality, it's her memory. With an internal sadness growing rapidly, Eve begins to form tears of sorrow. Making her way over to the tree and kneeling at the side of her younger self, she looks as her mum picks up an excited and little version of herself. Looking on in sheer admiration at her beautiful mum, her wonderful, beautiful, life-fuelled mum as she places a little Eve on her lap, ready to open her special present, she hears her mums voice: "Are you ready my angel, Father Christmas left this one especially for you."

"For me?"

"Yes, my angel, for you. Here you go."

Little Eve can't hold back any longer as she begins ripping the colourful and carefully crafted wrapping paper from off the present, and in her excitement, she throws it on the floor. Once unwrapped, little Eve holds in her hand the most gorgeous, handcrafted, wooden jewellery box. This uniquely designed piece showcases the most elegant white-gold detailing. On the lid of this magnificent personalised box, Eve's name has been carved into the wood and sits proudly with the same, elegant, white-gold trimming. With her little face lighting up as every second passes, Big Eve's watching her mum once again as she speaks, "Evelyn Jade Honey, this is for you to cherish always. I made sure that Father Christmas got this especially for you to put all your treasures in. And, guess what, its extra special, do you want to know why, Evelyn Jade?"

"Why, Mummy?"

"Because listen…" She opens the lid of the box; a delicate, tiny ballerina appears and begins twirling around to the tune of Ring a' Ring o' Roses. "This was my favourite nursery rhyme when I was a little girl, just like you."

"Weally, Mummy?"

"Really, my angel."

In the final snapshot of this flashback, Eve sees her younger self hugging her mum tight.

"Dank you, Mummy, I wove it forever."

Snapping back into her entrapment, Eve's in shock. Still surrounded by darkness, her head begins spinning round and round as she's trying to work out why this is happening to her.

***

In the room down the hall, Matthew's becoming distressed as he begins struggling with the bedsheets in his sleep. Moaning louder and louder, he speaks. "Why... No – wait, why are you doing this to me, please. Don't take her away from me. Noooooo..."

As he shouts, suddenly he wakes from his seemingly intense and unwanted dream. Soaking wet with sweat, from head to toe. The room's dark. Grabbing the glass of water from his bedside table, he feels an unwelcoming, unnerving and eerie energy surrounding him. Placing the glass back on the side, Matthew turns; he sees Jess isn't in the bed. The light in the en-suite isn't on either. Wondering where she is, he shouts out, "Jess," but he gets nothing back.

Eventually climbing out of bed, Matthew's taking no chances as he pinches himself harshly in order to make sure he's not stuck in a cruel entrapment. Slowly making his way towards the door, Matthew's no longer feeling alone. Unexpectedly, a huge gust of wind blows within the confinement of the walls. Matthew instantly stops.

"Jess... Eve?" Once again, he gets no reply.

Looking over his shoulder, he feels as if someone is stood right behind him. But, as soon as he turns, he sees the reality: there's no-one there. Shaking his head and trying desperately not to let fear become his primary emotion, Matthew quickly makes his way over to the window to shut this. Standing back in shock, he gasps. The window is already shut tight. Almost tripping over his own feet, he rushes towards the door. Without wanting to feel too much like a coward, Matthew calmly opens this, and then bursts out onto the landing. Looking around, he sees no-one's present.

Standing alone but feeling as though he's being accompanied by entities unknown, Matthew shudders as he slowly makes his way towards Eve's bedroom door. Placing his ear to the wood, he remains extremely still. Hearing nothing but his own heart beating, he's relived as Eve's room is thankfully silent. No sooner has his heartrate regulated and begun to ease, he unexpectedly hears a noise coming from downstairs. Breathing in deep, he heads towards the staircase. With every single part of his brain sending alarm bells and telling him not to go towards the noise, Matthew bravely ignores this, conquers his fears and begins to make his way down the spiral stairs. Halfway down, he whispers, "Jess, is that you?"

Without a response, rustling can be heard coming from the kitchen. No sooner have these unexpected soundwaves vibrated through his eardrums, Matthew instantly loses his cool and becomes rife with fear. Struggling to regain control of not only his breathing but his thoughts too, he's surrounded by an eerie darkness. With his feet bare, he's standing on a single step in the middle of the staircase. The only slight shimmer of light is coming from the mirror at the bottom of the stairs. With the random rustling noise continuing, Matthew looks around to see what he can potentially use as weapon should he need to defend himself. Noticing the solid-gold picture frame on the entry table and trying to make as little noise as possible, he slowly tiptoes over, and grabs the object. Now closer than ever, Matthew plucks up his courage. With his voice sounding slightly shaky, he says, "Jess,

Eve, if it's any of you two in the kitchen, you need to answer me now." Still he hears nothing.

Closing his eyes, Matthew's about to charge his way in, when suddenly hears a humming, which instantly knocks him off track. Again, he says, "Jess?"

Practically shaking from head to toe, he slowly places one foot in front of the other, and is heading straight towards the kitchen, where the noise and the singing is originating from.

"Last chance, Eve or Jess, this isn't funny." Still with no response, he says, "Fine, have it your way. One, two, three."

With his final words, Matthew courageously charges towards the kitchen door. But as soon as his feet reach the doorway, a gust of wind blows. The gust is so forceful this instantly shoves him across the hallway. Falling onto his back as he lets go of the solid-gold picture frame, this flies across the floor at force and smashes to pieces. Landing next to the bottom step, Matthew's heart feels as though, at any moment, it's going to burst. Looking up, he sees a grey mist elegantly drifting from out of the kitchen; it's luring him into a false sense of security. This dark and seemingly impure grey mist sets about surrounding him as he remains stiff and locked with fear. Overseeing the events taking place before his sight, Matthew's eyes begin protruding from their sockets. No longer does he feel in control of his emotions or his movements.

Taking over the room, the mist begins to thicken. Circulating around his physique, and being unable to stop this, the energy travels deep into his mind. Frozen, Matthew hears a symphony. This calming piece of music is attached to the mist, which is making its way through his eardrums and taking over his sight. Once this deceitful mist is satisfied with the invasion of this petrified soul, its sends for its owner to appear. Standing in the doorway, *she's back*!

With her head down low, her jet-black hair hangs past her thighs. This eerie-looking appearance is unnerving. As she stands, her hair drips a thick, black, sinister bloody substance. Her whole existence is grey. With deep, black marks and internal rips present sporadically across her physique, these horrific forced rips ooze the same sinister, black bloody substance which slowly travels and rolls down her body, landing on the floor. Peering through the gaps in her hair, she has black lips which ooze the same sickening substance.

Remaining immobile and motionless, Mathew's locked tight. Unable to close his eyes, the only ability he has is his sight. Forced against his own will to watch the horrific events taking place before his eyes, the movements of his body are no longer in his control. Wanting to scream, run and lock himself away, Matthew, unfortunately, has no such privilege.

As the black, bloody substance lands on the floor, it slowly begins making its way towards him. Reaching his feet, this evil impure liquid takes over his once innocent skin tone. As her sinister DNA is attacking his physique, the Dark Empress turns her humming into singing.

"Ring a' Ring o' Roses – her soul is mine. Ring a' Ring o' Roses – she's been chosen for the dark side."

With the final lyric sung, this evil entity lifts her head. Her eyes are the deepest blood red, and, as she charges at Matthew, her grey sharp teeth launch towards him. The sickening black bloody substance gushes from her mouth. Throwing herself into his mind, as he screams and jumps with fright, Matthew's now breathing heavier than ever. Looking around, he sees he's back in his bed, soaking wet, and covered head to toe in sweat. In sheer panic mode, he instantly reaches out and turns the lamp on at the side of his bed. Patting his body to ensure he's in one piece, Matthew slowly looks to the other side of the bed. She's there. Matthew sees Jess; she's sleeping peacefully next to him. Feeling a huge sense of relief, he throws himself back on to the pillow in order to regain control of his breathing and heartrate. Unsure of why this is continually happening, his curiosity gets the better of him and, as he grabs the phone from off the side, he notices it's five a.m.

Desiring answers, Matthew types an internet search: *Realistic paranormal nightmares what do these mean*? The fourth heading down instantly grabs his attention. It says, "*Shadow Person – Wikipedia.*" Clicking the highlighted link, he's directed straight to the explanation. Which reads the following:

"A sleep paralysis sufferer may perceive a 'shadowy shape' approaching when they lie paralyzed and become alarmed.

"One subject says 'You don't see shadow dogs or shadow birds etc. You see shadow people. Standing in doorways, walking behind you, coming at you on the sidewalk.'"

Reading this, Matthew diagnoses himself and is now *convinced* he's suffering with a sleeping disorder. Totally drained, he can't take another night of this insane, horrific ordeal. And so, he decides there's only one thing for it: he's going to the doctors in the morning. Putting his phone back on the side, he lies facing Jess. Taking in her expression and features, he begins to smile, she's so beautiful. The locket around her neck hangs over her shoulder and is glistening away as she sleeps. He reaches out and tucks her hair behind her ear. Slowly, Jess begins to wake.

"Shh... Sorry, I didn't mean to wake you."

Opening her eyes, Jess pulls back as she looks at Matthew's appearance. Instantly she becomes confused.

"Why are you soaking wet?"

"Shh, go back to sleep. It was just a bad dream, don't worry."

Climbing out of the bed, Matthew heads to the ensuite for a shower. With the steam gradually beginning to flow into the bedroom, a moment passes, and Jess decides to follow him. Standing in the doorway, she's peering across through the mist at Matthew. Admiring the view, Jess flirtatiously places her finger in her mouth and gently bites this. As the bathroom becomes thick with a misty, hot steam, she's becoming aroused with every second that she looks on at this strong, handsome man, rubbing his hands all over his hot, soapy body, cleaning himself. With his back turned to the door, and his head tilted back slightly, Matthew remains with his eyes closed. He is yet to notice that Jess has entered the bathroom. Removing her ruby red, silk night dress, she steps into the shower cubicle. Making her way over to Matthew, she gently touches his skin using only her fingers tips. With his adrenaline still present, he jumps as he turns. Instantly their eyes lock. With the hot water spraying them softly in the face, droplets begin to fall from their lashes and roll down their features. Sharing the soap from Matthew's body, their skin becomes lubricated and slippery. Jess reaches up and, as she throws her arms around his neck she passionately kisses him. Using her suction methods and soft lips, Jess travels down his neck, and, as she's enjoying tasting him, she gains instant pleasure as she's watching and feeling him surrendering to the moment. Not only this, but he's surrendering to her desires. Kissing her way down his physique, she licks his lower abdomen. Matthew, unable to hold his voice in any longer, begins moaning out loud with pleasure. With her hands firmly grasping his thighs, Jess reaches for his hard, erect existence, and places him inside of her mouth. Sucking and allowing him to travel to the back of her throat, Jess is embracing the control she has over the passionate moment as she can hear Matthew groaning louder and louder with ultimate pleasure.

As he runs his fingers through her hair and grips this, he sets about tugging at the roots gently. Turned on by the pleasure and pain, Jess jumps up and without giving Matthew time to process her next move, she wraps her legs around his waist. Stumbling slightly as he takes her weight, he places one hand on the wall of the cubicle. Fully aroused, he continues to grow and becomes even harder as the events that are taking place develop. Engaging in an intense passionate kiss, Jess places her hand in the tight curls forming in Matthew's hair. Moaning out loud, she begins tugging hard at the roots and as she pulls his head back; he's now moaning louder with ultimate pleasure. Whispering directly into his ear, she says, "I want you. Give yourself to me, now, Mr Honey."

Breathing heavier and heavier, Matthew surrenders to his urge. Impassioned in the moment, he slides himself deep inside her. These two begin moaning with gratification as they receive and feel one another. Unable to control his urge, his need, his desire, he begins forcefully thrusting Jess as her sexual groaning gets louder. Embracing each second as she feels Matthew deep inside of her, Jess pulls his hair once more and says, "Give yourself to me."

Desperately trying to hold back, he can't do it. As she's sucking and kissing him on the neck, travelling passionately to his lips, Matthew surrenders and gives in to her desires and sexual commands. Letting out one final moan, he thrusts her hard for the last time and whispers, "I'm coming."

Feeling his erect penis pulsate inside of her as he lets out his release gives Matthew an intense sense of euphoria. As soon as Jess receives him, her eyes flame. Embracing and capturing his DNA as this travels around her internally, she's feeling empowered. Content with the events that have taken place, they both share one final kiss. Breathing heavy, Jess drops her legs and Matthew groans as he leaves her body. Regaining his balance, and as the cramp slowly begins to leave his physique, he squirts soap in his hands, and begins rubbing this all over Jess's body. They're both smiling. Kissing her once more on the neck, Matthew unexpectedly whispers into her ear, "I think I love you."

"I know."

Immediately, with regret, Matthew's embarrassed. He quickly washes the soap off his body and as he gets out the shower. In a panic he says, "I'm sorry, I don't know where that came from."

Wrapping the towel around his waist, he heads back into the bedroom.

Remaining in the shower, Jess smiles, but her smile seems untrustworthy and deceitful as she plays with the locket around her neck.

Chapter 12
"Doctor, I think I'm going insane."

Sitting on the stiff, red leather, built-in couch, Matthew's in the waiting room at his local doctor's surgery. Much to his horror, he's surrounded by poorly patients big and small, who are continuingly coughing and sneezing, infecting the once pure air. Trying to distract himself from the possible illnesses he might contract whilst waiting for the doctor to call his name, Matthew begins admiring the display of leaflets and general health advice neatly stapled on the walls. With a vast knowledgeable display surrounding the possible effects of type two diabetes, along with pictures showing general care tips, and sharing advice, his attention is suddenly drawn to the small, blue, ocean-coloured leaflet just at the side. With tiny, pastel, multi-coloured fish around the border. He smiles. Matthew sees "Little Fishes Parent and Toddler Group". As his thoughts begin to drift, this happy trigger has placed him back to a wonderful time within his life. A memory he had so sacredly stored away surfaces. Lauren's sat with Eve on her lap and, with her usual radiant smile plastered across her beautiful face, she's clapping a tiny Eve's hands together. It's circle time at the group and they're all sitting waiting for the song to start. The introductions begin and each child, along with their parent/parents pretends to be little fish whilst singing their names. Eve's giggling away and is becoming extremely hyperactive as she's watching her just as giddy daddy, who simply can't sit still and behave himself. Whilst the introductions have begun, Matthew's wriggling around Lauren and Eve pretending to be a little shark. Singing along with Eve, he reaches over and grabs at her tummy as she sings her name. Lauren joins in the fun and attempts to save a tiny Eve from the little daddy shark.

Hearing a sudden loud cough, and feeling a splutter down his neck, this disgusting toe-curling event snaps Matthew out of his enjoyment and shoves him back into his existing reality. Feeling physically sick, he can't help but think once he leaves the building he's actually going to be physically ill, as well as mentally challenged. With his patience wearing thin, and his stomach turning at the germs which are resting on his neck, Matthew walks across the full waiting room to speak with the receptionist. Unable to mentally comprehend how much longer he can tolerate sitting with a room full of contagious illnesses and germs, he's almost ready to walk out.

"Excuse me... Can you tell me how much longer the wait is please? I've been sat here forty minutes already."

Without moving her head, the receptionist looks up at Matthew above the frames of her glasses. With a very stern and blank expression upon her face, she peers at him and looks back at the screen. I think we've all been here before and can relate to the stare she so gracefully gives him, it's the what-do-you-want-me-to-do-about-it look.

"Name?"
"Matthew Honey."
"You're next."
"That's great, thank you."

Squirting a generous amount of sterile hand sanitizer onto the palms of his hands, and wiping the excess onto his neck, Matthew makes his way back to the waiting room. This time, he decides to sit well away from the serial sneeze offender. Looking around, he sees all walks of life, little ones that just refuse to sit still, teenagers continually tapping away on their mobiles, and the rest either look exhausted or have a magazine or book glued in their hands, potentially to hide from the chaos of the waiting room. As Matthew looks up, something grabs his attention. He sees another informative billboard, only this time, the knowledge is aimed at mental health. No sooner had he started to read the advice being given, he hears, "Matthew Honey, please."

There he stands, at last. Mid-forties, with a full head of thick black hair, along with a few cheeky greys peeping through, this casual looking doctor stands wearing brown loafers on his feet and navy-blue cord pants, with a white and blue floral-patterned shirt, with the top button loose. His energy seems relaxed and calming. Relieved, Matthew looks to the doctor and impulsively says, "Thank God for that."

Turning a slight shade of pink with embarrassment as everyone's eyes glare at him, he laughs nervously under his breath. He didn't mean to say the words out loud. With his dry sense of humour and, once again, without thinking before he speaks, he reaches out and shakes the doctor's hand. "Matthew Honey, don't worry doc, I'm not contagious, I'm just nuts."

Much to the doctor's delight, Matthew let's go of his hand. Without knowing whether to join in and laugh at the words he speaks or call for security to stand outside his consulting room, the doctor politely responds, "Not a problem. Mr Honey, would you like to follow me please, we're in room four."

As they both walk along the thin airy corridor, they are surrounded by walls that have been painted a pastel green. They appear neglected and look as though a coat of paint is long overdue. With tiny chips and multiple black marks, you can see where the children have run their mucky fingers across the wall. With no order, hanging at eye level, are a number of calming pictures. These images are showcasing the most wonderful sights of English scenery. Alongside these, the occasional medical helpline poster can be seen. Arriving at room four, placed on the brown mahogany door is a beautiful gold plaque. Engraved on this, with sophisticated detailing, it reads, "Dr. Lane, GP, BMA".

"Please, after you."

"Thank you."

As they both enter the room, which is extremely messy and totally unorganised, Matthew's OCD makes an appearance. With heaps of paperwork sprawled out everywhere, Matthew's struggling as he has a strong urge to put some order to the room. A white sheet has been rolled out across the medical bed in the corner of this small space. Not only this, but multiple different types of medical equipment can be seen just lying around the room unaided. Much like his appearance, this room has the same relaxed presentation. Clearly, you don't receive cleaning and organisational lessons when you qualify for educated letters to be placed after your name.

"Please, take a seat, I'm Dr. Lane. How is it I can help you today?"

"Erm, well, I don't know where to start really. Honestly, between me and you, doc, I... well, I think I'm losing my mind." Placing his head in his hands he continues, "I'm convinced I'm losing it. Have you read through my notes?"

"Yes, I am aware of your situation and can I say, my condolences to you and your family for your loss. It can be hard for anyone to process, when losing a loved one. I'm sure you're not losing your mind. Please explain, I'd like to understand what it is that's making you feel this way."

Watching Matthew's posture slump and seeing him take the deepest breath in, Dr. Lane can feel his apprehension to talk.

"Do you mind if I call you Matthew?"

"No, it's fine, I prefer it."

"Thank you. Okay, Matthew, let me just say, whatever is said in this room, I want you to know is completely confidential; please don't be nervous. My job is to help, not judge."

Biting the bullet, he speaks, "Lauren, my deceased wife, well, as you'll have probably read, she's been gone for some time now."

"Yes."

"Well, doc, since then, I've not... how can I say this... Doc, what it is, erm, since Lauren, I haven't, you know, *been* with another woman."

"Okay." Dr. Lane continues making his notes as Matthew's speaking.

"Well, a few days ago, *unplanned* and completely randomly, I met a woman."

"Okay. I see, and how do you feel about that?"

"Well that's just it, doc, I can't get my head around how I feel 'bout it because ever since, I've been suffering with terrible nightmares."

"Okay. What is it you actually mean when you say nightmares: bad dreams, sleep walking, that sort of thing?"

"Oh no doc, these nightmares scare the, pardon my language, shit outta me. And I'm a grown man. I wake up soaked from head to toe with sweat."

"Can you recall what any of these nightmares are about?"

"Yeah, doc, it haunts me, it's the same thing every night. The most horrific, demonic sort of woman appears. It feels real, it feels as though it's physically happening to me. I mean, look at my hand – right, so in one of the nightmares I had my chain with a cross on in my hand. The cross cut me. Doc, how's that happened, look, you can see these cuts are on my hand, here, now, in my reality. And, well, my daughter Eve, she's changing too, doc. I don't know what's gotten into her, she seems distant. I just can't explain it. Everything's changed so much in such a short space of time, ever since I met Jess. I don't know, maybe it's too soon, maybe I should just stay alone." Placing his head in his hands with frustration, he continues, "You see, doc, this is what it's like, I'm driving myself insane. I feel mental. I'm constantly arguing with myself."

Dr Lane stops typing.

"Matthew, you shouldn't use the word mental when talking about yourself. I can see that you're not mental as you put it. What you're experiencing is perfectly normal. The cuts, can I see them?"

Matthew passes his hand to Dr. Lane. "Normal?"

"Do you have any idea how you may have got these?"

"Well, the chain I had in my hand, it's now snapped on the side in my bedroom, it came off in the night."

"Matthew, there's really no need to panic. You must have been physically creating the movement whilst you were sleeping, and your mind has performed a reflection of the movement within your dream. Now, tell me Matthew, would you say you think about your ex-wife at all during the day, or at night?"

"Dr. Lane, I think about Lauren non-stop."

"I believe what you're experiencing is actually a step forward in the grieving process."

"Huh, a step forward..."

"Yes. You see, what you are doing, Matthew, is forcing guilt upon your mind; this is natural. You're doing this because, now that you're thinking of moving on and contemplating creating a new family lifestyle for you and Eve, as much as you want this, deep down somewhere, you don't believe you deserve this. You don't believe you deserve to receive this life, because your ex-wife, Lauren, doesn't have the same opportunity. It's perfectly normal. During the day your conscious mind is preoccupied and distracted by the day-to-day activities. It's a very different story during the night. Night time is when we use and encourage our unconscious mind to take the reins, so to speak. The unconscious mind is what we use as children a lot to daydream. This is where our imagination is located. Currently yours is choosing to process guilt and portraying your worst fears at night. Would you say you struggle to drift off to sleep?"

"Doc, that makes so much sense, I think you're right. Erm, I actually haven't struggled to get to sleep.

But, well, now I have a slight build-up of anxiety when it comes to going to sleep. It's draining me."

"Ah, I see. Okay, so we have two options, well actually three options: you can wait and I will refer you to the sleep disorder clinic, I can prescribe you some sleeping tablets to try and help you relax, which will hopefully settle your unconscious mind, or we can send you away with nothing and I will monitor you, on an as-required basis. Which would you prefer?"

Matthew thinks about this for a second; he's not big on the whole taking medication hype, but nonetheless he gives in. He's so exhausted and truly can't function whilst being sleep deprived.

"I'll take the tablets please."

"Do you have any known allergies to medication?"

"None that I know of."

Typing away. "Okay, so, Matthew, what I'm going to prescribe you is ten milligrams of temazepam for seven to ten days. You'll take one each night about an hour before you wish to go to sleep. They work extremely fast, so under no circumstances should you take them when driving, operating any heavy machinery or planning to cook a meal etc. The tablets can be addictive, so your course is seven to ten days *only*. I'm hoping this helps your mind learn to relax again, just whilst you're beginning to process living this new chapter of your life. Honestly, Matthew, it's quite normal. I'm not concerned, and neither should you be."

"I know. I just suppose I never thought my life would come to this. I thought I would have my wife forever."

Dr. Lane looks to the time on his computer and sees that he's gone over the appointment by five minutes.

As he hands Matthew the prescription, he continues with his professional advice: "Just so you know the side effects on these are drowsiness, tiredness, nausea, anxiety and headaches. It's extremely rare, but if for any reason you experience severe changes to your body, such as blurred vision, irregular heartbeat, stomach cramps, or if the nightmares continue, stop taking the tablets immediately and come back to see me. It's all self-explanatory in the leaflet you'll receive. We're open Monday through to Saturday and I'm here every day. I'm going to book you an appointment for around ten days' time."

Placing the prescription in his pocket, he shakes Dr. Lane's hand. "Honestly doc, thank you, I thought you were going to have me sectioned."

Dr Lane smiles. "Matthew, you're fine. It's a very traumatic experience what you've had to cope with. Not only losing your wife, but becoming a single father is a big change. I'd expect you to go through these processes. After all, we're only human."

Leaving the surgery, Matthew's feeling slightly more at ease about his current situation.

Driving into the garage, he sits alone with his thoughts. Attempting to process the doctor's words and comprehend the reality of his current situation, he glances to the paper bag from the chemist resting on the seat next to him. Reaching across, he pulls the contents out of the bag. Reading the details on the box of medication and, upon seeing his name, Matthew suddenly feels an intense sense of inner sadness and devastation.

"So, this is what it's come to."

This surge of sadness internally becomes too much for him to bear. Dropping the bag on his lap, as he cups his head with his hands, Matthew breaks down. He let's go of the internal strength he's built, he can't hold it in any longer. Gently sobbing, he sees images in his mind of his wife, his best friend, his Lauren. Being brave is a speciality of his, but the reality of starting this new chapter without her is beginning to process in his mind, and the pain, like a huge, electric bolt of lightning, travels directly to his heart. Wrapped up in confusion, he's utterly apprehensive and unsure of what the right, or wrong, thing to do is. Regaining control of himself to a degree, Matthew wipes his face and begins checking in the rear-view mirror to ensure that his minor outburst isn't visual. Getting out of the car, he begins making his way up the stairs. The house is completely silent.

"Eve... Jess?" He gets no reply.

As he makes his way towards the kitchen, he looks to the entry table next to the door. In disbelief and shaking his head, Matthew's trying not to freak himself out. As the doctor's words begin circulating in his mind, he's desperately attempting to reassure himself that it's all in his, head.

"There's surely a logical explanation. It's fine. Don't freak out. Whatever you do, Matthew, just don't freak out."

The reality, unfortunately, is right before his eyes. As he battles with his mind, Matthew's attempting to put the words running through his head into action, and not freak out. But the facts are too hard to ignore. The golden picture frame *has gone*. It's disappeared and there is no getting away from the reality of this. Trying to soothe his mind and comfort himself, he begins speaking out loud: "It's okay, just keep breathing. It's all going to be okay."

Attempting to retrace his footsteps from this morning, he struggles. Being so embarrassed, he was in such a rush to get out of the house after the words he so thoughtlessly blurted out to Jess, he didn't even think to look to the table. Entering the kitchen, he quickly pours himself a glass of wine. Looking to the clock, Matthew doesn't acknowledge, or care, that it's only slightly past midday as he guzzles a mouth full of wine via the bottle. This cold alcoholic beverage is urgently needed. Regaining control of his thoughts after the pep talk he gave himself, Matthew takes his phone out of his inside pocket and rings Eve. Almost instantly, it goes to voicemail.

"Yeah, it's Eve, leave a message, or don't, not really bothered."

Beep.

"Eve, it's Dad. I've just got back to the house, can you let me know where you are please? I love you darling."

Matthew hangs up the phone and tries to ring Jess. But, much like Eve's, her phone also goes straight to voicemail.

"Your call has been forwarded. Please leave a message after the tone."

Beep.

"Hi Jess, it's Matthew. Listen, I hope what I said this morning hasn't freaked you out. If it has, then I just want to say that I'm sorry. It's all new to me. Take care, special one."

Putting the phone back into his jacket pocket and grabbing his wine, along with the bag containing the medication, Matthew makes his way upstairs. As he enters his room, he's standing virtually in the doorway when his mind decides to be unkind. No sooner has he placed one foot into the bedroom, instantly his thoughts are forced into a very sudden and intense flashback from this morning's events. Seeing the steam circulating around them both, looking deep into her eyes, and feeling the connection of bodily fluids as they intertwine with one another, Matthew hears the words he spoke: "I think, I love you."

With a knot building in his stomach, and a wrench in his heart, Matthew shakes the image out of his sight. With a face full of guilt, he breathes in deep. In one great big gulp, Matthew throws the wine in the glass to the back of his throat. Walking over to his bed, he places the bag from the chemist and the now empty wine glass on the bedside table. Sitting on the edge of the bed, he reaches for the silver cross and chain. As he's admiring the piece for its beauty and the memories it holds, Matthew slowly looks up. Smiling with his mouth, but with his eyes remaining heavy, he's desperately trying to regain control of not only himself, but his emotions. Embracing the moment, the peace, the tranquillity, the gentle vibrational energy as he's living the memories flashing in his mind. The vision of this stunning and pure piece of jewellery represents more than just an object or a possession; it has meaning, it carries love.

As his attention drifts, suddenly it clicks: the *cameras*! Placing the cross on the side, Matthew rushes out of the room and makes his way to his home office. Unable to comprehend why he didn't think of this before, Matthew's practically running up the stairs when, almost instantly, he gets a strong sense that he's being followed. He isn't alone. The house is empty, and yet Matthew feels a huge presence behind him. Standing still, and hearing the sound of his breath leaving his body, Matthew hesitantly speaks, "Eve?"

With no response, shaking his head and continuing with his mission, Matthew's desperately attempting to ignore the anxiety building in his mind. But again, he can't help it, he feels as if someone's run up behind him and is now standing over his shoulder and staring intently at his face. Stationary, he's too scared to turn around. Not only is his mind feeling this presence, his body feels this too as a huge gust of wind forcefully blows past him. Holding a sub-zero temperature, this energy carries a strong stench of death. Shuddering, as this not only makes the hairs on his body stand to attention, the stench irritates his nostrils and travels to the back of his throat, making him feel nauseous. Seeing the breath leaving his body, the hallway becomes dark and remains cold. Slowly, he turns. Matthew's eyes remain wide open and all his senses are heightened. Feeling as though he's being accompanied by entities unknown, and not the friendly kind, as he apprehensively turns around he sees there's no-one there.

Slightly relieved at the confirmation that his imagination is once again running wild, Matthew lets out a big sigh. Without wanting to allow the feeling of fear to take over and become his primary emotion, but tripping over his feet slightly, Matthew, attempting to be brave, shrugs this off and heads to his office. The eerie energy is not giving in, and still feeling as though he's being followed, Matthew looks behind himself once more as he arrives at his office. Checking over his shoulder, he sees nothing, and no-one. Turning his attention back to the task at hand, as he looks straight ahead, he begins to smile. Proudly placed, he sees the plaque Lauren had made as a gentle reminder to them both of how it all began. When they originally decided to set up their own business and embark on this new adventure together, Lauren performed a grand unveiling of the plaque to mark this huge stepping stone in their life. Shimmering away in all its glory, and made with the brightest gold, this classic addition to the dark oak wooden door is perfect, along with its thoughtful personalised engraving on it.

Creation Station
The Honey Empire
♣ ♦ M ♦ & ♦ L ♦ ♣
Masterminds busy doing what they love

As he enters the office, Matthew sits at his desk. Breathing once again, and placing his head in his hands, he feels exhausted, drained and confused. After Dr. Lane's diagnosis, he's saddened and unaware of the reasons why his mind is being so cruel. As he switches on the computer, his thoughts become overpowered by the unknown and, without having any answers, Matthew's apprehensive about the practicalities of looking for them. Entrapped by anxiety, and unsure about what he may see on the footage, Matthew knows that the cameras never lie, and this scares him more than anything. As he's about to type in his password, suddenly his phone begins vibrating in his pocket. It's a call from an unknown number.

"Hello, Matthew Honey speaking."

A male voice speaks with a slight foreign accent. "Hi, Mr Honey, how are you today sir?"

"I'm fine thank you. Sorry, I'm a little bit busy right now, can I help you with anything at all?"

"Yes, certainly sir, I am Rahul calling in relation to your broadbanding there. Can I ask, Mr Honey, who is your current using provider?"

Rolling his eyes. "Hi Rahul, thanks for your call but I'm actually fine as I am. Thank you for checking though."

"That is great news what I am hearing sir, but did you know that actually we are the cheapest in the world? You are being the lucky one today, Mr Honey. I would like to be helping you to be getting these savings of money, yeah."

"Look, I'm sorry, I don't want to waste your time…" But before he can finish speaking Rahul hangs up. "Hello… As if, bloody cold callers."

Putting his phone on the side, as he begins to type in his password, once again his phone rings. It's defiantly not Rahul. Matthew sees Hades Account flashing. With an air of urgency, he stands from his chair as he answers the call. "Hello, Matthew Honey speaking."

Matthew hears a familiar and somewhat eccentric voice at the other end of the phone. "Hi Matthew, it's Bill, Bill Hades. I've been trying to get hold of you."

"Yeah, Bill, sorry about that, it's been hectic recently."

"So, I believe business is booming for both of us. Generate the wealth, ha-ha. Keep the pot growing, so to speak. These lavish luxuries and private jets won't buy themselves. Ha-ha, aye, Matty boy."

"Ha-ha, yeah, something like that, Bill."

"Look, I wanted to arrange a meeting with you. We're launching a new clothing brand globally and I need you to produce our adverts ASAP. I'm busy now but get that Danny of yours to call Vera and set up a meeting. I need this brand launching into the world urgently. As always, Matty, you're the man for the job."

"Yes, sure, don't worry Bill. I'll get Daniel to set that up straightaway."

As they both hang up the phone, Matthew, with a sudden burst of excitement steps away from his desk and heads out of his office. His mind's circulating with elation and his sole focus is on the positive contribution life has just presented him with, and nothing more.

Making his way back downstairs, as he enters the day room, Matthew stands at the huge window gazing out at the beauty of the beach. He's taking in the moment for its unique productivity. Reaching up high as he's embracing his success, Matthew feels amazing. Aware that the meeting needs to be set up immediately, he rings the head office.

"Good afternoon, Honey Productions, it's Daniel speaking."

"Daniel, it's Matthew."

"Hey Matthew, I've just got an email from Vera, you know, Bill Hades's PA. I was literally about to reply to her now."

"That's great. Daniel, do me a huge favour and fit them in as early as you can. I don't care if it's a weekday, or a weekend, this is urgent business. This job is massive, and you know what Bill's like, he wants everything three weeks ago."

"Yeah, of course, not to worry, I'll get to it, like, now. Oh, who's attending?"

"I presume the usual suspects, me, you, Christina, Bill and Vera. I think this one's tight knit, so unless we're told otherwise we'll keep it small."

"Okay, so you'd like me to liaise with Christina too, not a problemo, consider it done."

"Oh, don't forget to book the meeting room, and give the usual caterers a call once you've confirmed. Daniel, I'm counting on you, please do what you have to; just make this happen. The Hades Account is our biggest. And we've got the summer Honey P Party coming up, clay pigeon shooting and the ultimate barbeque. I promise to give you all extra clay to shoot at and prosecco on tap if we get this contract. How's that sound?"

Daniel needs no further encouragement. "I'm on it, best service, biggest smiles and exquisite food. You are coming into the office today?"

"I've got a few things to sort out, so probably not. Any problems just call me; oh, and as soon as you've sorted the appointment send an email, copying all attendees in, as well as put it in mine and Christina's diaries."

"Sure, will do."

"Thanks Daniel."

"You're welcome, pleasure as always."

As they end the call, Matthew puts his phone back into his pocket and immediately sets about performing the victory dance. The Hades Account is worth a fortune and is one of Honey Productions's main revenues of income. Heading back into the kitchen with ownership of his new emotional high, Matthew once again pours himself a glass of wine; this time, it's in celebration. Looking to the floor, he shakes his head in complete astonishment. What is happening, how has his life become this whirlwind rollercoaster ride? Unsure of the answer, as he places the almost-empty bottle back in the fridge, Matthew returns to his previous task at hand and makes his way up the stairs; this time, the glass of wine he holds is victorious.

Remaining locked within his unstoppable high, and buzzing with excitement as every second passes, he's not giving any of his attention to the energy circulating around the house, which remains eerie. As he enters the office, he sits at his desk and, without any interruptions, successfully logs on to the computer. Stopping for a brief moment, Matthew once again feels slightly apprehensive of what he might uncover. With the practicalities circulating around in his mind of what he may find, and how this could shift his current high, Matthew rests his elbows on the desk deep in thought; he places his palms together and crosses his fingers. Resembling an individual deep in thought and prayer, like a whirlwind, Matthew's trying to process the pros and cons of viewing the footage from last night. In no order, these thoughts are travelling round his mind at a rapid rate. In a desperate attempt to conclude the debate in his head, Matthew strongly believes that if he at least watches the footage, and indeed sees nothing, which after his visit with Dr. Lane he's sure will be the reality, then he's certain he will no longer remain stuck questioning the unknown.

Starting this new chapter is a huge step forward, and in order to complete this transition, he needs closure on the strange happenings of the night. With this, his final thought, Matthew's set, and he decides he's going to watch the footage. Guiding the mouse, he clicks on the folder marked "CCTV Spy Cam". Instantly a split screen appears but wait – it's black on both sides. It can't be. Matthew's confused. Searching every file on the computer to ensure this hasn't been recording in a different format, Matthew has no joy. He is unable to locate the footage from the cameras. Even the live footage that should be filming now. Standing from his chair, he heads out of the office. Making his way over to the camera on the edge of the picture frame facing Eve's room, reaching up, straightaway he sees the huge error he's made. In his impulsive momentary decision to use the cameras, and without wanting to get caught out whilst rushing, he forgot one important thing. Matthew forgot to turn the camera on. Walking into his bedroom, he does the same check, and no surprise, once again he sees the camera isn't switched on. Feeling slightly insane, Matthew laughs to himself as he sits on his bed. Staring blankly, he's unsure of how to feel.

Opening the draw on the bedside table, he pulls out a strip of tiny keychain-sized pictures. As he's admiring the images he lies back on his pillow. The strip has multiple black and white photo-booth images on it. The purity shown is a young Matthew and Lauren. These innocent images were taken the night he proposed to her. Lauren's proudly waving her hand in the air, showcasing her ring which cost Matthew a tiny expense of twenty English pounds. Lauren's unaware of the value and doesn't care. All you can see in these tiny images is the true love and happiness that has been captured. Tears once again form in Matthew's eyes as he's reliving the memory. As the emotion-filled teardrops fall, one after the other, onto the pillow, Matthew wipes his face. Placing the strip back into the drawer, he makes his way back into the office and switches off the computer. Grabbing his phone from out of his pocket, Matthew attempts to ring Eve.

"Yeah, it's Eve, leave a message, or don't, not really bothered."

Beep.

"Eve, it's Dad, call me when you get this darling."

Suddenly, the front door bangs!

Chapter 13
"Let's start again..."

Rushing down the stairs, Matthew sees Eve and Jess stood in the hallway surrounded by shopping bag after shopping bag. They both look extremely pleased with themselves. A slightly relieved Matthew smiles as he makes his way over to Eve. Squeezing her tight and kissing her on the head, he instantly feels her happiness.

"Darling, I was getting worried, your phone kept going to voicemail."

"Sorry, Dad."

"It's okay, you're home now; where've you both been?" Making his way over to Jess, he reaches out and gently kisses her on the cheek. "Hey you."

"Hey handsome."

"Oh, my, goodness, Dad – we've literally had the best time. Jess took me shopping and helped me pick out some new clothes. Then we had lunch and, oh, sorry, my battery died. I didn't take my charger."

"Evelyn Jade, I wish you'd change your voicemail message."

"Why, what's wrong with it?"

"Erm, yeah, it's Eve, leave a message or whatever, not bothered."

"Dad, what you see is what you get. I'm as blunt as they come." Laughing, she continues, "Plus it's the truth, I'm not bothered. You always told me never to lie. So technically it's your fault."

"It's always somehow my bloody fault." He gently shakes his head. "What have we got here then, looks like you two have been on a mission, wow."

"We really have had a lot of fun together, haven't we, Evelyn Jade?"

"The best."

"So, come on then, show me what you've spent my money on."

"Oh no, Dad – Jess bought all this."

Mortified, Matthew says, "Wow, Jess, erm, thank you so much for the gesture, but please, how much do I owe you?"

"Don't be silly, Matthew, please, it's my treat."

Eve's smiling away. "Dad, let me show you what I've got."

Making her way into the day room, Eve can't help herself as she's continually pulling out the items with excitement. Stopping in his tracks, Matthew turns to Jess and grabs hold of her hands. Looking deep into her sight he says, "Thank you. Honestly, I haven't seen Eve this happy and chatty in a long time. Please let me take you and Eve out this evening, it's my treat. Actually, I'm not taking no for an answer."

"Thank you, Mr Honey. I mean, Matthew; that would be lovely."

As they enter the room Matthew and Jess can hear Eve wittering on to herself, she's pulling out all the items in the bags and placing them on the couch.

"Eek, I forgot I got that. Dad, you've got to see this dress that Jess picked out for me, it's ruby red."

"They're all amazing, darling. Listen, I've decided I'm taking us all out this evening, maybe you can wear one of them beautiful dresses since I missed the ultimate changing room catwalk show, which of course I've become accustomed to."

Shoving the items back in the bag, she says, "This day's just getting better and better." Making her way over to her dad, as she kisses him, Eve continues, "Oh, look, here's what we got for you."

Eve pulls out a solid gold picture frame and passes this to her dad. Beautifully positioned inside the frame is the picture which had gone missing from the entry table. Holding the frame in his hands, Matthew's unsure of what to say, or do, next.

"Look, see, I put the picture in for you already."

"Darling, where's the old frame?"

"Well, I went to get breakfast this morning and the old one was broken on the kitchen side; the glass was shattered and everything." Holding her hands up in the air, she says, "I didn't do it. It was Jess who suggested we should get you a new one as a surprise."

Looking at the image inside of the frame, and trying to digest Eve's words, without wanting to look too shocked, he says, "Yeah, of course, that's great, thank you darling."

With all her new possessions crumpled up and shoved back into the bags, Eve piles these up in her hands and begins making her way upstairs. With her energy beaming brighter than the stars and remaining full of life, Eve's practically skipping up the staircase. Smiling, Jess goes to follow and as she reaches the door, Matthew holds her arm, gently stopping her in her tracks.

"Jess, can I have a word please?"

"Yes, of course."

Looking out into the hallway, Matthew shuts the door. As he puts out his hand, he says, "Please, sit down."

As Jess sits she becomes slightly alarmed and confused by Matthew's actions.

"I wanted to say something about my choice of words last night."

"Oh, Matthew, honestly, it's fine. You really don't have to explain anything."

"No, I do. Really, I do." Taking in a deep breath and preparing himself for the words he's about to speak, he continues, "So, I haven't been myself recently. I truly thought I was getting to a point where I was rebuilding my life in all areas and, well... not fully, but slowly beginning to accept and move forward from the murder of my wife. Yet the more I've thought about this being my reality, the worse my state of mind has become."

"Because of me?"

"Oh, good lord no, not because of you. No, no, no, no, no. Please don't think that. It's not coming out right at all this. What I'm trying to say is, well... erm, since I met you I've not been sleeping too great. This isn't to do with you, honestly." Holding her hands, he continues, "Today I decided enough is enough and I went to see the doctor. I haven't been to the doctors for a long time. Do you remember last night when you asked me why I was soaked?"

"Yes."

"Recently, I've been experiencing bad dreams of sorts, but they feel real. The broken picture frame, well... I broke that last night whilst I was sleeping." Gently shaking his head as he knows this is making no sense and making him sound slightly insane,

Matthew continues, "Look, I don't want to go into too much detail, but I think I'm sleep walking. I'm hoping I've now found a solution, so I guess why I'm telling you this is because I'm truly surprised you've not run a mile; both me and Eve haven't been the easiest to deal with. And I suppose I just want to thank you for your graciousness."

Throwing her arms around his neck, Jess gazes deep into his eyes, and as she climbs on top of his lap, she leans over and whispers onto his lips, "All is forgiven, Mr Honey."

Kissing him with an immense sense of passion, these two are now becoming increasingly aroused as they receive one another's energy. Running her fingers through his hair and feeling him growing inside of his pants, Jess whispers into his ear, "*Mi temono.*"

Suddenly, Matthew feels an unknown energy radiating at a rapid rate throughout his body. His nerves are awakened by this mysterious and unexplainable tingling sensation. Feeling both pleasure and pain Matthew's confused as he's trying to accept this new-found orgasmic energy which is taking over his existence. But it's hard, his natural urge seems to want to fight against this, but his body, which is surrendering, won't allow his mind to take control. Powerless, Matthew begins moaning out loud as Jess tugs at his hair. Gradually giving in to this intense sense of euphoria, with his eyes remaining closed, he's unaware of the reality before him. As Jess sees and feels his submission, her eyes start to change. Her deep black pupils appear to have taken over. No longer can you see a patch of white. Like gaping holes in her face, she's taking possession of Matthew's soul, bit by bit, and she's now absorbing him through the windows of her eyes. Spontaneously, an intense, grey, cloudy mist surfaces. Its formation is slowly drawing from the darkest and deepest parts of her eyes. This cloudy presence outlines itself into a deceitful looking cross, a cross that appears upside down. Feeling his energy submissively embracing her presence and, as he becomes more aroused by the second, Jess showcases her true intention. Taking ultimate control of the moment, she unzips his pants and instantly places him securely inside of her. Grinding her physique on top of him, Jess leans and bites his lips. Drawing his blood, she embeds her teeth deep inside of his skin. Clenching her legs tight, she begins sucking the DNA from Matthew's body. With his blood travelling down her throat, and as they become one, the orgasmic pleasure Jess is receiving accelerates her into her true form. As Matthew's erect existence travels deeper and deeper inside of her, as soon as she's satisfied with its embedding, she commands, "*Aperto.*"

Instantly, Matthew opens his eyes. As she's about to lock his soul in deep, suddenly his phone begins vibrating. The strong vibration and loud beeping immediately breaks the connection which had been very calculatedly built. Not so much as a millisecond passes, and Jess's eyes resume back to her normal deep shade of brown. Snapping out of his entrapment, and looking somewhat confused, Matthew's unaware of how they have ended up having intercourse. Climbing off him, as his erect existence travels out of her body, and lands on his trousers, he moans.

Jess whispers once more, "Next time."

Regaining control of his mind, Matthew coughs. Shaking his head, he's trying to work out what's just happened. As he pulls away from Jess, his phone once again begins vibrating and beeping loudly. Reaching into his pocket, he sees he has an email from Daniel, and the heading reads: "Appointment Confirmation – Hades Account."

Making her way out of the day room, Jess leaves a very flustered and confused Matthew behind. Trying to regain control of himself, he clicks on the email, which reads:

Sent: Daniel Thompson
To: Matthew Honey, Christina Hart, Bill Hades, Vera Jenson
Subject: Appointment Confirmation – Hades Account

Dear All,

Re: Appointment Confirmation – Hades Account

Further to my conversation today with Vera, I am pleased to confirm the following appointment has been booked:

Date: Saturday 7th July
Time: 14:30
Location: Honey Productions, Canterbury
Meeting Room 5

On arrival, please make your way to the reception area and ask for Daniel Thompson.
If you require any further assistance, or if for any reason you need to rearrange the appointment,

please do not hesitate to contact me on either my direct dial or email.

With kindest regards,

Daniel Thompson
Receptionist
Honey Productions

Sent: Matthew Honey
To: Daniel Thompson
Subject: Appointment Confirmation – Hades Account

Hi Daniel,

Thank you for sorting this. Have you booked the caterer? Also, did you check Bill's food preference with Vera?

Kind regards,

Matthew Honey CEO
Film Director
Honey Productions

Sent: Daniel Thompson
To: Matthew Honey
Subject: Appointment Confirmation – Hades Account

Hi Matthew,

Yes, don't worry, I sorted this with Vera.

The menu's all sorted with the caterers, I'll leave a copy on your desk.
I ordered you your usual, shall I change this?

With kindest regards,

Daniel Thompson
Receptionist
Honey Productions

Sent: Matthew Honey
To: Daniel Thompson
Subject: Appointment Confirmation – Hades Account

That's great!

Thanks Daniel.

I'll be back in the office Monday. Please can you leave all messages and post on my desk, thanks.

Matthew Honey CEO
Film Director
Honey Productions

Sent: Bill Hades
To: Matthew Honey, Christina Hart,
       Vera Jenson, Daniel Thompson
Subject: Appointment Confirmation – Hades Account

Booked in the diary.

I will ensure we bring the storyboard for the new product. It's SaintsVill clothing range. We've got full branding and sample clothing etc... Vera will bring it all to the appointment.

Looking forward to seeing what that creative mind of yours achieves Matthew.

Regards

Bill Hades CEO
Hades Investments

Sent: Matthew Honey
To: Bill Hades, Christina Hart, Vera Jenson, Daniel Thompson
Subject: Appointment Confirmation – Hades Account

SaintsVill, sounds good!

See you and Vera on 7th July.

Regards

Matthew Honey CEO
Film Director
Honey Productions

Sent: Christina Hart
To: Mathew Honey, Bill Hades, Vera Jenson, Daniel Thompson
Subject: Appointment Confirmation – Hades Account

Confirmed.

Good choice of name Bill, I like it a lot.
See you all 7th July.

Kindest regards

Christina Hart
Executive Producer
Honey Productions

Unaware of the events taking place downstairs, Eve's wrapped up in her own delightful little world in her bedroom. Wearing a huge smile, which is plastered across her face, she's unloading all her new items. Carefully taking each expensive, designer piece of clothing out of the bags, she sets about placing the garments individually onto matching gold padded silk hangers. With her energy oozing excitement, Eve can't wait to add her newest additions to her already amazing clothing collection. Eve makes her way over to her gorgeous uniquely crafted, built-in, white wooden wardrobes which is positioned perfectly on the far side of the room. Opening the double doors, your sight is instantly attracted to how wonderfully organised the contents of this are. All Eve's clothes are arranged by not only colour, but season too. It's like a work of art. Admiring each individual piece as she places this in the correct order, Eve feels spoilt and completely fabulous.

Once her work of art is complete, and her new clothes have a confirmed spot in their new home, Eve grabs her diary and sits at her desk. The thick, red, leather-backed book, which is filled with all her deepest secrets and true thoughts, is her most sacred possession, and Eve is unaware that this has been unwillingly exposed. Flicking through until she lands at an empty page, Eve grabs her blue-ink fountain pen and begins writing a new entry:

"*Today I got my wish, today I got to spend the day with a woman!!! A woman who could very well be the figure I've been searching for. We went shopping, a real girl's day shopping, it has been amazing. I literally feel on top of the world.*"

But before Eve has time to finish her entry, a cold breeze presents itself within the confinement of her room. Shivering, Eve feels the hairs on her body quickly standing to attention. The sub-zero temperature is unnerving, and it carries not only a freezing altitude, but also attached to this is a nauseating stench. As this substance hits the back of her throat, Eve begins retching from her stomach with sickness. All her senses are awakened by this overpowering, disturbing manifestation, which is developing at a rapid rate. Dropping her pen onto the page, Eve splashes ink across the paper. Suddenly she no longer feels alone as she remains seated at her desk. No sooner has the anxiety travelled through her mind, Eve feels someone breathing over her shoulder and blowing directly down her ear. Taking in a deep breath, she slowly turns, and as soon as she looks over her shoulder, she sees the reality: there's no-one's there.

Exhaling with relief, Eve gets up from her desk and walks into the en-suite. Switching the light on, she makes her way to the ceramic white sink. Turning on the taps, Eve splashes the freezing cold water at force into her face. With her head in her hands, Eve slowly begins to hear a symphony of humming. The water which is flowing freely from the tap and is gathering in Eve's hands unexpectedly turns black. Jumping with fright as the black liquid takes over her once innocent skin tone, Eve hears the hummed tune being repeated over and over, getting louder and louder. Suddenly, the light begins to flicker on and off. She's standing completely stiff as her sense of fear takes over and becomes her primary emotion. Alongside this eerie and yet enchanting rhyme, Eve can hear the sound of each deep breath as it leaves her body. With the light remaining off, it feels as though the darkness she's surrounded by is now her new light. Too frightened to speak, and aware of the unnatural energy radiating from behind her, Eve's unable to contemplate running out of the bathroom. She's stuck stiff.

The bathroom suddenly becomes filled with light, and no sooner has Eve looked up, she freezes with fear. Staring at her reflection, Eve sees that the mirror tells no lies. Behind her stands the most horrific and terrifying demonic grey woman. Her jet-black hair is hanging heavy either side of her face, and black blood is oozing from the cracks around her mouth. Not only this, her whole existence is traumatic and oozing the same black substance: she's back!

Chapter 14
"Medication time"

Night has fallen. The village of Hythe, just a few hours ago, was filled with laughter and life – now, the same pathways are silent and still. Not a soul is present on the streets, or a seagull in the sky. No form of visual life can be seen. The lampposts are lined up symmetrically and one or two of these are flickering. Grey waves begin mounting with each gust of wind that flows, becoming fiercer and stronger with every decent as they crash against the sand. The tide is firmly in and pushing closer to the man-made grey brick wall that stands solid and separates the beautiful English beach from the streets. Beaming up high, the moon is out. Established within the jet-black sky, this magnificent sphere within the universe is captivating as it's grasping all the attention, alone, without a star in sight.

Inside the Honey residence, a dark energy is making its way around this silent building. The mood throughout the house is eerie and although Matthew, Jess, and Eve are sleeping, the hairs on their bodies begin standing to attention. Travelling at a rapid rate, this dark energy has made its way into Eve's room and is once again circulating its sub-zero temperature in readiness for the arrival of the Dark Empress. Suffering with fright, and being taunted by terror, Eve's becoming unsettled in her sleep as she mumbles, "Mum..."

Continually fidgeting, she's getting tangled in the bedsheets as she sets about pulling these up to her neck in her sleep. Trying desperately to shield herself from the freezing energy circulating her room, Eve remains psychologically unaware of this cold unpleasant existence which is gradually invading her space. Once formed, an unexpected vibration originates. Not only can this energy be felt, it is also seen as the walls in the room absorbs the vibration. These sturdy foundations set about shaking and this unidentified energy develops stronger and more powerful as it travels through the floor. The solid, wooden bed also accepts the mysterious tremor, and mirrors the movement of the walls. This well-built piece of furniture stands no chance as it violently rocks back and forth. Eve's body, at force, is shaking in-sync with the movement of this aggressive vibration and she looks as though she's having multiple seizures, one after the other.

The grey, deceitful mist once again begins circulating and taking ownership of the room. Oblivious to what's happening to her and her surroundings, Eve's locked deep within her unconscious mind. Presenting itself, this powerful, unnerving manifestation is becoming thicker with each second that passes. The entity that is forcing its way through the cracks surrounding the door and trickling through the golden keyhole is dark and unwanted. Eve's powerless. She's unable to wake and remains trapped against her own will, a victim to her own mind, being thrown at force around the bed. Unexpectedly, the rocking stops and the bed, along with Eve, becomes still. With no visual help, the curtains, which hang heavy, begin sliding open.

Unaccompanied, and peering through the glass on the windowpane, is a single, black raven. This intimidating creature stands stiff and is staring intently at Eve. Almost as big as the window itself, and with eyes that are the deepest red, this creature is a true reflection of its proud owner; the raven abruptly begins pecking at the glass. Eve's hearing initiates. Becoming sensitive to the loud tapping and emotional at the disturbance, she cries out, "Mum!"

A dulcet, eerie female voice develops and can be heard alongside the incessant strong pecking. Lay with her head on the pillow, Eve's expression begins changing. She's unable to breathe in her sleep. With her hands around her throat, Eve's reacting to the voice that can be heard in her mind.

"It is time, my child. *Non temere di me.*"

Struggling to take a breath, Eve's body is now limp. The vibration in the room once again takes over Eve's bed and forcibly shakes the frame. Throwing her lifeless physique aggressively from one side to the other, as the spoken words develop in her mind, the evil energy attached to the sound begins circulating. Registering its existence, this unknown entity is taking ownership of Eve's living cells. With the transition almost complete, her facial features spasm and, as they set about twitching, Eve, no longer holding her throat or being thrown around the bed, is lay with her eyes open, motionless. Foaming at the mouth. A grey tinge begins to spread rapidly across her once pure skin tone. This shade, which is unknown to the human world, begins travelling around her body and taking over her identity. Eve is no longer Eve. Her features slowly begin to showcase the evil that has devoured her soul. A deep crack spontaneously appears through the centre of her face. With its power over her soul, the development progresses as this takes over and begins ripping its way through her grey, lifeless lips. With its final formation, black blood oozes from its reality. This sinister thick substance slowly drips down Eve's face and sets about rolling under her chin. Calculated and devious, this thick black liquid travels like a magnet to the necklace and locket hanging around Eve's neck. Embedding itself all over this precious piece and taking over its purity, ensuring this no longer glistens, much like its owner, this object has been tainted by evil.

The mist, now thick, is continually spreading its unwanted manifestation and this once light, airy and innocent room is riddled with an unknown entity strong enough to make your soul crawl deep inside you. Suddenly, a wicked and cruel form appears... Once again, waiting for the timing to be perfect, she's back!

Walking through the wooden mahogany door, this evil and dark spirit begins making her way to Eve. With her presence now locked in the room, the raven at the window is pecking fiercer than ever and flapping with frustration. This female form with her soulless expression has her head low. Her bone-straight, jet-black hair hangs equally either side of her face and drips the same eerie, sinister black substance as her body. Leaving its unwanted materialization wherever it lands. This substance has a nauseating stench of death attached to it. With her neglected, unloved grey face, she peers through the gap down the centre of her hair. Eyes that are the deepest red. These traumatic-looking body parts are an exact match to the mysterious raven. Moving only her head slightly, she begins looking across at the window. With a sudden sharp movement, she twitches her head – instantly, the window opens and the huge black bird glides into the room. Flapping her wings and content with her surroundings, this creature forcefully positions herself on the headboard of the bed. As the demonic empress begins singing her possessive rhyme, this intimidating and deceitful bird stands strong and proud, admiring Eve's acceptance of the carefully calculated possession.

"Ring a' Ring o' Roses – your soul is mine. Ring a' Ring o' Roses – you've been chosen for the dark side."

With the final word spoken, Eve's body, which has lost ownership of its soul, shoots up and sits forward. Her eyes are deep black and appear as gaping bottomless holes in her face; not a glow or a shade of white can be seen. With her grey horrific existence, Eve is indefinitely no longer Eve. The mist has now formed thicker and as the raven flaps her strong, black, glossy wings, deep red blood bleeds from the surrounding gaps present in her tiny eye sockets. The bird, much like her creator, is gaining energy and pleasure at the ownership of its newest member. The chosen one has finally accepted her fate. The wait is over. As her face remains grey, Eve's appearance is rapidly transforming. Deep internal cracks begin forming and ripping sporadically through her flesh. With wounded gashes all over her face and body, once their formation is complete, sinister black blood oozes from each individual manifestation. Her non-human form, her new identity, is horrific. The demonic empress, with her head remaining low, slowly begins stepping towards Eve's bed whilst continually singing her possessive rhyme with her deep dulcet tone.

"Ring a' Ring o' Roses – your soul is mine. Ring a' Ring o' Roses – you've been chosen for the dark side."

Eve is taking in every second of this possession. Hovering her demonic, impure grey hand over Eve's face, the demonic empress is ensuring the implantation and acceptance over this young girl's mind, body and soul. Controlling and capturing every cell as this secures and travels through her DNA, taking over its purity. Reaching out to Eve's submissive and grey face, with her cold, neglected finger, she collects the black substance which drips from the wounds in her flesh. Bringing her finger to her mouth, she begins ingesting the sinful element and with ultimate pleasure she speaks. "Soon you will shine, my child. The timing is almost right. We will finally be one, we will finally live our purpose. We, together, will unite and using the vulnerable, the impure, and the weak, we will build our empire. And the world will pay, as the universe becomes ours. *Non temere di me.*"

Eve's transforming into a mirror image of the demonic empress with every second that passes. Whilst she stands by, watching with pride, the deep satisfaction this evil entity is internally feeling begins to appear upon her presence. Raising both her arms over her head with euphoria, she's embracing the moment. With her head held high, you can now see the terrifying reality of her facial features. This sight is traumatising. Her eyes are the deepest blood red, surrounded only by black. Deep grey skin, with its black marks and forced rips present upon it. These unnatural wounds ooze a sinister black substance which rolls down her physical form. In its final resting place, this deceitful manifestation stains wherever it lands.

Opening her mouth, she proudly showcases her grey, stained teeth. The black, bloody, sickening substance gushes from her mouth and drips off each razor-sharp tooth. Flowing down her chin as she's squealing with ecstasy at her victory. She spits the black liquid across the room. Her prized possession, Eve, is now mirroring her evil, tainted and unsaveable features on her face. With the same black substance gushing from out of her mouth, Eve appears impure but empowered, by the events that are taking place.

The raven abruptly flocks to the ceiling and, as she comes back down, she lands on Eve's shoulder. As the blood that's bleeding from the Raven's eyes begins trickling down her feathers, this dark creature focuses her sight on Eve. Satisfied with her vision, she showcases her acceptance by pecking at the black blood present on Eve's face. Receiving her energy and feeling empowered, this intimidating creature loudly squawks as she ingests the substance. Standing at the side of the bedframe, the demonic empress, with her evil intentions, desires to share the acceptance of this soul. Leaning forward, using her black, coarse tongue, she licks the same wounds. Satisfied with the taste of the sinister substance, the demonic empress begins drinking this. As she's extracting the possessive liquid from Eve's body, she's gaining strength with every drop. Sat in the bed accepting her fate, Eve's embracing each soul-draining draw as the blood's felt departing from her body. Without a soul present in her physical form, and no emotion upon her face, Eve's voice is deep and no longer sounds her own. Unexpectedly, and with black liquid gushing out of her mouth, she speaks, "I'm ready... Mum..."

A bang is heard outside the room. Not long after, a sudden creak in the floor. This instantly startles the demonic empress and her evil accomplice.

"Eve... Jess?"

Standing half-naked in the hallway, Matthew's wearing only his black pyjama bottoms. Shivering as he feels a huge draft of cold air presenting itself on his body. His skin develops goosebumps and the hairs on his arms begin standing to attention. With confusion and fear, he notices a significant cloud of smoke seeping from the cracks surrounding Eve's bedroom door, which is slowly disappearing as the hallway progresses into the darkness. Staring attentively, and trying desperately not to freak out, Matthew slowly places one foot in front of the other and, with an air of caution, he makes his way over to the room. Feeling each pump as his heartrate is fiercely pounding against his chest, the only sound he hears is the sound of his breath as this leaves his body. Tiny beads of sweat form on his forehead and roll down his flesh. The hallway is dark, gloomy, and Matthew doesn't at all feel alone. With his anxiety heightened, he is no longer in control of his thoughts. Playing cruel tricks, his mind continues to send off signals telling him that someone is standing right behind him. But when he turns, he sees there's no-one there.

Desperately attempting to gain answers, he bravely shouts out, "Eve, Jess, is that you?"

Waiting in anticipation for a response, Matthew receives nothing. The picture frames on the walls are creating lurking-looking shadows which are spreading around the hallway, resting on the floor. The anxiety and the fear of the unknown within his mind has made the hallway appear haunting and long. With every step, he continues to hear his breath as this is leaving his body. Rife with terror, he doesn't want to enter the room, but he knows he has too. His daughter could be in danger – unable to control his emotions, Matthew gathers his strength, breathes in deep and, as he grabs the doorknob, suddenly his fear initiates. Jumping back with hesitation, he doesn't enter the room. Remaining trapped, he's stuck feeling an overwhelming sense of anxiety and is completely unable to stop his mind from racing. The smoke continues to surround him, and he can only just make out the door, along with the hallway, as it has now been taken over. Approaching the bedroom door for the second time, Matthew closes his eyes tight, grabs the doorknob and, as he breathes out, this time he courageously thrusts this open. Bursting into the room he shouts, "Eve!"

With a sub-zero temperature, the room is clear. This freezing element is circulating rapidly along with an unnerving deadly stillness; every inch is overcome by darkness as the night has taken over. Matthew's senses are on high alert. Seeing a sudden movement from the corner of his eye, his attention is immediately captured. Eve's curtains, which hang separated, are blowing rapidly. The window is wide open, and the strange cloud of smoke isn't present within the room. It's as though the unnerving, eerie mist never existed. Heading to the huge window, he battles against the wind as he shuts this tight. Shivering, he makes his way to Eve. Sleeping peacefully, she looks innocent, pure and beautiful. A mirror reflection of her mum.

Kissing his daughter on the head, he smiles. Placing his cheek onto hers as he gently kisses her soft, warm, skin, and feeling a sense of relief as he gradually moves away.

Eve suddenly mumbles, "Mum."

Smiling with sadness in his eyes, but feeling content with his observations, Matthew convinces himself that it's all in his head. He must be experiencing a side-effect from the tramadol he's taken. Still mumbling, Eve turns on to her side. As soon as she moves, Matthew's OCD instantly makes an appearance. He notices a black smudge the size of a fifty pence piece on her pillowcase. Reaching over, he touches this, and like glue, the liquid attaches to his skin. Embedding into the prints on his fingertips, the texture of this thick, sticky liquid is nauseating and freezing cold, with its sinister black tone and sub-zero temperature. Pulling his face, Matthew's attempting to work out what this is and, as he reaches his finger up to his nose, he sniffs this. His nostrils are instantly awoken by a pungent stench which forms a strong metallic bloody taste at the back of his throat. Quietly retching so he doesn't wake Eve, he's struggling not to vomit whilst grabbing the hand sanitizer from off the bedside table, along with a tissue. Squirting the sterile liquid onto the tissue, he sets about using all his power to remove the unknown substance from his stained skin. But the more he rubs, the deeper this liquid embeds. With a strong resemblance of black ink. Matthew glances to the floor next to his bare feet and notices a similar-looking drop present on the ground. Searching with his eyes, he sees another, and another, and another. No sooner has he spotted these disturbing-looking black marks, they suddenly set about disappearing. With a slight vibration, the floor is absorbing of each droplet.

With his thoughts racing and all his senses remaining heightened, Matthew's full concentration is focused on working out what this is, when suddenly he jumps with fright. A huge bang, along with a loud squawking noise, comes from the direction of the window. Straightaway, Matthew looks up; there's nothing and no-one there. But the window is once again open. Taking a deep breath in and bravely placing one foot in front of the other with caution, he makes his way to the window. With his adrenaline kicking in, along with the cold sea breeze rapidly hitting his body, the combination of this sets him shivering. Peering round the curtain, he sees, on top of a flickering lamppost, standing proud, the biggest black raven. Continuing to look in disbelief, the eyes on this huge bird are horrific, and they stand out like red flames. No sooner has he locked his sight on this intimidating looking creature, she begins flapping her strong, glossy wings with force. Frightened, Matthew drops down to take cover. The huge raven *swoops* down to Eve's window, almost hitting him. Stumbling back slightly, as he stands, he sees the black bird has mysteriously disappeared.

Slamming the window shut and pulling the curtains tightly together, Matthew turns and sees Eve shivering in her sleep. Making his way to her, he pulls the loose bedsheets over her body. Staring at her beauty, as he moves her hair from out of her face and tucks this behind her ears, almost instantly Matthew becomes confused. The black stain on the pillowcase has gone! Gently, he removes the pillow from off the bed without disturbing Eve and begins searching the fabric front to back. Still he sees nothing. The black marks on the floor have also disappeared. Convincing himself it's definitely a side effect, and that actually it's not a big deal at all, reaching for the hand sanitizer, this time Matthew coats the entirety of the skin on his hands. With his attention taken, he leans over to remove the hair from out of her face. Tucking her hair behind her ear, he reaches across and picks up Gregg, placing the scruffy-looking bear next to her face. Looking above her bed, he stares at the heart-shaped, colourful collage of pictures. The beautiful shrine of the family he once had. Embracing the moment, as Matthew turns to leave the room, he reaches for the door and begins to pull this shut. Remaining unsure and cautious, he changes his mind and decides it's best to leave the door open.

***

Arriving in his room, Matthew sees Jess. She's tucked up and is back in bed sleeping. Heading straight to the sink in the en-suite, he turns the cold tap on and continually throws ice-cold water onto his face. Catching his breath, he grabs the hand towel from off the side of the sink and gently pats the water off his face. Breathing deep as he gathers his thoughts and lifts his head, suddenly the bathroom light flashes on and off. Instantly Matthew freezes. In his reflection, he sees, standing right behind him, the demonic woman. She's back! With her jet-black long hair hanging equally either side of her grey face, her existence is traumatic. Black blood is oozing from the cracks surrounding her mouth. Deep rips are sporadically present upon her flesh and covering her body. These impure-looking wounds are oozing the same sinister black blood. With her head low, she quickly twitches her body and, as her face spasms, Matthew sees her true identity. She has evil eyes that hold secrets you'd never desire to know. Black, thick tears roll down her face. Tainted by evil, her eyes are the deepest shade of red, surrounded entirely by black. Staring in complete shock, Matthew is frozen. Separating her lips, as she speaks, the black liquid begins gushing out of her mouth, and with her deep, dulcet voice, she quietly says, "Let's play a game... It's time, you will see; she is mine."

The black bloody substance is continuing to gush down her chin. Matthew, not wanting to accept this vision, blinks so harshly his eyelids feel as though they're about to bleed. Opening his eyes, he sees she's gone. No longer frozen, he once again bends to the sink and cups the freezing cold water. He sets about rapidly throwing this in his face; it's so cold it instantly takes his breath away. Gasping for air as he lifts his head, his nerves are shattered. Looking down at his hands, he sees they're uncontrollably shaking. Walking back into the room, a sudden movement is seen from the corner of his eye. It's Jess. She's sat upright in bed. Mentally unprepared for this sight, Matthew jumps. With his adrenaline travelling at a rapid rate around his body, this time as he jumps he practically throws himself across the bedroom.

"My god! Jess – you gave me a fright."

"Is everything okay? You seem on edge."

"Yes, I'm fine – just a bad dream."

Holding his chest to help regulate his breathing and slow down his heartrate, Matthew reaches the bedside cabinet and grabs the packet containing the pills Dr. Lane prescribed him. Desiring answers, he unfolds the tiny leaflet, which was inside the box. Scanning through this, he quietly begins speaking to himself. "No, not that, where is it – I swear these pills must cause some sort of hallucinations that he forgot to tell me about." Rustling the paper in his hand, he quickly becomes agitated. "Where is it?"

"Matthew – what is it you are looking for?"

"I knew I should have listened to my instincts. I don't take pills."

"Matthew, what's wrong?"

"Bloody hell... These pills."

"The pills to help you sleep?"

"Yes, the doc said they'd help to keep me asleep."

"Look, calm down, pass it here."

"Jess, you know I said I've been sleep walking?"

"Yes, I remember."

"Well, recently... erm, I'm not too sure how to word this, but I've not just been sleep walking."

"Okay."

"I've also, well... been seeing, things."

"Seeing things... What do you mean, like what?"

"I can't explain it. The doc says it's normal, when moving on emotionally."

"Moving on, with me?"

"Well, yes, but I don't know, maybe it's too soon."

"It's never too soon to try anything. Tell me, I'm intrigued. What is it that has you wound up so tightly?"

"Never mind – please, just forget I said anything."

"Try me, or I could help you release some of that tension." Whispering, she continues, "Inside of me."

With her leading words, and Matthew really not wanting to go into detail, he takes the leaflet out of her hand and places this back on to the bedside table. As he lays his head on the pillow next to Jess, he says nothing and gazes at her beauty. Looking deep into his soul. Jess is seductively tucking her hair behind her ear. The chemistry between these two individuals is extremely strong. Without wanting to hold back any longer, their bodies are still spiritually intertwined and are calling for each other's existence to become one. Moving closer to her, Matthew makes his move and leans in. With her urges answered, they both begin to engage in a lengthy passionate kiss.

Holding Jess's head in his hand, he tugs at her hair with his firm grip as she begins moaning under her breath. Slowly he places one leg over her slender body and mounts on top of her. Jess, wearing nothing but her black-lace underwear, embraces Matthew's toned physique as he places all his weight on top of her.

Running her hands round his back and holding him tightly in her arms, she digs her fingernails into his skin. Captured in the moment for its purity, he kisses her gently on the neck and gradually makes his way down to her chest. Jess moans louder as the intense powerful urge and desire to have Matthew inside of her begins to drive her internally wild, like a sex-starved mistress.

Placing her hands on his head, she grips the slight curls present in his hair. With his face at her lower abdomen, Matthew's gently tickling her skin as he's kissing his way down. Tugging at the lace French knickers she's wearing, he begins pulling these down. Jess lets go of his hair and places her hands behind her head, grabbing the sheets as she starts to gyrate her body on the mattress. Looking up, Matthew sees the enjoyment present on her expression. Removing the lace from her body, as he's kissing her existence, his warm breath begins leading a tingling sensation through all her senses, driving her wild. Unable to contain herself any longer Jess shouts, "Matthew, I want you inside me!"

Immediately responding to this command, he licks her as she becomes wet with pleasure. Removing his boxer shorts, he places himself deep inside her. "Oh, Jess, you feel so good."

"Give yourself to me, Matthew."

Receiving every inch of him inside of her and feeling empowered, Jess suddenly wraps her legs around his body tight. As he thrusts, she's holding him deep. Passionately kissing him, Jess feels every individual pump of his heart beating on her chest. Looking deep into his sight, she's captivating his soul and begins absorbing this. Matthew's breathing rate has unexplainably changed and is now heavy. Guiding him with her seductive energy, she rolls him onto his back. Still remaining locked in eye contact, she kisses him one last time. As Jess begins moving up and down on Matthew, he moans with great satisfaction at the intense amount of pleasure he's feeling as he says, "Oh, Jess, you're so tight."

"Give yourself to me, Matthew, I want you to let go inside of me. I want you to leave yourself inside of my body."

As she's gyrating faster and faster on Matthew's hard erect existence, he surrenders as his body is no longer able to contain his orgasm. The build-up has become too intense, and as he moans once more, he grabs her hips and pushes Jess's body down. Holding her still as he lets go of his semen and releases himself deep inside of her. Feeling the arrival of his DNA, Jess chooses to stay in the moment of power she has and remains on top of him. Matthew, still feeling the after effects of his orgasm, is lay back embracing the body-tingling pleasure, and yet he's blissfully unaware and not ready for what's about to happen. Leaning in, Jess whispers directly into Matthew's ear, "Your soul is mine."

With the words circulating around his mind, his eyes transform and turn into a deep grey mist. Looking deep into the windows of his soul, Jess is taking over his sight, his mind and his existence.

As she's breathing him in, whilst remaining inside her, Matthew pulls himself up. Jess, now sat on his lap, sees his eyes have turned black. With the transformation almost complete, she says, "Welcome to the dark side."

With these possessive words spoken, Matthew's mind begins to spin at a rapid rate. His breathing increases. Out of breath he says, "Why?"

"I am Jezebel, and she was never yours to keep!"

Unable to control the movement of his lungs, Matthew sees a flash image of the demonic empress; with this, his final vision, he passes out cold on the bed. No sooner has he embraced the heavenly pleasure of the natural release of his orgasmic indulgence and feels as though he is in heaven, he's back, submitted to hell... But why?

Chapter 15
"Defy the odds: 7/7 at 7"

"How long's left until they arrive?"

"Erm, I think we've got around an hour or so."

"When's Christina getting here? We need an urgent prep meeting."

"Erm, not sure Matthew, shall I give her a call?"

"Yes please, and have you called the caterers?"

"Yep, they should be arriving any minute now."

"Well, they ain't here, so call them again!"

A bag of nerves and anxious about whether he has the ability to concentrate or not, Matthew's recent terrifying delusional events are continuing to play on a loop inside his mind. Standing alongside Daniel in the immaculate, glass-paned boardroom, they're both waiting in anticipation for the arrival of Bill Hades. Glistening spotlights are beaming bright on the ceiling, creating a warming glow throughout the room. Ten high-back, solid, dark-oak chairs stand alongside a huge matching dark-oak table in the middle of the room. This extravagant piece of furniture showcases a centrepiece which is of the expensive kind. A modern crystal-clear art deco vase stands proudly, filled with ten of the whitest lilies.

Across the way and built into the wall is a huge seventy-two-inch television. Underneath this, and matching the table, sits a dark-oak cabinet which contains a hidden built-in mini fridge. Matching the number of chairs around the table and spotlights on the ceiling, on top of the cabinet, in an organised fashion, lie ten Honey Productions personalised pens, pencils and notepads.

On the edge of the cabinet, perfectly parallel and turned upside down, are ten stunning expensive crystal tumblers, along with the boardroom phone. Every item sits with precision and isn't leaning so much as a centimetre out of place. This organised and stunning room is immaculate; not a fragment of dust can be seen, nor a smudge on any of the glass. Rushing around, Matthew and Daniel are ensuring the room's presentation is pristine in time for the arrival of Bill and Vera.

Sorting through the objectives of the day and finalising the memos, Daniel's placing everything that's required out onto the table in readiness for today's meeting. Matthew, still on edge, jumps as the boardroom phone begins ringing.

"Hello, Daniel speaking. Oh, that's great. Yeah, sure, tell them I'm coming downstairs to meet them now. Yep. Okay. Thanks Kirsty."

"Who's here? It can't be them, I've not met with Christina yet."

As she enters the boardroom, Christina says, "You've not met with who yet? What are you getting in a tizzy about?"

"Christina, thank God for that. What time do you call this?"

"Erm, plenty of time before the meeting is what I call this."

"That was the caterers by the way, they're in reception. I'll leave you both to have your prep meeting. Be back shortly." As he's leaving the boardroom, Daniel whispers to Christina, "Good luck, he's been a right stress head all morning, not sure what's gotten into him."

Leaving the boardroom, Daniel closes the door. Waiting for him to go out of sight, Matthew sits at the table and places his head into his hands.

"Matthew, what's wrong?"

Struggling to speak out, his appearance is slumped as he's looking to the floor.

"Matthew, please, talk to me. What's got you so wound up, is Eve okay?" Making her way across the room, she sits beside him. "Matthew – please, I beg you, speak to me, I'm getting worried. I haven't seen you like this since, well, since Lauren died. Is Eve okay?"

"Yeah, Eve's fine."

Shaking his head, Matthew's quick to wipe away the single tear that's rolling down his cheek. Reaching out, Christina holds him tight and gently says, "I miss her every day, too. I really do; she was the only best friend I had for all my life." Pulling back and holding onto his shoulders, she continues, "But Matthew, it's time. You can move on. No-one will judge you and I'm sure Lauren would want you to be happy. Please, stop doing this to yourself; no matter how much we would love her to be around again, it's not going to happen. Lauren isn't coming back."

Clearing his throat and wiping his face, Matthew speaks. "I know. I'm sorry. I'm just tired. I haven't been sleeping too great recently, and it's draining me. My memory's going, my nerves are shot, and I'm being told by the doc that it's normal. It doesn't feel very normal, Chris."

"I know. Listen, we all know your heart will always lie with Lauren. She was amazing, she truly was. But look at what you actually have present in your life now. Eve seems to like this Jess, which is your biggest challenge of all. She's been raving to Melissa about her. The best advice I can give you is to just relax and stop being so hard on yourself. Enjoy this for whatever it is; no-one's saying go away, have babies, get married and buy a house..."

Matthew interrupts. "Don't even joke about that."

"Matthew – look, see, stop being so serious, it's not what we're all saying. Life goes on; it's a fact. How do you think my mum and dad felt? They buried their child, the other half of me, my twin... it's been so hard on everyone, and we all just want you to be YOU again. Maybe without this Jess, or with her, but whatever it is, you must decide fast or you're going to make yourself ill. You look exhausted."

"I haven't slept. I can't sleep. I keep seeing this woman. I can't explain it because I can't remember all the details, but she's just constantly taunting me at night. I know it sounds mental, and I'm telling you this because, well, what have I got to lose, really? Nothing."

"Thank you."

"Thank you for what?"

"For speaking to me. I know how hard this is for you. Matthew, it's such a traumatic thing we've all experienced, you and Eve more than most, but just look at it this way, the reality is, your mind is clearly playing cruel tricks on you. I promise. Maybe you should head back to the doctor's after the meeting today."

"Can't. I've got to go straight home from here, there's something I need to check back at the house. Hopefully I'll get some closure. I promise, if it carries on, I'll go back. I think I'm just going to cool it off with Jess for a while. Stay friends. I only hope Eve doesn't freak out."

"I'm sure she'll understand. Now, off to the toilet and sort yourself out before Daniel comes back and Bill and Vera get here."

"Thanks Chris, I'm lucky I have you." Matthew heads to the door and, as he opens this, he turns and says, "You truly are like her in every way, you know. Like you say, the other half."

Smiling as he closes the door, Christina sits at the table and sighs with relief.

Arriving at the toilets, he heads straight for the sink, turns on the taps and continually throws the freezing cold water onto his face. Gasping for air as the water's dripping from his features, with his head remaining low and his arms spread out either side of the sink, Matthew's desperate to return back to normal. Wiping the excess water from off his face and straightening his tie, his mind unexpectedly throws him back into a happier time of his life.

Toddling around their favourite clothes shop is a tiny Eve. She's pulling at her mum's arm, rushing to the tie rack. Lauren's smiling, Eve's giggling and Matthew's not too far behind them both. Gripping the ruby-red, silk tie with her hands and ripping this from the tie rack, Eve mischievously runs off to her daddy. Passing this to him, she says, "Daddy's tie."

Snapping back into his existing reality, Matthew's wearing the ruby-red tie from his vision. Taking a deep breath in, suddenly the light in the toilets flashes off and quickly flashes back on again. No sooner has he regained his sight, he's frozen stiff. She's standing right behind him. The Dark Empress has returned. As she lifts her head, black blood gushes out of her mouth. The light once again flickers off, and this time, when it comes back on, she's gone! Breaking down, Matthew sobs into his hands. "Please, just stop."

He's had enough. Curled up into a ball on the floor of the toilet, Matthew's ability to feel sane has disappeared. He can't cope with the mental torture he's enduring anymore. Physically drained, he begins uncontrollably crying with exhaustion.

***

Unaware of her dad's suffering, Eve's backstage getting ready for her final ever production at the school theatre. She's been nervously practising all morning with her fellow musicians. All different ages, from all different school years, congregate in the designated practise areas. All the students are getting excited in readiness for their dress rehearsal, and then the big finale, which is fast approaching. This year, Eve has her very own solo performance and she's reviewing her notes, alone, in the corner of the dressing room. Satisfied with her understanding of the chosen piece, and with her mind beginning to wonder, she's confused by the thoughts that are racing throughout her head. All the other girls, grouped together, are extremely giddy. They're all loudly giggling and chatting away to each other in the middle of the dressing room.

"That was the best we've ever done it. Girls, we're going to rock this."

"I know, I'm emosh, this is our last ever show. I'm gonna miss spending this time with you ladies. Group hug?"

"Group hug."

"Eve... Come on. Eve... Eve, are you ok?"

"Huh? Oh yeah, I'm fine. Sorry, what were you saying?"

"Georgina was saying we're going to rock this. Group hug, come on, get in."

"No, I'm all right thanks, I'll stay here."

Making her way across to Eve, concerned for her friend, Emma once again speaks. "Are you sure you're all right, you've been on another planet all morning?"

"Yeah, sorry, just thinking."

"About what?"

"Nothing really."

"Well, I don't think it's quite nothing, you've barely spoke to any of us all morning. Eve, I know we haven't been close for some time now, and God only knows I've tried to be there for you, but you won't let me in. Please, don't do this, you're not alone. Speak to me."

"Emma, you won't understand, and I can't explain it anyway."

"Try me."

"Okay then, but you're gonna freak out."

"Like I said, try me."

"Something's coming."

"Huh, what's coming?"

"Argh, see, it's hard to explain."

"Well at least try."

"The voices inside my head. Emma, they keep rambling on about my purpose."

"Voices?"

"Yeah, voices."

"So, I still don't understand, what's coming? Your purpose? I'm confused, what does that even mean?"

"I'm not sure. Look, come over here."

Grabbing Emma by the arm and dragging her over to the clothing rail where all their wonderful costumes hang in size order, Eve pulls Emma in between the items and hides. She doesn't want anyone to see them or hear what she's about to say.

"This should be safe. Okay, be quiet and don't tell anyone."

"I won't."

"Emma, promise me?"

"I promise. Eve, you're scaring me slightly."

"Emma, it's serious. I keep hearing this voice. It's constantly whispering to me, telling me that my time has come, and saying that my purpose is greater than this, greater than me."

"Okay, that's a bit strange. Eve, I think that maybe you should go and speak to someone."

"I can't, Emma, I must trust the process."

"Trust the process? Eve, what on earth has gotten into you? Listening to these voices and letting them in? I mean, come on, that's not exactly normal, you must see that."

"Define normal, Emma?"

"Not that."

"You don't understand. I get it, it's fine, you're a clone and you'll always be a clone. Go on, off you go, get back to your group hug."

"Don't be mean, Eve. Why do you have to push people away all the time?"

"Push people away, why, how close have you all been for me to push you away? I think you'll find you've stayed well away from me for a long time."

"No, I haven't! You wouldn't let me near to help."

"That's a load of crap and you know it. You dropped me at my time of need. My mum died, and we'd been friends since nursery. Ten years of friendship, for what? My mum made you tea and looked after you when you came and stayed over at our house, then you drop me when I need you most."

"Eve, I tried to help you. I can't believe you think that. You turned so nasty, what was I supposed to do, allow you to keep having a pop at me cause my mum and dad are still alive and together? You made our friendship impossible."

"Impossible, ha-ha, don't make me laugh, shows your commitment to our long-standing friendship."

"Whatever, Eve, seriously, don't ruin this for us; we've all worked hard for this and it's our last one. Just because you're unhappy doesn't mean the rest of us should have to change and tip-toe around you."

"Unhappy, you lot don't understand the meaning of the word unhappy, with your protected lives. You'll soon see. I can't wait for my day. You'll all see. It's not far away and then, well, I don't need to say what's going to happen next. I'll show you all."

"Whatever, Eve, I'm done trying to make you feel okay. Enjoy your misery."

"Yeah, enjoy your fake friendships. Pfttt…"

Separating the clothing and stepping back out into the dressing room, Emma joins the group of girls, leaving Eve on her own.

"What's up with happy over there?"

"Oh, the usual everything's got to be about Eve. I give up trying."

"I don't even know why you try. I wouldn't give her the time of day after the way she treated you. Emma, you're better off with us anyway."

"Thanks Georgie. I love you."

"I love you too, my beaut. Now, everyone, let's do this."

Once satisfied and feeling better, Emma, along with the group of girls, sets about mischievously creeping around backstage. Peeping through the huge, heavy, red-velvet curtains, they're all getting excited as some of their parents are beginning to take their seats. On the front row of the theatre, Eve's reserved two seats. One for her dad, and the other for Jess. Making her way backstage, as the girls move on, Eve glances through the curtains and sees that neither her dad or Jess are sat in their seats. With the production starting in less than thirty minutes, she's left her phone at home and is unable to call either of them to confirm if they're coming or not, and so she doesn't hold out much hope.

"Eve, come on, quick."

"Huh."

"You're spacing out again. Mrs Mastalerz is looking for us."

Being pulled by Layla, they both set about rushing into the dressing room and each girl quickly grabs their instruments. Greeted by their teacher, who's a beautiful, fun and unique woman. Mrs Mastalerz, a free spirit, is the complete opposite to all the other teachers. The investment in her student's is personal and inspiring. This is just one of the many reasons why Eve's talent in music has flourished. Mrs Mastalerz has so much love and respect for all her students; they're not just a grade, or an alphabetical statistic on her register, they're her life. Music, and teaching, is her life. Having spent many hours and lunchtimes with Eve, along with after school lessons since her mum died, Mrs Mastalerz has a real soft spot for her and pushes Eve to achieve her maximum potential. She sees the capabilities she has and encourages her to take her talent and musical career as far as the bright lights of Hollywood.

Standing in the packed-out dressing room, and with her mind beginning to drift, Eve's once again spacing out. Drifting off into a happier time in her life, she's back in the classroom with Mrs Mastalerz, alone. Housing the talent of the school, each drama, music and dance room has a grand wooden-built stage. Standing on the stage in her music room, Mrs Mastalerz has a cardboard self-made Grammy Award in her hands.

"And the winner is... Evelyn Jade Honey for her outstanding production and contribution to the music industry. Congratulations, Evelyn Jade, come and collect your award."

Cheering and clapping her hands whilst making enough noise for a crowd, an overwhelmed Eve takes centre stage and collects her cardboard Grammy Award.

"Thank you, wow. What an honour this is. I would just like to thank my dad, and everyone who's been involved in my career progression and, most of all, I want to thank the public, for without you, I am nothing. Every single one of you believe in me, and so I believe in me too. Also, I just wanted to say, my high school teacher is the reason I am here today. Mrs Mastalerz, if you're watching this, wherever you are in the world, I thank you. This is for us... we did it."

Often performing role play and using their imaginations, Mrs Mastalerz inspires Eve to see her name in lights with her very own Hollywood star. But the greatest gift of all for Eve was when she got to be alone with her favourite teacher. This was the only time she truly felt free to be herself, no pressure, no name calling, no laughing or pointing, just free to be Eve. Hearing her teacher's voice, she snaps out of her flashback and straight back into her existing reality.

"Right everyone, settle down, settle down. Can everyone hear me, hello?" *Cough, cough.* "Everyone! That's better. Okay, thank you, so does everyone have their instruments?"

The whole group of students, in-sync, speak out. "Yes Mrs Mastalerz."

"Okay, the parents are now arriving and we're about to start at any minute, so I want you all to get in your outfits. First production team, where are you?"

The group of twenty students put up their hands, Eve included.

"Okay, can you all quickly get changed and line up over by the curtains on the correct side to which you are to be seated. And please, be quick, you're our opening act."

The curtains are closed. The conductor has just taken his bow, and he is now standing at the front of the stage with his back to the crowd. As the final parents take their seats, the huge, heavy, red-velvet curtains open. Anxiously sat in her starting position, Eve looks to the front row. The seat she's reserved for her dad is, as predicated, empty. With disappointment and anger building up inside of her, suddenly, she looks to the seat at the side – astounded, she sees Jess. Sat smiling, with her head held high. Their eyes lock.

Tapping his baton on the edge of the wooden stand, the conductor begins the musical performance.

With the production almost over, the audience are clapping and cheering with pride at all the amazing pieces of music they've been blessed to hear from their talented children. Performance after performance after performance; before you know it, it's time. Eve's moment arrives. Mrs Mastalerz proudly makes her way to the front of the stage.

"How great have they all been? I'm blown away and so very proud of them all. Now, as many of you know, this is the last production for most of the students here as they leave school in a couple of weeks and will start the newest chapter of their lives. Many of them have bravely elected to perform a solo for you this afternoon, and so it is my greatest pleasure to introduce to you, on piano, the amazing, multi-talented Evelyn Jade Honey. Please, put your hands together as we welcome her to the stage."

Walking out nervously, Eve once again looks to the front row; she's so angry. Her dad still isn't sat in his seat – he hasn't bothered to turn up even though he knew how important this was to her. With the voice on loop inside her mind, this incessant whispering is repeating the same words over and over. Standing alone, she looks to Jess and bows. As she sits on the stool at the huge, black, grand piano, no sooner have her fingers graced the keys, suddenly her thoughts are taken over. She's given into this whispering and the last pure molecule of her soul has surrendered. With this submission, her eyes instantly become overcast and grey. Feeling as though she's about to throw up, her head begins uncontrollably spinning. Under her breath, like a command, Jess whispers, "Your soul is mine."

Instantly, Eve passes out on the stool and violently hits her head off the keys on the piano as she falls on the floor. Whilst repeatedly convulsing. Mrs

Mastalerz attempts to run to Eve's aid, but as soon as she reaches the piano, an unforeseen force awakens around Eve's shaking body and this throws Mrs Mastalerz across the stage. As she lands in a heap on the ground, Mrs Mastalerz lies motionless with her eyes wide open. Her soul no longer looks as though this is present in her physical form. Before anyone has chance to tend to both Eve or Mrs Mastalerz, unexpectedly, all the lights go off and the theatre becomes dark.

Panicking, the parents begin grabbing their children and fumbling around in the dark. All of them desperately attempt to rush for the nearest exit. Upon hearing the news, all the students behind the stage become hysterical. Everyone individually starts screaming, and the noise of each scream combined becomes ear-piercing. People of all ages, both young and old, are radiating fear. The energy circulating in the theatre becomes daunting, and the evil entity that has taken control of the room is feeding from the distress and is gaining strength with every second of its overpowering manifestation.

Strangely, a single light appears at the front of the stage. This spotlight is reflective and is focused only on Eve as it begins lighting up her surroundings. Fearful of the unknown, all the conscious minds within the theatre are freaking out, all that is, except one!

Standing calmly from her seat, Jess's sole attention and focus is fixated on Eve. With eyes that hold secrets and are filled with deceit, Jess's energy is not symbolic of the current situation. She appears calm and looks victorious. As Eve's still uncontrollably and violently convulsing on the floor, black foam begins oozing from her mouth, when suddenly, her body comes to an abrupt holt and she now lies motionless. Making her way to Eve, Jess, slowly placing one foot in front of the other, is transforming with every inch that she gets closer to Eve's body. Her true form is proudly taking shape.

With the lights remaining off, and the only tiny spot of light beaming at the front of the room, the parents, along with their children, are unaware of the transformation taking place on the stage. Continuing to climb over one another in a desperate attempt to get out of the building, as soon as each of them reach the exits, they're quick to learn that all the doors and windows have been locked tight. There's no escape.

***

"Atticus, it was great to meet you. I'm sure following in your uncle's footsteps, you're going to be a great success."

"Thanks, Christina. Actually, film production has always excited me and so when uncle Bill invited me to this meeting, there was absolutely no way I was passing up this opportunity."

"Oh, bless you, well, what I will say is Matthew's usually more alert than this. And so normally, you would've received more informative knowledge, but he's just got a lot on today, haven't you Matthew?"

"Huh?"

"I was saying to Atticus that you've got a lot on today."

"Oh, yeah, a lot on today."

Standing from their chairs in the boardroom, Matthew, Christina, Daniel, Vera, Bill and his nephew Atticus are gathering their notes from today's meeting. Content with the decisions that have been made regarding the finalised advertisement for SaintsVill clothing, Bill looks to Matthew. "You all right, Matty lad?"

"Huh?"

"I said are you all right, Matty lad?"

Waking up slightly, as this is the second time he's had to answer the same question twice, a more alert Matthew replies, "Yeah, sorry Bill, I've just got some stuff going on I need to sort out after here. But it's fine. Anyway, yeah nice to meet you, Aaron."

"It's Atticus."

"Oh, sorry, yes, my mistake; it is, isn't it?"

Putting out his hand, Atticus says, "It's been a real pleasure to meet you Matthew, and I was just saying to Christina how much I admire the film production industry."

"Atticus, I tell you what, to make up for today as I've got a lot on, why don't you get Daniel's email address and arrange to come in, so you can see a day in the life of Honey Productions? Maybe get you on as an intern or something."

"Aye, Matty boy, you best be coughing up a finder's fee for him, or better still, let's say, a free advertisement, aye Matty boy, ha-ha, that should cover it, right?"

"Aye, Bill, is this your secret weapon – get a freebie using this one and keep the wealth? Haha. I tell you what, if he's half as good at business as you are, the lad will be worth every pound."

"You sussed me, Matty boy. I tell you, fine lad is our Atticus. I assure you he's made with a great genetic build-up. Raised well, aren't you, lad?"

"Thanks, Uncle Bill. I learned from the best."

"You've paid him to say that, haven't you, Bill?"

"Aye, cheeky, forgot you were here. Christina, come now, bring it in for a hug."

Looking to his watch, Matthew sees the time's six p.m. Gathering his things in a rush, he says, "I'm gonna have to shoot. Daniel, don't forget to type the minutes and send them out to everyone, oh and pass Aaron, sorry, I mean, Atticus, your email cause he's going to come in on an intern thing. Right everyone, it's been a real pleasure, but I must go."

***

Back at the house, Matthew's in the kitchen, swaying slightly. He's had enough! Like an alcoholic drinking straight from the bottle, he's throwing back the contents of wine it holds. His ties pulled down and his shirt's hanging out of his pants. No longer resembling the strong man he once was, Matthew looks a mess. His hair's sticking up and his whole appearance is neglected. Slightly drunk from the amount of wine he's consumed in such a short period of time, he stumbles out of the kitchen and begins making his way up the spiral staircase to his office.

Pushing the door open with one arm and waving his bottle of wine around with the other, Matthew sits at the desk and, as he turns the computer on, he sets about slurring his words as he talks to himself. "Operation bump in the night, ha-ha. I like it. So, now then, now then, now then… what do we have here? I know I turned you on this time, ha, you can't outsmart Matthew Honey."

Gulping back his wine once more, Matthew manages to log in and opens up the CCTV camera file. "Now —" caught off guard, he unexpectedly hiccupped, "—let us see what's going on then—" once again, not in control of his bodily functions, he hiccupped, "—nanny cam, and, login—" With the alcohol having a clear effect on his system he hiccupped a further time before continuing, "—kaboom, CCTV camera. Oh hello, lookie, what is it we have here then! So..." Taking another gulp of his wine from the bottle before finishing his sentence, Matthew continues, "We've decided to play ball this time have we.".

Clicking the link, the live footage currently recording begins playing. Completely intoxicated and almost tumbling from his office chair whilst dramatically waving his arms around, Matthew nearly falls into the solid dark-oak cabinet which is holding his library of books. Laughing somewhat hysterically to himself, he says, "Whoopsyyyyy."

Regaining his balance and placing the virtually empty bottle of wine down on the edge of the desk, suddenly he feels a huge draft flowing down the back of his neck. This cold progressive gust of air carries a sub-zero temperature which makes the hairs on his skin stand to attention. Looking up, the office door is closed, but it's not shut tight. Standing from his chair and stumbling over to the door, peering through the gap, Matthew looks out into the empty hallway which is embracing the darkness.

"Eve... Jess?"

With no response and content that he is, in fact, alone, Matthew ignores the shiver and again stumbles back over to his desk. Looking to the time on his computer, he sees it's 06.47 p.m. on the 7/7. Distracted by the events that have been taking place, Matthew's unalarmed and completely unfazed about the fact he's not spoken to his daughter all day. With a look of confusion fast spreading across his features and slightly shaking his head, Matthew's trying to figure out where he was up to. Reaching for the mouse next to the keyboard and once again swaying slightly, Matthew remains unsteady as he's seated in his office chair. Losing his balance once more, this time he almost knocks the bottle off the edge of the desk as he carelessly begins directing the mouse towards the pre-recorded footage from last night. Forwarding the recording to the time when Eve went to bed, Matthew begins observing, as he can see his daughter sleeping. Looking her usual angelic and innocent self in her pure white bedsheets. He smiles as he's watching her sleeping peacefully. Once again, he begins forwarding the recording. Eve's body is now moving around in her bed at a fast-forward pace as the hours minutes and seconds tick by quickly. Feeling content as the room remains normal, no sooner has he embraced this, something mysterious catches his eye.

Stopping the recording at 3.07 a.m. he sees an unexpected change within the room. Staring intently at what he believes is smoke seeping from around the doorframe, Matthew leans closer to the monitor. Pressing play once more, he's fixated on this spot and is watching as the grey mystified smoke seeps thicker and thicker into Eve's room, becoming established. Looking to his daughter, Matthew sees she's completely unaware of this presence surrounding her as she's sleeping in her bed. As the footage is continuing to play and, unable to comprehend what's actually taking place in his daughter's bedroom, Matthew's frozen stiff and can no longer believe what he's seeing. Things like this don't happen in the real world. This is surely wrong; someone's edited the footage as a prank!

Gliding through the closed wooden door, as though this sturdy foundation never existed, is the same demonic grey-looking woman he's being taunted by in his mind, except this time it isn't in his mind. This recording tells no lies. She's there as clear as day in his daughter's bedroom.

Unsure if he should feel relieved that this is confirmation he's not going insane, or petrified at her true existence, Matthew, suffering with shock, releases a single silent tear which falls slowly down his face. This image disturbs him so much it literally shocks the alcohol out of his system and pushes him right back to being sober. Watching as the events unfold, he sees her true horrific form; he sees her grey body and her long black hair which is dripping a black substance everywhere she lands. With her head down low and the grey mist circulating in the room. Suddenly, Matthew sees Eve's sleeping body shoot up. Eve, now sat up straight in her bed, has her eyes wide open.

Once again, Matthew leans closer to the monitor, with instant regret and a look of horror on his face. He sees Eve is no longer Eve. She's a mini mirror reflection of this demonic entity. With eyes that resemble gaping black holes in her face, black blood is oozing from the surroundings of her eye sockets. With a skin tone that is unknown to this world, Eve's body has been taken over and is showcasing the same dark shade of grey. Her flesh has deep rips spread sporadically all over it and black blood pulses out of each one. Trying to come to terms with the horrific image of his daughter, Matthew slumps back in his office chair when, unexpectedly, he sees appearing on the footage a huge, black raven. This sinful-looking creature lands on Eve's shoulder and begins pecking at her face. Eve doesn't flinch or react to this. Watching from the side of the bed, the grey demonic entity makes her way from the doorway across to Eve to join her evil acquaintance. With the raven on one side, the demonic entity leans over to Eve's face and with her black tongue she licks and begins ingesting the substance oozing from Eve's existence.

Feeling a vibration on the table from the soundwaves of the recording, suddenly this develops a repetitive and rhythmic vibration. The demonic entity's mouth is moving. Whilst sat up in her bed, Eve appears to be embracing the words spoken. Rewinding the footage, once he's content with its positioning, Matthew turns the volume to its highest point. Through the distorted recording he continues to struggle hearing the words she speaks, but what he can make out is a tune. Grabbing his headphones from out of the drawer, he plugs these in and once again presses play. Closing his eyes, Matthew hears it! It's a nursery rhyme. With a dulcet and eerie tone, he hears the demonic entity singing Ring a' Ring o' Roses, but the words aren't quite right. Fiddling with the settings, Matthew rewinds the footage and listens again; this time he hears, "Ring a' Ring o' Roses – your soul is mine. Ring a' Ring o' Roses – you've been chosen for the dark side."

Almost instantly upon hearing this rhyme, it sparks a sense of familiarity within his mind. He's heard this before. Continuing to watch in disbelief, Matthew feels numb. The raven suddenly flaps her huge wings and goes out of sight. The demonic entity looks straight to the door. Appearing startled, a sudden transformation begins taking place. Holding his breath, Matthew can't believe his eyes. He can't process what he's seeing. It's her... it's...

"Matthew, what are you doing?"

Jumping, this time he successfully knocks the virtually empty bottle of wine off the desk and onto the floor. Matthew looks like he's just seen a ghost. With his eyes open wide, and breathing at a rapid rate, he's frozen stiff to his chair.

Standing in the doorway, Jess once again speaks. "Matthew, what's wrong?"

"Jess... I... Erm..."

"You what?"

With his voice low and his eyes still wide he says, "Where's Eve?"

Looking to the monitor on the desk, she smirks as she makes her way closer to him and continues, "So, now you know."

Rife with fear, Matthew is unable to move. "Where is she, where is my daughter?"

"Don't you worry, I told you, Mr Honey, I always take good care of my pieces. Evelyn Jade, come here please."

Entering into the office, Eve stands directly at the side of Jess.

"Eve, come here, get away from her. Get away from her now!"

Attempting to stand, Matthew's quick to work out that he's stuck to his chair. "Please, I beg you, don't do this; she's all I have."

"You see, that's the problem, she's actually all you never had. Selected from billions of souls, I mapped out your fate; I created your destiny. You should know something, Mr Honey. I might as well tell you now that the truth is out. I have been watching you for years – many, many, many years. Your first and only born, Evelyn Jade, way before the point of conception, had been chosen for a great purpose. She was always a possession of mine. Did you think that your choice of gift for Lauren all those years ago, you know, the solid silver locket from the old gypsy lady's stall, and the fact I had the other, that these lockets were just simply a coincidence? Did you really believe the fact that I had the only twin of this necklace was just by chance?"

"Eve, come here please. Eve, listen to my voice, it's me, your dad."

Choosing not to answer the question which Jess has just asked, Matthew's desperate to get his daughter away from this evil individual. He's totally unprepared for what's about to come next.

"Bless you, Mr Honey and your innocence, or should I say your desperate and weak mind. You see, you were so obsessed with your dead wife that you totally missed all the signs. I'm calculated, but you're stupid. You've made this so very easy for me. I couldn't have you taking off with my chosen one. The locket your wife fell so desperately in love with, this was my hunter, my tracker so to speak, I have always been watching, watching every single move you've each made. You see, I always knew I was up against one teeny tiny problem…"

Eve's still standing in the doorway. The transition is beginning as her skin tone is changing to a slight shade of grey. Jess slowly makes her way closer to Matthew. Leaning into his ear, her breath is ice-cold and has a strong pungent stench attached to it. Leaving a strong metallic taste at the back of his throat, this instantly makes him feel nauseous. Empowered by her current situation, Jess continues, "Unfortunately, you both got too attached to something that never belonged you. I was faced with a dilemma, so to speak. I was faced with the fact that my possession, my creation, my chosen soul, had two very strong keepers who loved her very much, and so I decided that one of you had to go. Yes! It was I who killed your poor little Lauren. It was I who ripped your world apart and made you weak and vulnerable. Now, Mr Honey, I'm taking what's rightfully mine! Did you really think you could keep her from me? Ha! I killed your wife and you're lucky I don't kill you, too, now that you've served your purpose. The clock is ticking; my demonic empire will be unleashed upon the world. I am the Dark Empress and the universe will be mine. This is just the beginning."

Silent tears fall rapidly down Matthew's motionless face as he realises what she's saying; it's worse than he could have ever imagined. All his worst fears and nightmares are coming true.

"I am Jezebel. And she is mine. Let's have some fun. Do you like to play games, Mr Honey? Ring a' Ring o' Roses…"

With these final words spoken, both Jezebel and Eve begin showcasing their horrific true demonic forms. With a new sensation present in her body, Eve feels tiny electrical shocks, along with an immense sense of deep internal pleasure with every millimetre of this evil possessive takeover that's tingling its way through her veins and entering into every tiny cell of her DNA. A thick substance appears at the back of her throat and Eve's nostrils are awakened by a strong pungent stench. This substance empowers over all her senses and with each second that ticks, the development of this manifests a metallic taste which quickly takes ownership as it travels deep into her taste-buds. Eve suddenly chokes as she's attempting to welcome this strange texture at the back of her throat. Instantly, a black, thick substance begins dripping from the cracks present and surrounding the outline of her grey lips. She coughs as this thick sinister substance commences its evil intention and rolls down her chin and begins resting on her chest.

The silver necklace and heart-shaped locket hanging around Eve's neck is suddenly embodied by the black substance as this covers every inch of the irreplaceable piece of memorabilia and destroys the beauty that this item once represented; the weight of this hangs heavy and snaps the chain, and this precious piece of jewellery falls slowly to the floor. The final piece of the puzzle, the final item to remind Eve of the life she once had, has now gone! As this lands on the floor, the Dark Empress and her chosen soul are united at last, standing strong side by side. With their transformation complete, the pair throw themselves at Matthew and begin dragging his soul deeper and deeper into the dark abyss of his own mind.

The time has come; it's the final game.

Chapter 16
"The final game"

"Eve... Eve... Eve!"

"Yes Father?"

"Eve – where are you?"

"I'm here, Father."

"*Where?* I can't see anything."

"Father..."

"Listen to me, princess, I don't want you to panic, just follow my voice. I'm coming to find you and we're going to get out of here together and go home."

"Help me, Father, please, save me, you must before it's too—"

"Eve! Eve! Eve! Before it's too what?"

As the echoing of his voice disappears and the silence becomes deafening, Matthew's desperate to hear his daughter's voice. Holding hope in his heart that she's still within his vicinity he shouts out, "Darling, everything's going to be all right. I'm coming to find you."

Bravely taking one step forward whilst being surrounded entirely by black, Matthew's completely unaware that he's been trapped inside the darkest depths of his own mind. He's standing alone and as the fear that's circulating in his thoughts fast becomes his primary emotion, Matthew's feeling exposed and vulnerable. Hearing only the sound of his breath as this leaves his body, he's suddenly caught off guard and an excruciating pain circulates around his wrists. This strangulating unknown force is cutting through his soft flesh as his arms are mysteriously ripped apart and raised above his head. Screaming out in agony, he's forcefully being pulled from off his feet. Coming to an abrupt halt and left dangling from what he can only begin to imagine is a great height, his ankles begin to feel the same excruciating pain as they're also ripped apart and restrained in the same manner. Unable to see what, or who, is doing this to him, Matthew's battling against this strong powerful force in a desperate attempt to free himself. But the fiercer he pulls the tighter the grip becomes.

Giving in and remaining still as the movement creates too much pain for him to bear, Matthew drops his head as his energy levels run low. An eerie silence manifests, but he doesn't feel alone. The dark energy embedded inside this stillness begins toying with his thoughts. With his sight gone, his hearing becomes strong and, as a sudden twitch is felt inside his ears, a repetitive tune circulates inside his mind and sets about taking over his thoughts. Absorbing the haunting, eerie version of Ring a' Ring o' Roses which is being hummed, he suddenly hears, "Do you like to play games, Mr Honey?"

Desperate to release himself and not engage in these torturous mind games he shouts out, "Why are you doing this to us? Where is she? Eve, Eve!"

"Wrong answer, Mr Honey. I hope you're ready. Let the games begin."

As an intimidating and insane laughter circulates in his mind alongside the incessant nursey tune that refuses to stop, his surroundings unexpectedly become lit. As his sight adjusts to the brightness of this spontaneous spotlight, Matthew looks at his current unfortunate state. He's suspended inside a huge, thick, rope-made spider's web. Struggling as he's attempting to free himself, he hears Eve's desperate cry. "Father, help me."

Looking down, he sees Eve dressed in her mother's nightie, on her knees, helplessly staring up at him. Reaching out she says, "Father, please, I'm dying."

"Eve! No, I will not lose you, don't worry, I'm coming darling."

No sooner have these words left his mouth, as he's fighting with all his might against the strong power of the tight restraining rope, the web unexpectedly begins violently shaking. Peering up above his head, Matthew sees approaching him from out of the darkness, intimidating, evil, blood-red eyes which are getting closer and closer to him. Attached to these sinister-looking eyes is a huge, thick-legged, monstrous tarantula the size of a t-rex. Tripping over its long legs and making its way towards Matthew at a rapid rate, this monster-sized creature spits venom from its pincers as they surface. Before he has time to react, or hit out, Matthew hears, "*Mi temono.*"

Instantly released from his entrapment, he's once again falling into the darkness. With his final decent, and landing in a heap, he's curled up. Rocking back and forth whilst firmly holding his head in both his hands, Matthew's attempting to protect his body as he's just smashed his skull off the ground he's landed on. Petrified of the unknown and screaming out loud with agony, he's confused, frantic and attempting to allow his mind to process what's happening. Beginning to pat his body to ensure he's in one piece, and searching his surroundings, Matthew's inattentive to the fact his wrists and ankles are wounded, and blood is gushing out.

"Eve, where are you darling?"

Night has fallen and not a single star can be seen. It's as though his surroundings are lost deep within the universe. The dimly lit streetlamps are vaguely lighting his parameters. It's freezing cold. Matthew's breath can be seen leaving his body. Hearing the chiming of bells, he sees the outline of a cathedral across the way. The desperate cries of his daughter begin echoing alongside the vibration of the chimes. Matthew looks up high at the ruins of the castle that stands at the side of this strong house of God; he sees Eve at what was once a window. She's calling out to him: "Help me, Father, I want to go home."

"I'm coming for you, darling, stay there."

"Hurry, Father, she's coming for me."

Without so much as a second thought for his own safety, or indeed his life, Matthew runs towards the castle and attempts to force his way through the huge wooden-built door with its steel fixtures and bolts. Almost instantly, he's unsuccessful, but that's not going to stop him. Running around to the other side of the castle, Matthew's confronted with another challenge: an unsteady, manmade grey-brick wall stands before him and is being supported by a thick, razor-sharp, metal fence which is almost half the height of the castle. With the clinking sound of metal as he throws himself at this, Matthew grips onto the gaps and begins fearlessly climbing. One leg after the other, like a rocket he launches himself over the top. The razor-sharp metal rips through the layers of his clothing and gashes deep into the flesh on his leg. Falling from the top onto the floor, with his adrenaline surging throughout his veins, he doesn't notice the blood that's gushing from not only his head, but any part of his body.

Stumbling up onto his feet, Matthew's not giving up. Feeling an electrical and powerful surge of energy as he charges at the castle, he's determined to save his daughter and break free. Scaling the wall of this huge structure, he finally makes it high enough to throw himself through one of the unprotected gaping holes on the side of the castle. Matthew's finally inside. Instantly, his heart begins racing. He may be inside but now he's got an even bigger challenge on his hands: he's got to find his daughter in this dark haunted-looking building without any light, and he doesn't think for a second, it's going to be easy. With the odds stacked against him, the only tiny reflection into the castle is coming from the streetlamps outside.

Covered in blood, Matthew's current physical state has become somewhat life-threatening. He's rapidly losing blood and his body is getting weaker with every second that passes. Allowing his attention to fixate on finding his daughter, Matthew's heart is strong and the love he has for her is empowering him enough to ignore his body's signals of surrendering and urges him to keep fighting.

"Eve? Eve? Where are you, darling?"

"Father, I'm here."

Following the vibration from the soundwaves in her voice, he's frantically running around the castle.

"Eve?"

"I'm over here, Father."

Tripping over his feet as he is struggling to keep up with himself, finally Matthew reaches the room, where he hears her voice. Without any hesitation, he walks down the grey-brick stairs. Unable to see the step ahead, Matthew kicks the debris, and this begins bouncing down each step. The sound of the crumbling falling rocks echoes throughout the castle's parameters. The internal structure of this historical building isn't as sturdy as it looks. With his heart racing he peers into the dark, empty, stone-walled room which has one streak of light beaming in from the streetlamp outside. Closing his eyes and breathing in deep, on his exhale with his voice low he says, "Eve?"

"Here, Father."

"Eve, oh, my princess, there you are."

Walking into room, he turns and sees Eve. She's cowering in a dark corner. Running over to his blessing, Matthew instantly begins crying as he reaches out to comfort and hold his daughter. But as soon as he reaches her an unforeseen force awakens and throws him to the other side of the room and well away from the exit. She's gone. Jumping up with shock, Matthew attempts to run, but he's quick to learn he's unable to do so. Suddenly he hears an unfamiliar, spine-shivering, daunting voice, "Ring a' Ring o' Roses – I've been chosen for the dark side."

Looking to his left, Matthew sees Eve. She's still wearing only her mother's nightie which is covered in grey dust, dirt and rips. As she's slowly crawling down the same stairs he's just walked upon himself, once again, she sings, "Ring a' Ring o' Roses."

Unexpectedly she stops and looks towards Matthew. Staring directly at him with her head tilted, again with her voice deep and not sounding her own, she speaks, "Are you scared, Mr Honey, is this better?"

Feeling physically sick but unable to throw up, Matthew hears the crack from her bone as she abruptly snaps her own neck. With her head hanging low, she says, "Help me, Father."

With her body raising from off the step, she's levitating up high. Her eyes are as black as the midnight sky and sit as gaping holes in her face. Showcasing her demonic form, Eve is no longer Eve. She's a true reflection of the sadistic owner of her soul. Remaining at a great height, with no visual help, her body begins jolting and twitching as she's dislocating her bones one by one! A black, thick substance gushes out of her mouth and as this lands on the floor it rolls and travels towards Matthew.

"Help me Father."

Letting out an insane laughter, the entity that's taken ownership of her body and soul is dragging Eve closer to him. Frozen stiff and attempting to process what's taking place before his eyes, Matthew's unable to blink. With his chest rapidly moving up and down, his breathing rate has become erratic and out of sync. Not only this, his heart feels as though, at any minute, it's going to pop.

"Help me Father – Ring a' Ring o' Roses."

With these final words Eve violently throws herself at her dad. With his mind spinning out of control and as he screams out loud, Matthew's again released from his entrapment and thrown directly into another.

Continuing to get weaker by the second as he's still rapidly losing blood, Matthew reluctantly checks his parameters. He's surrounded by crispy autumn-coloured leaves which are smothered with dirt. Not a building can be seen, just tree after tree after tree. The sky remains black and there's not a single star in sight. A grey mist begins to present itself and as this circulates around the sturdy trees, it quickly covers the ground he sits on and rises to his neck. Slowly stumbling onto his feet, Matthew's attempting to hold himself up as he leans against the tree trunk trying to catch his breath. This deceitful mist is entering into his body. Attacking his organs and suffocating him internally. Matthew begins uncontrollably panting. Leaning with his back on the tree he huffs, "Eve."

Almost falling back down on to the ground, he begins retching as the mist has a nauseating stench of death attached to it.

With his eyes closed, he hears the crunching of the leaves making its way towards him from out of the distance. Getting louder and louder. Matthew's taking no chances as he hobbles in the opposite direction trying to get as far away from whoever is making the noise as he possibly can. The trees all look the same and the branches begin pulling at his arms in order to restrain him. Scratching his face, one of the twigs catches his eye. Blinded, he falls to the floor. As soon as he's landed, these impure branches wrap around Matthew's body and tightly restrain him from having the ability to create any movement. Slowly drifting in and out of consciousness, Matthew's lay half-dead! The sound of the crunching leaves and snapping twigs has stopped.

"So, now do you like to play games, Mr Honey?"

Lay without a single molecule of energy left within his body, Matthew's breathing slow and his body is motionless; only his eyes remain half-open.

"Shame, I thought you might have put up a little more of fight than this. I must say, even your wife was a stronger advocate than this. Pathetic."

Slowly, making her way around his body, Jezebel, in her true demonic empress form, is teasing his soul. The mist that's circulated is getting thicker and thicker. Surrounding both Matthew and Jess until they can no longer see what's in front of them, no sooner has this developed it quickly disappears. With a slight slit still present in his eyes, he sees Eve. She's once again Eve. Precious, innocent and pure. As water forms in the corners of his eyes, these teardrops filled with love fall down his face. Slowly he whispers, "Eve..."

With a glow surrounding her, she resembles an angel. Matthew's levels of strength and life gradually begins to rise as his heart warms at this vision. He begins to question deep in his mind. Decision made, he isn't going to give up and let this evil woman win. There's no way she's ripping his life apart any more. She will not win. Clenching his fists together, and tightening all his muscles, Matthew groans as he stretches out and rips all the strangulating branches from off his body. Smiling with deceit at his attempt to free himself and save Eve, Jezebel is watching and allowing him to use up the last of his life's energy on a pointless task. Freeing himself, Matthew stumbles onto his feet and, as he's crying with around ten percent of his life left, he's feebly making his way towards his daughter. But as soon as he gets within reaching distance she disappears, and Jezebel stands before him. Reaching out to Mathew with her horrific existence, she violently throws herself at him and drags him to his death.

Passing out, Matthew slowly comes around. Unable to move his body, he sees he's lay alone on Lauren's grave. Completely losing consciousness, he's out!

Hearing the beeping of machinery, Matthew wakes. Looking to his body, he sees it's wounded, bruised and covered in fresh and dried blood. The room is dimly lit and he's wearing a hospital gown in a hospital bed. Looking to his body once more, he notices all the wires and machines that are attached to him. Taking these off one by one, he hears the machines begin uncontrollably beeping as they lose their readings. Suddenly, two nurses frantically burst into the room.

"No, no, no, you mustn't do that; just lie back, please."

"Eve, but Eve…"

"You can see Eve when you're better."

"I must… I need… I have to…"

"That's all well and good, Matthew, but you're at the moment too unwell to do anything now; lie back please."

She injects him with relaxants. Matthew slowly begins drifting off. The last words he hears are from the nurse. "Who's Eve? Do we have their contact number on his records?"

"No, we can't find any contacts on his records."

Chapter 17
"You've been here before"

The house is no longer a home. All the curtains remain closed and are no longer opened. Neglected, filthy and with an energy circulating that is unknown to this structure, the Honey residence resembles a derelict building.

The walls are dirty, the contents are smashed to pieces and the only item that stands strong is the golden mirror that was once proudly placed at the bottom of the stairs where it no longer sits. With the paint chipped throughout the house and the carpet black from dirt, this property is unrecognisable.

The day room is dark, dim and daunting. The mirror stands against the closed curtains at the front window. Matthew sits in a wooden rocking chair and is slowly rocking back and forth, back and forth, in a timely manner.

Wearing dirty, faded, black ripped jeans and black boots that are thick with dust, Matthew's appearance is unrecognisable from the strong man he once was. With his head tiled he resembles a sedated medical patient.

Looking to his hands in the mirror, Matthew gently smirks as he sees what he's holding. In one hand he has a 9mm pistol with a sleek black silencer fitted perfectly to this. In the other hand he holds a golden picture frame. The image inside the frame is of the family he once had. Matthew Honey, Evelyn Jade

Honey and Lauren Honey. The Honeys. How sweet their life once was, but no more.

Hanging around the picture frame is the locket that both Lauren and Eve once wore. The hunter.

"Whatever my fate, I ask you to free me. If death is in my cards, please let my soul know she's gone with no return. If life is in my cards, please let my soul live free and tell me how I can bring her back."

Continuing with his rocking, Matthew is no longer, Matthew. He's a broken man at the depths of despair, with nothing left to live for except the hope that one day he'll be reunited with his daughter; she is still living after all. And what does he have to lose? The only thing to fear is death and death doesn't seem so bad given his current cursed life.

"I will find her…"

Picking up the pace as his rocking gets faster and faster, he looks to the mirror and speaks. "I won't lose you, Eve."

Letting out an insane laughter, the room suddenly goes dark as he shouts, "So you want to play games, do you? Let the hunt begin. I'm coming for you, Jezebel. Eve, I promise on my life this time I won't let you down."

The insane laughter continues… And so, the hunt begins… Until next time…